VIXENS OF...

As Sunil Gupta left the laboratory he stopped in his tracks. He could hardly believe his eyes as he gazed at Dr Diana Graveney standing stripped to the waist, her head thrown back, her hips swaying as she fondled her bare breasts.

'Come to me, Sunil,' she breathed, her pouting lips curling into a smile of welcome.

He saw the grey-green pebble between her fingers and the strange luminescent tracks it left on her skin as she caressed herself. She unfastened her skirt and he watched as it glided down her thighs to form a dark pool at her feet.

Underneath, she wore nothing but her holiday suntan and a pair of tiny high-cut briefs . . .

Vixens of Night

Valentina Cilescu

HEADLINE
DELTA

First published in 1997 by
HEADLINE BOOK PUBLISHING

A HEADLINE DELTA paperback

10 9 8 7 6 5 4 3 2 1

ISBN 0 7472 5582 2

Typeset by Avon Dataset Ltd, Bidford-on-Avon, Warks

Printed and bound in Great Britain by
Cox & Wyman Ltd, Reading, Berks

HEADLINE BOOK PUBLISHING
A division of Hodder Headline PLC
338 Euston Road
London NW1 3BH

Vixens of Night

Background to the Story

Andreas Hunt and Mara Fleming have been forced to assume new identities as right-wing MP Nick Weatherall and vampire-slut Anastasia Dubois, loyal servants of vampire-sorcerer, the Master.

The Master's lustful slaves feed on the sexual energy of their victims. Many of the country's elite have already succumbed to the deadly erotic lure of Winterbourne Hall, the finest whorehouse in the world. But the Master craves yet more power. He has been elected leader of His Majesty's Opposition, and 10 Downing Street is only a step away.

Faced with an impossible situation, Andreas and Mara have already resorted to desperate measures – saving the world from a mad magician and reducing the Eiffel Tower to rubble in the process.

The danger of discovery is never very far away. Although the Master has so far failed to guess who they really are, how much longer can their luck hold out? And there is worse to come. The Master now has a new prize in his sights, one which will take Mara and Andreas to the limits of erotic endurance.

Prologue

There was something funny about the little grey-green stone. In fact, Diana Graveney had never seen anything quite like it.

It was getting late, and most of the staff at the National Geological Archive had left for home hours before, but Graveney couldn't take her eyes off the tiny stone in the yellowed cardboard box. She checked the details on the label: Sample 312, Unidentified, Origin Unknown.

An enigma.

Picking up the box, she tipped the stone off its bed of cotton wool and into her palm. Its coldness was surprising, exhilarating, like the fizz of chilled champagne poured over a lover's naked skin. She shivered, suddenly and inexplicably excited; and as she caressed it, the stone seemed to sparkle a little more intensely.

'Exquisite,' she murmured, although only moments before she had been on the point of dismissing the stone as not worth cataloguing. How peculiar. She could have sworn that it was . . . changing, becoming very slightly translucent, its very essence mutating even as she held it, though she knew that was impossible. Yet its coldness was definitely growing more acute, becoming the knife-sharpness of Arctic meltwater, gushing and bubbling over naked, upturned breasts.

Such wonderful pictures were dazzling and dancing in her mind. Erotic pictures, images bound to incredible sensations. If she closed her eyes for a moment, she could believe

3

that she was caught in a breathless swirl of ever-changing colours, a kaleidoscopic vortex in which there was no escape from the shivering, moist caresses of countless invisible fingers and lips and tongues.

With a shudder she forced her eyelids open. Dizzy with pleasure, she stumbled in sudden light. Looking down at the stone clutched in her hands, she saw that a clear, shimmering brightness was flooding out of the heart of it, bathing the whole of the basement archive in white and gold and sea-green luminescence.

The play of the light on her skin was like the gentle lapping of water. She felt as though she were swimming, floating, her body arching and offering itself delightedly to every new caress.

Questions chased each other inside her head. What was happening to her? Why was her mind suddenly flooded with images of glorious nakedness? Why was her body aching with this urgent, undeniably lascivious need?

The stone seemed to be whispering to her, coaxing and beckoning. There was no resisting its seductive messages. *Do it, do it, do it.* Yes. Why not? Why resist pleasure? In one impetuous movement, she tore open the front of her starched white blouse, pressed the cold gem to her skin and began rubbing it over and around her aching nipples.

Oh, but it felt good. Soooo very good, like an ice cube only much, much nicer. She moaned and sighed in her secret, stolen pleasure, her voice low and husky with excitement. And thrusting forward, she began to grind the base of her belly hard and rhythmically against the lock of the old roll-top desk.

It was about half-past nine when Sunil Gupta finished in the laboratory. He was just passing the top of the ironwork spiral staircase which led down into the archive when he heard noises. Strange noises. He stopped and bent over

4

the balustrade, peering down into curious, shifting patterns of coloured light. What ever was going on down there . . . ?

'Miss Graveney?' he called hesitantly from the top of the stairs. 'Diana?'

There was no reply, but Gupta could hear soft moans, interspersed with harsh, rasping gasps and a kind of heavy, rhythmic grating sound, like furniture bumping across old tiles.

'Diana?' he repeated, although somehow he knew she wasn't going to answer.

He started down the twisting staircase, the flooding light almost blinding him so that he had to shade his eyes. It wasn't until he was halfway down that he had his first sight of her, and even then he could hardly believe his eyes. Doctor Diana Graveney was standing half-naked in front of her desk, her head thrown back, hips swaying and her usually neat black hair hanging down her back in wild rats' tails.

Gupta stopped in his tracks, his eyes widening.

'*Diana*?'

Turning her head, she smiled at him, her moist lips curling into a smile of welcome. Her hands went on circling and kneading her bare breasts.

'It's . . . beautiful, Sunil. Beautiful. Can't you feel it?'

She didn't need to explain. He felt it. There was an incredible sensual magnetism in this cold, brilliant light. It was coaxing him down the last three steps into the archive, the heels of his Timberland boots making a dull clunking sound on the open ironwork.

The floor felt as treacherous as quicksand beneath his feet.

'Diana, I'm not sure I should . . .'

'Come to me, Sunil.'

He could hardly believe her lips were framing those words, seducing him, urging him on, offering him what he'd never dared to crave.

'Don't be afraid, it feels incredible.'

He saw the tiny grey-green stone between her fingers, couldn't tear his gaze away from the luminescent tracks it left on her skin as she used it to caress her nakedness. As he watched, she unfastened the side button on her skirt and wriggled her hips, so that it glided easily down over her thighs to form a dark pool at her feet.

Underneath, she was wearing nothing but her holiday suntan and a pair of black high-cut briefs, trimmed with lace.

'Sunil. *Sunil*, please.' She beckoned to him, and he felt as though she was drawing him on into the very centre of the light, begging him to ease the pain of her frustration.

A faint but frantic voice shrieked a warning in the mad darkness of his lust. Stop this right now, Sunil. You scarcely know this woman. Oh, you've asked her learned opinion about interesting rocks, you even had an argument once about radiocarbon dating . . . but that was work. This is something else and so is she . . .

And now here she is, stripping down her panties and rubbing her sprinkle of dark pubic moss against the brass catch on the front of that roll-top desk. And she's doing it just for *you*. Are you sure this is what you want? Another voice laughed back, I'm a man aren't I? And she's naked and voluptuous and willing. Of course it's what I want.

Gupta's lips were dry, his throat parched. His knees trembled and threatened to give way as he walked slowly towards her across the cracked tiled floor. What he was going to do next, he really wasn't at all certain. All he knew was that his comfortable chinos had suddenly become very constricting, half strangling the burgeoning throb of his too-sensitive prick.

Gupta was a modest man, timid even. He couldn't believe he was doing this, couldn't imagine what madness could have made him reach down and rub the crotch of his pants, cradling the beautiful hardness in his shaking fingers.

He was almost close enough to touch her. One step further and there'd be no going back. He hesitated, he wasn't sure why.

'D-Diana?'

Graveney's moist lips parted; and then she growled at him.

Growled? Gupta blinked, not quite sure that he had really heard that guttural, animal sound rasping out of that pretty white throat. Then, to his amazement, he opened his own mouth and growled right back.

He wasn't Sunil Gupta any more, and she wasn't Doctor Diana Graveney. They weren't cool-headed scientists. They were caveman and cavewoman and, as if it understood, the basement room began to change and mutate around them. The floor beneath their feet became rutted and muddy, the brilliant light dimming to a dull red glow that illuminated rocky, rough-hewn walls and stalactites that dripped sweet-scented juices onto their hands and faces. Everything was melting and flowing, changing into the mirror image of their lust.

They embraced, their bodies writhing snake-like against each other, their fingers rending the useless clothes from their bodies. In a mad rage of lust, Gupta seized Graveney in his arms and hoisted her aloft, both hands under her backside. Sliding her onto the top of his desk, he pulled open her soft wetness and slid her down hard onto the fiery dart of his prick. As they coupled, her fingers uncurled and the tiny gemstone fell to the ground, rolling in sparkling circles until at last it came to rest, winking up at them like a knowing eye.

With her legs about his waist, Graveney rode him like a she-cat, hissing and spitting, the spiked heels of her shoes digging into his hips and leaving deep, dark indentations.

Gupta ran his fingernails down her back, scoring her with the force of his need; and he lavished savage kisses on her breasts, drinking the sweat as it coursed into the deep valley between their wobbling, quivering mounds. She felt like silk; hot, wet, slippery silk wrapped tight as a whore's kiss about his exultant shaft.

The sudden slash of Graveney's red-tipped claw took him unawares. As it pierced the soft, smooth flesh of Gupta's cheek, he let out a hiss of pain. Yet the ooze of blood felt astonishingly warm and seductive on his skin, and its honey-sweet scent filled him with an excitement he couldn't even begin to understand.

Graveney was in paradise. She was a sensual gourmet, but this pleasure was more intense, more piquant than anything she had ever known before. Gupta was nothing; an irrelevance, a minor diversion – yet screwing him felt like one long, unbearably intense orgasm.

Her wetness oozed and gushed, its sweet, aromatic stickiness constantly renewed as she used Gupta's body for her pleasure. She tightened about his prick, holding them both on the edge of orgasm until at last she heard him cry out and felt the fountaining heat of his come . . . then she let go, her ecstasy tumbling down bright steps into an endless, sparkling ocean.

A moment, and then she would begin again. Graveney felt the source of all sensual power within her, and knew that this pleasure could last for as long as she wanted it to. Which might be a very, very long time. But first, she told herself, there was something she needed to do. An urge that demanded to be satisfied.

She slashed her sharpened talon across Gupta's cheek. He mewled like a scratched kitten, but his blood sprang up in fat crimson beads, invitingly ruby-dark and sweet. Graveney let out a long, blissful sigh. As she smiled, her sharp canine teeth glinted in the unearthly light and she nuzzled into the crook of Gupta's neck, putting out her tongue-tip to lap up the first drop of honeydew.

First, she must feed.

Chapter 1

'Holy shit.'

Andreas Hunt caught a glimpse of his face in the mirror, and nearly jumped out of his skin. It didn't matter how long he'd been occupying Nick Weatherall's body. He'd never get used to being grinned at by somebody else's reflection – and the reflection of an obnoxious right-wing MP at that.

Shaking black thoughts of the Master out of his head, Andreas slid out of bed and put on his dressing gown. He homed in on the splashing sounds coming from the ensuite bathroom and called out hopefully, 'Don't suppose you're getting lonely in there?'

Mara's laughter was soft, sweet and huskily seductive. He could picture her stretched out in the bath in a cloud of pinkish-white suds, her breasts now exposed, now hidden as she worked up swirls of creamy lather then rinsed it slowly and languidly from her perfect skin. Mmm. Nice.

'It's a lovely big bath,' she teased.

'Big enough for two?'

'Why don't you come and find out?'

He would have done just that, only at that very moment – right on cue – there was a knock on the door of their hotel room. Bugger room service. If this was breakfast, frankly he wasn't interested. The only cream he wanted with his morning coffee was the luscious ooze from Mara Fleming's adorable pussy.

He cursed silently, willing his erection to deflate.

'I'll get it.'

Tying the belt of his robe, Andreas padded barefoot to the door and lifted the latch. He stood and stared, open-mouthed. What the . . . ?

Mara's voice called faintly from the bathroom.

'Who is it?'

Good question. And one that Andreas found himself unable to answer right away. The petite young woman with the long black hair and the silver fox coat pushed the door wide open and swanned past him, into the room. She couldn't have been more than five foot three, yet she filled the room with her presence.

Andreas stood and gaped. The woman sauntered into the centre of the bedroom, surveying it in a single sweep. Then she turned to face him, fixing him with glittering, nut-brown eyes. She wasn't saying much – and it wasn't difficult to see why. Her full, plum-juicy lips were pierced by two small, emerald-green rings which sealed them, binding her to silence. Not that she seemed at all disconcerted by this unusual adornment, thought Andreas as he watched her open her fur coat and send it slithering to the carpeted floor. In fact, she seemed to be revelling in her power to titillate and shock.

Beneath her fox fur, Andreas's uninvited guest was naked except for a pair of skintight shorts in fine black rubber, shiny as glass and clinging like a coat of paint to her trim, athletic body. The stripes of a recent whipping criss-crossed her breasts with deep magenta. Andreas couldn't take his eyes off her. He couldn't even speak. All he could do was stand and stare, and lick his lips like a starving fox looking into a chicken coop.

He cleared his throat, but no sound came out. Beads of sweat were breaking out, cold and clammy, on his brow. Something very peculiar was happening to him. What was it about this girl that compelled him to devour her with his eyes? Now, Andreas Hunt lusted after women as much as the next man (and the three men next to him), but this one was doing things to him that he couldn't begin to fathom. If there was such a thing as sexual magnetism, this girl obviously liked to buy in bulk.

The pierced lips curved into a coldly wicked smile; but Andreas wasn't looking at the girl's face. His eyes were fixed on the spidery letters scrawled in greenish-grey kohl pencil across her small, spherical breasts.

'FOLLOW HER.'

The smile grew colder still, more icily sensual. Turning round, the girl swept aside her hair and bared her back to Andreas. On it was written the message:

'BUT FIRST ENJOY HER. M.'

So this was the Master's doing. He might have known. Another of the Right (Dis)Honourable Anthony LeMaître's little games, devised with Sedet's complicity to keep his acolytes on their toes. He wondered what this game was supposed to prove.

Normally, Andreas would have resented being tested yet again. Today he felt positively grateful. This girl was one hell of an unbirthday present, and he wanted to unwrap it with a violence that astonished him. For fuck's sake, Hunt, he reminded himself, this girl isn't even remotely your type and her tits are like little apples. Not one bit like Mara's luscious handfuls . . . but lust strangled his doubts at birth and his hands knew exactly what to do. Already they were stripping off his dressing gown, flinging it on the bed, and following it with the pair of silk boxers he'd only just put on.

Andreas's prick knew what to do, too. The girl's silent smile grew perceptibly brighter and more knowing as her eyes caressed the stone-stiff rod that thrust out from the dark thicket at the base of his belly. And he could have sworn that the greenish-grey writing on her breasts glowed

13

with a faint yet strangely compelling luminescence.

Enjoy her. Enjoy her, do whatever you want to her, she's yours. The memory of the Master's exhortation throbbed to the pulse of his swelling need. Perhaps nobody could be *all* bad, not even undead vampire sorcerers with a world domination fetish. And hey, the girl didn't even need to be told what Andreas wanted her to do. Without a word passing between them, she sank to the ground, positioning herself on her knees before him like a devoted worshipper.

Excitement washed over Andreas like warm, tropical surf. He stroked his hands covetously over the girl's dark, sleek hair. He sensed a dangerous electricity within her, a fire that crackled and consumed, yet something reckless inside him wanted more and more of it. He longed to claw and bite and fuck and possess, and frankly, at this moment, he didn't feel much like Andreas Hunt at all. Not even lusty Nick Weatherall MP, the empty-headed bonking machine whose identity he had 'borrowed' without anybody noticing.

Right now Andreas Hunt was an animal. A pleasure-seeking missile. An engine of unstoppable desire.

Tilting forward his hips, he cupped the girl's small, apple-hard breasts and squeezed them hard about his dick. Her flesh was hot but slippery with cooling sweat and he slid between her tits with a delicious ease.

'Sexy bitch,' he murmured, transported by the sudden mainline hit of sensual exhilaration. 'Oh you horny little slut.'

She placed her hands over his and began moving slowly back and forth, masturbating him between her breasts. All the time her eyes were locked to his, fucking him with her mind, inviting him to share the filthy secret film show of her imagination.

Andreas shivered to the intense sensations rippling through him, beginning with the very tip of his prick and spreading almost instantaneously to the heaviness of his sap-filled balls, the ache of his tensed thighs and belly, the fluttering excitement in the pit of his stomach. Mara was only in the next room, but for once he wasn't thinking about Mara, only about the girl with the velvet tit-fuck and the refrigerator smile.

'Tighter,' he hissed.

And he felt her fingers tense, pushing her small breasts even harder about his shaft, her clawed fingernails digging into the backs of his hands. He was trapped in silk and steel, sliding harder and faster with every thrust, listening to the quickening harmony of their synchronised breathing. And he was loving it. And now the girl was moaning, her eyes half closed, the muted sounds of need escaping from between her pierced and sealed lips.

He could feel it coming, rolling down upon him like a bow-wave, turning the leaden need in his balls to boiling, bubbling pleasure.

'Yes. Oh hell yes.'

The bite of her nails into the back of his hands caused a sharp, violent pain which pushed him over the edge into pleasure. His tribute to her skill spurted out in thick white gobbets which spattered her breasts, her throat, her face, his hands, and dripped in long, lazy trails down over the girl's bare belly.

If he thought she had finished with him, he was wrong. If he had thought he was in control, he was even more mistaken. As she rolled over onto her belly on the floor, he felt his lust return a hundredfold. He had to have her, he had to have her now.

He ripped down her tight rubber shorts and scythed into her, clutching her upthrust buttocks and pulling them apart. She was as soft and warm as melted butter and took him inside her with an animal growl of welcome. He was on top, forcing his desire on her, but he had the strangest feeling that she was at the controls of the sex machine. She was fucking him, her backside rising up to

15

meet him, dictating the speed at which he would take his pleasure.

Somehow it didn't matter. All Andreas cared about right now was the girl's divine arse, and the smooth, sweat-streaked back that begged to be bitten and licked and thrashed and . . . oh, oh, oh, it was happening all over again, more powerful than ever.

He took her a third time and left her curled like a sleeping kitten on the Chinese silk rug, her lust spent at last. Stepping over her – and not quite sure whether to be proud or ashamed of his behaviour – Andreas went into the bathroom.

Mara was dozing in the bath, her eyelids sleepy and heavy. The whirlpool was roaring, surrounding the sublime swell of her breasts with rushing eddies of foamy water and making the firm flesh quiver irresistibly. Andreas's appetite was instantly revived.

He reached over and turned off the whirlpool.

'There's a naked girl in the bedroom,' he commented.

Mara pushed her damp hair back from her face. Her green eyes narrowed, but he knew she wasn't jealous. Mara believed in sharing – and telling. Jealousy was for people who didn't trust each other.

'Well, it's a novel twist on room service,' she commented with wry humour, teasing Andreas by playing with the dollops of lather which obscured her rose-pink nipples. She grinned. 'Do they do naked men as well? I'll have two, please, with a side order of chocolate mousse.'

Andreas dodged as Mara threw a blob of lather at his nose. It landed on his ear and he scraped it off.

'I'm serious!'

'I suppose there's a first time for everything.' Mara picked up the soap and started washing one long, slim leg.

Andreas sat down on the edge of the bath, eyeing the bar of soap as it slid lazily up and down Mara's thigh. She was a wonderful tease; he wondered what on earth he'd seen in that other girl.

'I could do that,' he commented hopefully.

'Oh yeah? Well if you're very good I might let you.' Mara rinsed off some of the lather, in the process exposing one pink-tipped breast. 'So who's this so-called naked woman then?'

'The Master sent her.'

'Is that what she said?'

'It's hard to say anything when your lips are sealed together.' Andreas trailed his fingers in the water. 'She brought a message. God only knows what the Master's playing at. We're supposed to go with her.'

'Where to?'

'Fuck knows.'

'Do we have to go right now?' Mara's emerald eyes coaxed so winsomely as she slid her right hand down, brushing away the scented foam from her hard-tipped breasts.

Andreas surveyed the alternatives on offer. The Master didn't like being disobeyed, in fact he tended to get quite touchy about it. On the other hand, he *had* told Andreas to 'enjoy her first'. Who was to say he hadn't meant Mara?

'Later,' Andreas decided with a grin. And, slipping into the bath with Mara, he rediscovered the pleasures of playing hookey.

It was over an hour later when the girl – now wearing her fur coat again – led them out through the hotel lobby and into a waiting limousine. She ushered them silently into the back, then got into the front with the driver and the car roared away into the rush hour.

Mara was gazing out of the window and Andreas took the opportunity to take a good long look at her. He wasn't much good at all that New Man crap, but she'd gone awfully quiet all of a sudden, and that bothered him.

'Something's wrong, isn't it?' he hazarded.

Mara turned to look at him. She laid her hand on his

thigh and slid it tantalisingly upwards until it was almost – but not quite – touching his balls. She pulled a face.

'Let's see. I'm trapped in a sex vampire's body, you're supposed to be dead and the Master's on track to be the next Prime Minister. Oh yeah, and while we were trying to save the world we accidentally melted the Eiffel Tower. I guess you could say something was wrong . . .'

'Not that. You know that's not what I mean.' He squirmed uncomfortably. 'Give me a break, Mara, I'm trying to be sensitive and caring. And it doesn't come naturally.'

Mara smiled.

'I know. Nothing's wrong, not really. I just worry sometimes . . .'

'What about?'

'The way Brabant was able to control my mind like that. It was so easy, I couldn't fight him. He just took me over completely.'

'Brabant's dead.'

'Yes, but . . . what if it happens again, with somebody else? What if my psychic powers aren't strong enough to protect us both from the Master?'

'Of course they're strong enough.' He lifted his wrist and the dragon's-eye talisman jingled reassuringly. 'If you hadn't powered this thing up for me, the Master would have found me out months ago.'

'What if . . . ?'

Andreas silenced her with a kiss.

'Stop worrying. Sex vampires never worry.'

Mara pouted prettily, back to her old self again.

'Unless they're not getting enough sex.'

Andreas let his hands roam down from her throat until they were cupping the twin treasures of her breasts. Oh but they were wonderful breasts. If he had anything to thank Anastasia Dubois for, it was that the body she'd donated to Mara was so deliciously pneumatic.

'Then I'll just have to make sure you do, won't I?'

He'd have considered doing it right there and then, but the limo was slowing down; and when he glanced out of the window he realised that they were turning into the high-tech moonscape of London Docklands. Leaning forward, he rapped on the partition and it slid back.

'Sir?'

'Why have you brought us here?'

'Mr LeMaître gave strict instructions, sir. We'll be arriving shortly, if you'd just like to relax and make yourselves comfortable.'

The partition slid back and piped music filled the compartment. Andreas exchanged uneasy looks with Mara. Relax? Sod that for a game of soldiers.

'You don't suppose the Master's rumbled us?'

"Course not.' Mara sounded less than one hundred per cent convinced, but her fingers stroked the amulet at Andreas's wrist. 'This will protect you, as long as we keep empowering it.'

'And what about you?'

'I'm a white witch, remember? I always get by.'

The car skirted Canary Wharf and turned right, drawing up outside a dazzling construction in white marble and tubular steel. Somewhere to the right, a blue and red train was whizzing along the light railway to a riverside station. The rear passenger doors of the limousine clicked open, and the girl was at Andreas's side, beckoning to him and Mara to get out.

She led them up the front steps and into a high-ceilinged foyer, much like any foyer in any brand-new office block. A uniformed security guard sat behind the reception desk, but he gave only the briefest of glances to the newcomers and they walked swiftly past.

At the end of a faceless, featureless corridor was what appeared to be a blank wall. But a simple touch on a button raised a four-inch-thick steel door, revealing what lay beyond.

'Well bugger me with a breadstick,' whistled Andreas, peering into the vastness. The whole of the bottom three floors of the building had been gutted and lavishly redesigned, to produce a huge and perfect reconstruction of an Ancient Egyptian palace, complete with painted friezes, pillars, a sunken pool and scantily clad serving girls with serpent headdresses and gossamer filmy robes.

'So you finally decided to honour us with your presence,' snapped Sedet, the Master's queen, rising from her gilded throne to glare down at Andreas. Behind her, hologrammatic representations of the Valley of the Kings, projected across the windows, cut out any faint reminder of the modern world outside.

The Master waved his queen aside. His expression was one of sardonic good humour. He, apparently, was in one of his rare good moods.

'Did you enjoy my little gift, Weatherall?'

'Yes. Master,' Andreas added hastily.

'Good. And you found Graveney . . . how shall I say – *stimulating*? She excited your lust?'

Andreas searched for the words the Master would want to hear.

'She was very satisfactory, Master. Remarkably so, in fact. Thank you, Master.' The words stuck in his throat, but he couldn't afford to risk punishment or – worse – disclosure. One day soon he was going to pay the bastard back with interest, but until that day he would grovel with the best of 'em.

'You would say that her charms were irresistible?'

'Well . . . yes, Master. In fact, that is why we are late. We . . . er . . . lost track of time.'

'Excellent. It is just as I thought.'

The Master beckoned the girl to him. She went to him like a lapdog, joyful to be called yet slightly fearful of incurring his displeasure.

'Kneel, slut. And unveil yourself.'

20

She knelt, letting the fur coat fall away.

Bending over the girl, the Master placed his index finger on her lips. Before Andreas and Mara's eyes, the two green rings melted away, dissolving into tiny snakes which writhed and slithered onto the Master's finger, where they changed once more into rings.

'Thank you, Master. Blessings upon you, Master,' breathed the girl, taking the Master's hand and pressing her lips to it in passionate kisses. He shook her away like an irritating child.

'Explain.'

'I did as you commanded, Master. I went to the hotel room and offered myself to Weatherall. He was unable to resist me.'

'And why was that, Graveney, my devious little slut?'

Graveney's brown eyes sparkled with grateful devotion.

'Because of the rings with which you pierced me, Master. And the magical writing upon my body.'

'Ah yes, the rings.' The Master held out his hand to Andreas. 'Rather unremarkable objects, wouldn't you say?'

Andreas peered at them. Even now, on the Master's finger, they seemed to emanate some kind of power . . . a sexual force . . . something indefinable, yet compelling. The Master rubbed them and a greenish-grey powder smeared his fingers. The same powder which had been used to write on Graveney's bare skin.

'I feel . . . drawn to them . . .' Andreas admitted, reaching out to touch them; but the Master turned away.

'Quite so.' The Master smirked. 'Unremarkable at first sight, yet the powder which coats these rings is most un-usual. It was ground from a fragment of a rather exceptional stone. Explain, Graveney.'

'I am a geologist,' Graveney began. 'I was working at the National Geological Archive, cataloguing old specimens, when I came across one I had never seen before. No one knew what it was, or where it had come from. I touched it . . . it made me feel—'

Sedet cut in, her violet eyes flashing with contemptuous fire. The spiked heel of her boot ground Graveney's hand very prettily into the stone step on which she knelt.

'Mistress . . . !' squealed Graveney, hissing with anger as she tried to free herself. 'Mistress, I have done nothing to offend you, I have done nothing to deserve this indignity . . . !'

'Be silent,' snapped Sedet. 'Or I will have your mouth sealed up again.' She turned back to Andreas and Mara. 'Now *I* shall tell our dear friends how that stone made you feel. It broke through all the bounds of your self-restraint, it raised your lusts to such a level that you disobeyed your Master's express command to exercise discipline over your appetites.'

Graveney hung her head, ashamed of the irresistible impulse which had driven her to prey upon the hapless Sunil Gupta; an incident which had taken some skilful covering up by the Master's acolytes.

'Yes, Mistress,' she whispered.

'Enough, my queen,' sighed the Master. 'You may have the slut for punishment later. For now, there is important business to discuss.'

The Master snapped his fingers and a beautiful youth in heavy eye-paint stepped forward. He held out a small jewelled box, balanced on a cushion.

'Slut.'

Mara met the Master's gaze.

'Master?'

'You may look.'

She peered inside the box. All she could see, lying on the bed of pink velvet, was a small sphere of greenish-grey stone, polished and lustrous as metal. Lying next to it, shaved from one side of the sphere, lay a tiny splinter of the same stone, needle-sharp and glittering.

22

'What is it?'

'As yet I do not know. Even expert scientists have been unable to analyse or identify it.'

There was something wonderfully fascinating about the tiny greenish-grey stone, something which made Mara long to touch it. Energy seemed to emanate from it like multicoloured fire.

'It looks so ordinary. And yet . . .'

'And yet it contains a source of unmatchable sexual power, which I fully intend to possess. This sample, of course, is far too small to be adequate for my purposes. So you are going to get me more of it.'

The blood drained from Mara's face.

'*Me*, Master?'

'You . . . and Weatherall.'

Oh joy, thought Andreas bitterly. Oh pure, unfettered rapture. Another of the Master's 'special assignments'. Being the Master's trusted accomplice was almost worse than being on the wrong end of his displeasure. But only almost. He tried hard to look really, really pleased.

'After all, you two work so well together.' The Master's lips twitched slightly at the corners. 'But this time, try to be a little . . . tidier. People don't take kindly to having their national monuments reduced to rubble.'

For a moment, Andreas almost thought that the Master knew. Knew everything, and was simply playing with them for his own amusement. Then the irrational fear faded as quickly as it had come; paranoia was such a waste of time. Grovelling was a much more profitable investment.

'We will not let you down, Master,' he heard himself promise, rather rashly. 'But . . .'

'But what?' demanded the Master.

'How will we find the stone?'

'The details are for you to decide,' replied the Master coolly. 'Or are you inadequate to the task?'

'N-no. We'll find it.'

23

'Naturally you will. And quickly. Is that clear?'

Andreas swallowed. 'Perfectly.'

Sedet draped herself over the gilded arm of the Master's throne and ran the tip of her tongue seductively along the length of her index finger. Manipulative bitch, thought Andreas, but his politically incorrect cock twitched treacherously in his pants.

'I hear they have rebuilt the Eiffel Tower,' commented Sedet langorously. 'Since your little . . . accident with it.'

'As a matter of fact, it is being reopened next week,' said the Master. 'Along with the three or four arrondisse-ments which have had to be rebuilt on account of your carelessness.'

There's gratitude for you, thought Andreas. If it hadn't been for us, the entire world would have gone down the tubes, vampires and all. But he just shuffled his feet and tried to look embarrassed.

'I have decided,' announced the Master, 'that you and the Dubois slut will attend the ceremonies in my place, as representatives of His Majesty's Opposition. The following week, you will begin a fact-finding tour of developing countries.'

'But . . . ?'

'Shut up, Weatherall, and listen. What you will really be doing is looking for more of this.' He indicated the tiny fragments of grey-green stone.

The Master looked at Mara and smiled. Andreas follow-ed his gaze, and was puzzled to see that Mara was staring fixedly at the box in the Master's hand. She seemed mesmerised by it, and the tip of her tongue was flicking across her parted lips in small, quick, snake-like movements.

The Master snapped his fingers, and Mara looked up, her expression slightly dazed and confused.

'M-master?'

'Slut. You are not paying attention.'

Mara coloured slightly. 'I . . . I'm sorry, Master. I . . .'

'It fascinates you, doesn't it?'

Mara's eyes returned lovingly to the tiny stone in the box. She nodded her head dumbly. Still smiling, the Master held out the box, coaxing, enticing, tempting.

'Why don't you come and touch it? You'd like that, wouldn't you?'

Mara walked slowly and deliberately towards the Master's outstretched hand, her eyes never leaving the small carved box in his palm. Something about the expression on her face made Andreas feel profoundly uneasy. It was obsessive, almost carnivorous; a vampire look that transformed her from the cheeky, sexy, defiant Mara Fleming he knew into something that made his blood congeal with cold.

He watched her intently, wondering what force could do this to her, wanting to intervene and break the spell but knowing he mustn't. She moved like a sleepwalker, her body fluid and sinuous beneath her white skirt suit, more like a hungry prowling animal than the Mara he knew. Her stockinged thighs brushed together with a gentle swish of sheer nylon as she moved, her rounded backside mobile yet firm beneath the short white skirt. Andreas loosened his shirt collar. Was it him, or was it getting hot in here? Mara wasn't the only one with an appetite that demanded to be satisfied.

'You want to touch the stone, don't you?' smiled the Master.

'Yes.'

Something tensed in the pit of Andreas's stomach. That voice . . . it sounded different, far away, not . . . not like Mara's voice at all.

Mara's trembling fingers stretched out for the stone, but Sedet snatched at it and held it tantalisingly out of reach.

'Later perhaps,' smirked Sedet. 'If you are very, very good.' Her voice was a tiger's growl. Andreas caught a spark of anger in Mara's green eyes, but she made no attempt to take what she craved.

'Here, slut.' With a snap of his fingers, the Master summoned Mara to his side. She climbed the last two steps to the dais. 'Stand there, in front of me.'

Mara obeyed, taking up her position in front of the Master, with her back to him. Andreas watched the Master's ringed right hand snake around her waist and slide up her skirt. Stocking tops and kissable thighs were revealed, millimetre by tantalising millimetre, until the white triangle of Mara's panties shimmered into view, veiling the red-gold curls beneath.

Her lips parted and she let out a faint, shivering sigh as the Master began to masturbate her through her panties, rubbing with circular movements that tantalised far more than they satisfied. Slowly her hips began to move in time to his finger-fucking, swaying and tilting as though coupling with an unseen lover.

'Feels good, doesn't it?' breathed Sedet, her voice syrupy with mocking laughter. 'Poor little slut, you're such a slave to your appetites. You have no self-discipline at all.'

Unbuttoning her silky cream blouse and sliding it down over her shoulders, Sedet bared her plump, buoyant breasts. Their bare, uptilted nipples bobbed eagerly, stiffening at the caress of cool air on bare flesh.

The fine sliver of green-grey stone glinted dully as Sedet took it from its carved box. Raising it to her lips, she kissed it then put out her tongue and ran it over the needle-sharp tip.

'Delicious,' she murmured. 'Don't you wish you could taste it?'

Mara moaned softly. There was no denying her excitement. Andreas ached with jealous need as he looked at the spreading patch of wetness, oozing into the crotch of her panties and making them transparent. He wanted to taste, too: not the stone, but the sodden white satin which held the essence of Mara's sex.

The Master pressed harder on Mara's pubis. She squirmed at the touch, but he would not let her go. On the contrary, with his free hand he began to explore the pleasure ground of her backside, probing underneath her panties, sliding between her arse cheeks to the winking eye between.

Mara's whole body shook as she surrendered to the overwhelming power of her lust. And all the time, her eyes remained fixed on Sedet, following hungrily as the Master's queen began to pleasure herself with the tiny, mysterious stone.

'It feels so good,' breathed Sedet. 'Its touch on my skin . . . exquisite. Wouldn't you like to feel it too?'

'Please . . . please,' gasped Mara. Sedet smiled cruelly at the torment on Mara's face. Favoured slut or not, all other women were rivals in Sedet's eyes, and she adored making them defer to her superior sensual powers.

'Very well,' said Sedet. 'You *shall* feel its kiss.'

The Master's fingers circled Mara's sex, sometimes lightly, sometimes with a sudden and brutal hardness which forced apart her labia and turned the warm ooze of pleasure juice to an abundant trickle. Mara's hips worked back and forth, now forcing herself against his fingertips, now pushing backwards so that the index finger of his other hand nudged into the tight pout of her anus.

Sedet's gloved fingers made short work of Mara's white jacket, tearing it from her in one savage movement. Underneath, Mara was naked save for the crystal pendant which the Master had given her as a mark of his favour. Sedet jerked it from Mara's throat and held up the needle-sharp stone, inches from Mara's face.

'You want it?'

'Yes.' That strange voice again, Mara's and yet not Mara's.

'Let me hear you beg.'

'Please. Oh please . . . I can't bear it.'

But the full force of pleasure was far more unbearable.

Taking Mara's right breast in her hand, Sedet squeezed it into a hard white sphere, until the nipple stood out in a swollen magenta stalk. The fine, razor-sharp tip of the stone pierced Mara's nipple in a swift stabbing movement that drew a single drop of dark crimson blood.

'Ah! Ah no, no I can't!'

With a scream that chilled Andreas to the core, Mara climaxed, a great rush of honeydew inundating the Master's fingers as she fainted clean away.

Sedet stood over Mara's prone body, limp and unconscious on the steps of the Master's throne. She licked the smear of blood from her index finger with obvious pleasure.

'Interesting,' she observed, nudging Mara's bare breasts with the pointed toe of her boot. 'I had always imagined the Dubois slut was more . . . resilient.'

Andreas's heart pounded. He'd never seen Mara like this before, so cold and still.

'Is she . . .'

The Master regarded him with a raised eyebrow.

'Is she what, Weatherall? *Dead*?' He laughed drily, the joke pleasing him. 'Have her taken away, question her when she recovers. I must know everything about the powers of this stone.' He took it back from Sedet, like a precious plaything from a careless child, and placed it firmly back in its box. 'Everything there is to know.'

The room was in darkness, the heavy curtains drawn to block out all but the faintest glimmers of light.

Torches flamed dull red in distant corners of the room, and an all-pervading scent of burning incense filled Andreas's lungs with a sweet, sickly heaviness, making his head swim. It was a great honour to be granted the Master's private suite, but frankly Andreas would have preferred to be back with Mara in their nice, anonymous hotel room.

He sat beside Mara, her naked form still and white on

the deep pile of mink and sable pelts. As he stroked his hand across her brow, he felt her stir at his touch.

'Mara?'

She murmured, rolled to one side then back again; and her eyelids flickered.

'Andreas.' Mara's voice was not sleepy, but wakeful and seductive.

'Are you all right? I thought . . .'

'I need . . . a drink.'

'I'll get you a glass of water.'

Her hand met his, pulling him back down beside her as he attempted to get to his feet.

'Not that kind of drink, Andreas. Don't tell me you don't understand.'

She pulled him down onto the bed of furs, made him straddle her, reached up and unzipped his pants. He was already hard for her.

As her lips parted to take his dick into her mouth, she smiled. And that was fine . . . or it would have been, except for just one thing.

It wasn't Mara Fleming's smile.

Chapter 2

'Mara . . .'

'Mmm?' Mara didn't turn round. She was busy admiring herself in the British Ambassador's eighteenth-century mirror, smoothing her hands over the sleek curves of her body.

'Mara!'

Mara swung round and stuck out her tongue at Andreas. She looked like a naughty fifth-former in that unbuttoned silk shirt and short grey kilt, thought Andreas.

'What?'

'Don't you think you'd better do yourself up?' His gaze wandered inexorably downwards, into the snug valley between Mara's pushed-up breasts, so white and luscious inside that red lace bra.

Mara laughed; a low-pitched, husky-voiced chuckle that set Andreas's cock twitching hopefully in his sober suit. Her nails caught the light as she fastened the bottom two buttons of her blouse; they were dramatic talons, long shaped ovals freshly laquered in metallic yellow. Not really Mara Fleming's style at all, but Andreas supposed every woman liked to change her image now and then.

'Why? Don't you like looking at my tits, *Andreas*?' Her lips framed his name with delicious deliberation, as though she was uttering some wicked secret. He caught her arm, pulled her to him and shut her up by covering her mouth with his. Her body writhed against his like a randy snake's and his dick danced in harmony; he wanted her, wanted

31

her real bad . . . and this was a real bad time.

'Not so loud,' he hissed, kissing her neck. 'Do you want everybody to realise that Nick Weatherall MP is really Andreas Hunt?'

Mara smiled. That same, disturbing smile she'd given him in the Master's private chamber. It reminded Andreas of somebody else's smile, somebody . . . if only he could remember.

'None of us is *always* what we seem,' she purred. He caught a meaningful glitter in her eye. 'Come to bed.'

'But . . .'

'Now.'

Andreas cursed his common sense.

'We're due at the reopening ceremony for the Eiffel Tower in ten minutes,' he protested. 'If we're not there, the Master will want to know why.'

'Screw the Master.' Mara ran her hand down the side of Andreas's face, his neck, under his jacket and down his belly to the too-tight waistband of his suit trousers. Her hand felt cool as stone through his shirt, lapping up his heat, feeling the determined thump-thump-thump of his racing pulse.

A man has only just so much self-control, and Andreas had less than most. His hand slid round Mara's waist and held her tightly against him, pushing the swollen hardness of his dick against her pubic bone.

'All right, you little tease . . .'

His fingers were just easing up Mara's skirt when there was a knock at the door. The spell broken, Andreas and Mara sprang apart. Mara even had the good grace to look shaken.

'Is something wrong?'

She shook her head. Snapped at him – which wasn't like Mara at all.

'Why should anything be wrong? I'm fine. Just a bit . . . dizzy.'

The door opened and a diplomatic flunkey stuck his Brylcreemed head into the room.

'The cars are waiting, sir, madam.'

'Er, yes. Right.' Andreas exchanged looks with Mara. Funny, she seemed perfectly normal now, her usual self. The weird smile had gone. 'Lead on, we'll be right behind you.'

As phallic symbols went, the Eiffel Tower had been through some pretty extensive cosmetic surgery.

As the convoy of diplomatic limousines cruised along the Champs Elysées, Andreas and Mara contemplated the wonders of modern French architecture.

'It's very . . .' commented Andreas, stumped for exactly the right word.

'Blue,' said Mara. 'It's very blue.'

Julian, the flunkey, cast a dispassionate eye over the thousand-metre-high structure which stuck up like a flaming arrow from the heart of Paris. He yawned elegantly.

'Well that's the French government for you,' he commented. 'Not like the British. Can't leave anything the way it used to be.'

'It used to be a heap of twisted metal,' Andreas remarked drily.

'Ah, but in Britain it would have been reconstructed using the finest traditional materials and techniques, restoring it to an exact replica of the original tower.' He sighed. 'And they used to say the Pompidou Centre was a pile of tat.'

Andreas tried to be impartial about the new Eiffel Tower. It wasn't very easy. Frankly it looked like something between a blue neon skyrocket and the helter-skelter at Skegness – only bigger. Slide down this bugger on a doormat and your arse would burst into flame. At the very top was a huge flashing Tricolore, and underneath it, not much smaller, a yellow and red McDonald's advertising hoarding. Even art had to move with the times, and the Americans had been more than generous in their donations.

The second-rate dignitaries of several dozen nations had assembled in the Champs de Mars for the inauguration ceremony. Limousines unloaded men and women in suits, flanked by gorillas with sunglasses. They weren't taking any chances this time.

Andreas turned to Mara. 'Coming?'

'Well, darling, that's the best offer I've had all day...'

She winked at him and uncrossed her legs. It was then that he realised she wasn't wearing any underwear. Her whisper-soft, eight-denier stockings stopped an inch above the hem of her kilt, and from there on up it was nothing but bare, smooth skin. In the dark triangle between Mara's thighs, Andreas made out the kissable frizz of her pubic curls. He looked at Julian. From the expression on his face, it was clear that he'd noticed too: he just couldn't believe his eyes.

Taking Mara's hand, Andreas pulled her out of the back of the car.

'Mara!'

She smiled into his outraged face and kissed him; whispering into his open mouth, 'I want you to fuck me.'

Andreas felt sweat gathering in tepid pools on his skin, making his clothes stick to him. He licked his lips nervously; they tasted salty. Despite his terror of discovery, his balls ached with a delicious, wicked anticipation.

'Mara, what the hell's got into you lately? Don't you care about blowing our cover?'

He saw a shadow of doubt creep across Mara's bright-eyed gaze, then it was gone. She giggled.

'Don't you care about fucking me any more, Andreas? If you can't satisfy me, I'll find someone who can.'

She turned and stalked off, Andreas following in her wake. Thankfully, the milling crowds of dignitaries and officials drew attention away from them. He was profoundly grateful for that; Mara wasn't exactly playing the shrinking violet, with that filmy silk shirt stretched provocatively tight over a red push-up bra, and that tiny grey kilt flouncing up and down as she walked. One decent gust of wind and the Eiffel Tower wasn't the only thing people would be getting an eyeful of.

They were ushered into their positions, in a specially built grandstand at the base of the tower. The guests were a real mixed bag: the Foreign Minister of Tanzania, the Saudi King's third cousin, a couple of heirs presumptive and fourteen cultural attachés. The Mayor of Paris droned on about international cooperation, tiny tots in red, white and blue lisped the Marseillaise, and Johnny Halliday and Jean-Michel Jarre thumped, bawled and gyrated their way through a ghastly version of the new European Anthem.

For the first ten minutes or so, Andreas did his best to look interested. His attention wandered. The Norwegian Ambassador's wife had the most spectacular breasts he had ever seen; he amused himself trying to guess her bra size. Forty-four D? No chance, double-D at the very least. Maybe even forty-six. A man could suffocate in there and die happy . . .

A sudden, extremely erotic sensation made him start. For a split second, he thought it was part of his daydream, but no. Mara, who was directly in front of him, was reaching back and running her long-nailed fingertips up and down the front of his trousers.

He froze. The sensation wasn't unpleasant, far from it. Mara had had him on the edge of madness all day long and all he wanted to do was throw her down on the ground, right there in front of the Regimental Band of the French Foreign Legion, push up that tiny, useless skirt and slide deep into her soft wetness. But here? Now? While the world's television cameras were watching?

'Mara,' he whispered into the nape of her neck. 'Are

you crazy? Not . . . here . . . !' But she simply looked at him over her shoulder. Smiling. Licking her lips.

Now – contrary to what the Master might think – Andreas Hunt was only human. His muffled protests were half-hearted at best, and the feel of Mara's cool fingers on his crotch was all the nicer for being forbidden. The crowd was packed tightly around them; no one could see what was going on, at least that was what Andreas told himself. In any case, they were all far too busy watching the topless cancan dancers to care about one Englishman and the cool white fingers unzipping his fly.

Julian was to his right, muttering something about 'yet more gratuitous nudity'. Andreas tried to listen and make the right kind of noises, but Mara's sharp-nailed fingers had burrowed their way inside his pants and were busy coaxing his hardness out into the warm circle of her palm.

' . . . might've guessed they'd get sex into it somehow . . .' sniffed Julian.

'Mmm?' grunted Andreas. He hoped it sounded questioning, but really it was a suppressed groan of agonised pleasure. Good as she had always been at hand-jobs, Mara had never before shown quite such an appreciation of the finer points of technique.

'Sex,' snapped Julian, turning his head towards Andreas. Andreas prayed his gaze wouldn't slip below waist height, thanking his lucky stars for the fat Belgian Ambassador whose corpulent buttocks were obscuring the view.

'W-what about it?'

'The French. They're obsessed with it.'

There was no answer to that, thought Andreas. If they *were* obsessed, he could quite understand why. Surely there could be nothing more compelling than the feel of silken fingers on a willing shaft; unless, of course, it was the feel of silken lips . . . of whichever kind.

As though reading his mind, Mara's fingers tightened, forming a firm sheath about his dick. She began working him back and forth with a slow, rhythmic deliberation which drove him to the edge of craziness.

'Of course . . .' droned on Julian, 'we're not like that.'

'We?' gasped Andreas.

He was losing the plot big-time. The spunk was boiling in his balls and he might reach the point of no return at any moment. He ought to be strong, push her away, not give into all these base urges. But he'd been away when they did moral fibre at school.

'The English. You don't catch us waving our genitalia in people's faces, do you?'

'Maybe it's the climate,' suggested Andreas weakly, his mind briefly filling with a picture of naked old-age pensioners strutting their stuff along Blackpool Prom in a force-ten gale. All those pink (and blue) floppy bits blowing about all over the place; strewth, it didn't bear thinking about.

The Parisian sunshine was hot and strong on the back of his neck, but it wasn't the weather that was making Andreas sweat. He was starting to shake, his whole body tense with the sheer inhuman effort of resisting pleasure.

'You reckon that's it? You could be right . . .'

Shut up, shut up, shut UP, cried a voice inside Andreas's head. Shut the fuck up, Julian, and watch the wobbling flesh, you know you love it really, you anal retentives are all the same.

He didn't reply to Julian's next question. He couldn't. Mara's nails were pressing with exquisite determination into the lust-hardened flesh of his dick. And that was all he needed to break down the very last barrier of his resistance. It took two, no, three quick strokes of her hand to finish him off, and it was all he could do not to shout out loud as the hot cream spurted out of him, all over . . .

All over what? Even as the last thrill of orgasm was dying away, panic gripped Andreas. What had he done? What trouble had he got himself into this time? His mind was filled with horrific imaginings: that Canadian bishop with a big wet patch up the back of his purple cassock; or the fat Belgian, wondering how he'd managed to get his trousers all sticky.

He needn't have worried on that score. Setting him free at last, Mara screwed her head round and – quite shamelessly and deliberately – raised her hand to her mouth. It was dripping and glistening with pearly white goo. She started to lick it off, as though it were melting ice cream.

The spell broken, Andreas fumbled with his fly and hurriedly zipped himself up. His heart was pounding in his chest; but maybe, just maybe, nobody had noticed what had happened.

Then he saw her. She was standing with the Caribbean delegation, a cool six-footer with skin like caramel and a tumbling mass of oiled black curls. A sort of black Cher, thought Andreas; high-cheekboned and almond-eyed. What, in his days as a tabloid hack, he would definitely have described as a Stunna.

And those dark eyes were fixed on him, her lips curled very slightly at the corners as if . . . as if she *knew*. He felt drawn to her, mesmerised by her though he knew nothing about her. And he might have stood staring at her for ever if she hadn't chosen that moment to turn her back on him.

His pulse steadied to a dull thump-thump. Julian wittered on about taste and decency and how unattractive testicles were when they bounced up and down like that. And Mara licked her fingers like a greedy kitten, lapping until every last drop was gone, as serene as if nothing at all had happened.

The Master contemplated his prize.

It was small, insignificant-looking and priceless; sitting quite innocuously at the centre of a pentagram, within a septagram, within a circle. You couldn't be too careful, not where unlimited power was concerned.

The curtains of the boardroom were drawn tightly shut, esoteric patterns drawn on them in blood. No ordinary blood, either; this had been taken from the soft, shaven pubis of a Romany woman with second sight.

One last drop of blood remained. Standing over the small piece of stone, the Master raised his finger. The droplet of blood hung from its tip, a trembling crimson bead. Without a word, he let it fall onto the stone.

At first, nothing happened. And then the room began to darken, as though the sky had become cloudy outside. What was that sound? A creaking, like the sound of rusty door hinges or old floorboards, sagging underfoot. Then the whole room lurched to one side, so suddenly that the Master had to put out his hand to stop himself falling over.

When the room righted itself, he realised that it was no longer the boardroom, but somewhere quite different; a place that he had once known very well. He was standing in the captain's cabin on his own slave ship, the *Plaisir de Mort*, many years ago when he had sought to build his empire of lust in the Indies . . .

A tumult of light and sound surrounded him. He waited a few moments, until his senses had accustomed themselves to this new environment. The ship was in full sail, running with the wind, rolling as she rode the choppy, sunlit waves.

The Master made to reach out and open the door, but his hand met no resistance and the next thing he knew, he was walking straight through the solid oak to whatever lay on the other side.

He found himself in the hold of the *Plaisir de Mort*. Row upon row of naked bodies glistened with sweat in the hot, foetid twilight; muscular backs heaving, wrists weighted with clanking chains. He caught his breath. For at the far end of the hold he saw himself as he used to be, in his old and as yet uncorrupted body. Hundreds of years before the sorcerers had duped him and imprisoned him in crystal; before his fugitive spirit had been forced to take refuge in the body of Andreas Hunt.

His body, his own, beautiful body. The body he had occupied for four thousand years. And yet . . . it seemed stiff and immobile. He glanced about him. *Everything* seemed frozen in time. He moved forward, disregarding everything but the lone figure standing before him. Such beauty.

'I had almost forgotten,' he murmured, 'how beautiful I once was.'

Desire stirred within him. His one-time self was magnificent in frilled white shirt, unlaced to the waist, tight fawn breeches and polished knee boots, a cutlass thrust through the belt. He yearned to run his hands over that perfect body, to kneel before it and strip down those breeches, to run his tongue over bare thighs and that smooth, thick shaft. To pay homage to his matchless self.

And more. Instinctively, he stroked his penis through his sober mohair suit. He imagined the sublime pleasure of being taken by his own self, by the only being worthy of penetrating his sublime arse. And the thought made his stiffened cock ooze moisture.

When he looked again at his old self, he realised that he was no longer alone. Recognition slashed through him like a sharpened knife blade. Kneeling before him, her head in his hands, was a golden-skinned Indian woman, a Zanzibar priestess he would never – could never – forget. She was exquisitely beautiful, high-cheekboned with almond eyes and oiled black curls that tumbled like lamb's fleece down her bare, caramel-smooth back.

Desire and loathing stirred within him, the one serving

only to strengthen the other. This was the woman who had led his slaves in rebellion against him, forcing him from Isla Venemo and concealing it forever from him with her cursed magic. He watched his old self, fingers claw-like about her face, twisting her hair, forcing her protesting lips down onto his erect prick. There was a look of joyful power on his face.

Such a beautiful prick. The most beautiful thing the Master had ever seen.

He extended his finger, to caress his old shaft once again; and as his fingertip made contact, he felt himself poured like hot liquid into his old body. Breath caught in his lungs. And then he felt sudden, sharp pain, as the woman closed her teeth on his penis.

'Bitch!'

The pain angered yet excited him. He gazed down at her. Her dark eyes blazed defiance. He kicked her away from him.

'Take her. Strip her, I intend to teach her a lesson in obedience.'

Rough men, *his* men, laughed as they took the woman and threw her down on the deck. Already bare from the waist up, she kicked and scratched and shrieked as they cut away her skirt and forced her naked backside into the air, pinning her down by the shoulders.

'She's good an' ready for you, Master.'

'Take 'er, Master. She's wet an' willin'.'

He stood over her, seizing her by the hips and forcing her wriggling backside higher, opening up her treasure chest with brutal fingers. The tight, chestnut-brown dot of her anus beckoned him, dared him, maddened him with lascivious hunger.

She screamed curses at him as he pushed his dick into her, making her take him right down to the balls, delighting in her humiliation as he stole her last virginity.

'Bastard! Bastard, burn in Hell . . .'

But he threw back his head and laughed. Hell? Let the foolish bitch threaten him with Hell, he knew more of that place than she would ever dream in her blackest nightmares. Hell was his dark soul's haven.

He had been waiting centuries for this delicious revenge. With each thrust of his hips he came closer to the ecstasy of triumph. The flesh of her arse-cheeks reddened to the squeezing and scratching of his devouring fingers and he watched with pleasure as her treacherous pussy began to swell and dilate, betraying her unwilling pleasure.

His climax came violently; in a single, shuddering jet of semen that stole his breath away and threw him into a wildly spinning vortex. He was dizzy, disoriented, lost . . . and suddenly, everything went black.

The Master awoke at the centre of his circle. The tiny, precious fragment of stone had been reduced to smouldering ash.

Slowly and stiffly, he got to his feet, his mind adjusting with difficulty to the present. In his many centuries of life, the Master had forgotten many things; but that incident on the slave ship was as fresh in his memory as if it had been mere seconds ago.

He reached down and ran his fingers over his dick, wincing. It was still sore from the priestess's teeth. And it was then that he realised. It *had* happened only seconds ago.

'You want to go *shopping*?'

'That's right, Andreas. I'm going to spend, spend, spend. This is Paris, remember! And I'm going to make the most of it while we're here.'

'Mara . . .'

'Fashion, jewellery, *objets d'art* . . .'

Taken aback, Andreas shrugged and sighed.

'OK then, I'll come with you.'

Mara kissed Andreas, her fingertips scratching lightly down over his back.

'No need, you'd only be bored. See you later.'

Andreas watched Mara skip down the steps of the Hôtel Georges V with a mixture of bafflement and suspicion. Mara? Shopping? The two concepts just didn't go together. She wasn't the type to spend a fortune on designer gear and, besides, she'd been behaving out of character ever since that day when she'd blacked out. Maybe it was time he tried to find out why.

The tiny part of Andreas Hunt that was still one of Britain's top sleaze journos nudged him into action. He gave her just long enough to get round the corner of the hotel, then slipped on his jacket and legged it after her, keeping close enough to see where she went but far enough behind not to draw attention.

He followed her with a newshound's cunning, darting behind lampposts and into doorways, blending into shadows, even grabbing a complete stranger and kissing her when Mara turned round unexpectedly and he was sure she was about to spot him.

'*Monsieur! Laissez-moi immédiatement!*'

'*Pardon, madame.*' He grinned cheesily. '*Ne parle pas français.*'

He hurried on up the street, in pursuit of Mara. Apart from a slapped face, it was all going quite nicely.

What wasn't so nice was the red-light district Mara led him straight into. Not that he felt at all uncomfortable there. In fact he blended into the crowd straightaway. Pimps, punters, sleazeballs and private eyes – they were his kind of people. But Mara's? Hell no.

He turned the corner and encountered a seething mass of humanity. Somebody had started a fight and it had spilled out of one of the strip joints onto the pavement, watched enthusiastically by half a dozen half-naked girls and a couple of men in string vests.

'*Excusez-moi, excusez* . . .'

He pushed his way through, but when he got to the other side of the crowd Mara was gone. Bloody hell. That was just plain careless. He imagined what his old editor at the *Comet* would have said. 'Hunt, face it; you're a useless cunt.' Well, that just about summed it up.

But wait a mo . . .

That couldn't be Mara. Could it? He knew in his heart of hearts that it was, though he could hardly believe it. She was walking down the steps of a whorehouse, bold as brass and dressed like one. The tasselled bra, leopardskin hot-pants and white patent-leather thigh boots left no room for ambiguity. Mara Fleming was dressed as a hooker; and if Andreas wasn't very much mistaken, she was on the lookout for business.

He didn't have to follow her much further. About a hundred yards down the street, she disappeared into a sex shop. Two minutes later, she emerged with a middle-aged, rough-looking bloke with a week's growth of beard. Andreas almost stepped out in front of her, asked her what the hell she thought she was doing in a place like this, but something held him back.

Mara and the bloke walked round the corner, into an alleyway where an old white Citroën was parked by the kerb. The bloke opened the rear passenger door and Mara slid in. She was laughing, Andreas saw; but her eyes seemed glazed and distant, not like Mara's at all.

The minute the bloke got into the back of the car with her, Mara was all over him, unzipping him and going down on him right away; not apathetically and mechanically, like a seasoned hooker, but hungrily like a ravenous beast. When she'd drunk him dry, she ripped down her shorts and wanked him back into hardness, straddling him and pumping down hard until his cock jerked and spat.

Andreas might have stood and stared for ever, if a sound somewhere behind him hadn't distracted him. Instinctively alarmed, he spun round and ducked, and brownish-white wings flashed over his head. Just a tatty-looking pigeon.

Relieved, he turned back towards the car. But it was gone.

And so was Mara.

Chapter 3

When Andreas got back to the hotel suite, the TV was droning out Canal+, but he could still make out an undercurrent of soft moaning, coming from the bathroom.

He followed the sound through the doorway and into the bathroom. He stopped dead in his tracks. Mara was half naked and covered in sweat, crouching on the floor. Her blouse was ripped open and her breasts were squeezed between her hands. Andreas realised with a shock that she was straining desperately to suck her own nipples. She was murmuring, whimpering, 'Please, please, oh I must, oh please . . .'

'Mara?'

She looked up at him, her face filling with hope and lust.

'Andreas! You've come! Where have you been?' Her hands reached up at him, clawing, drawing him down.

'I might ask the same thing,' he muttered uneasily, but Mara wasn't listening.

'I'm so glad you're here. Oh hurry, Andreas, I want you. I *need* you. I'm soooo wet.'

He had meant to get the truth out of her, there and then, only watching Mara getting it on with a stranger in a car had turned Andreas on more than he realised. Either that or it was a hot day and he hadn't had it in . . . oh . . . hours. At any rate, he found himself willingly sinking down onto Mara's generous breasts, burying his face between them, licking the salty, perfumed sweat which trickled between them.

'Suck me. Suck my nipples.' Mara's voice was hoarse with urgency. She took her pierced left breast and forced the hard, rubbery nipple against his lips.

He took it in, rolling it between tongue and palate, nipping it gently between his teeth, toying with the ring so that it turned round and round, caressing her flesh from within.

'Harder!'

He obeyed, but he was afraid of hurting her; and no matter how roughly he sucked and bit her, it didn't seem enough to satisfy Mara. Her hips bucked and gyrated, her whole body writhing and trembling, in the grip of a sexual frenzy the like of which Andreas had never seen before. And all the time she was ripping the clothes from his body, tearing at the zips and buttons, lavishing rough caresses on his aching manhood.

When he came up for air, Mara began kissing him, pressing her lips savagely all over his bare skin, leaving red imprints where her melting lipstick mingled with his sweat.

'Come between my breasts,' she whispered, and she slid onto her back on the tiled floor, pushing her breasts hard together about the sleek length of his shaft.

He enjoyed it, there was no denying that. But there was an undercurrent of something else; uneasiness? Fear? It was hard to give it a name. It was something dark that lingered just out of eyeshot, a chill breeze on a sweltering summer's day. But nothing dark enough or cold enough to stop the pleasure from leading him on, making him thrust again and again between her breasts, until pleasure could only be a matter of seconds away.

At the apex of every stroke, Mara put out her tongue, licking the juices from his glans. Sometimes she wriggled her tongue-tip, so that its point found its way into the small, deep well at the end of his cock. It was too much to bear and he came all over her face, watching her in curious fascination as she began to lick his semen from her skin with long, slow, lapping movements.

As Mara rolled onto her back and presented him with the perfect globes of her backside, Andreas allowed himself to relax a little. Maybe he'd been overreacting. When all was said and done, this was just sex; nice, normal, animalistic sex.

It was then that something on the TV caught his attention. A minor news item, so minor that it barely made the end of the early-evening bulletin. Something about the 'Paris Vampire'. He strained to catch the details, and almost wished he hadn't. For the second time in two days, a man had been found dead in his car, drained of all his juices . . .

Mara bit her lip. Her legs ached and trembled as she struggled to keep the lotus position, willing her mind to seek out some corner of tranquillity.

Around her in the darkened hotel room, candles guttered in an intangible breeze, raising the tiny hairs on the backs of her hands, making her shiver. She wasn't sure why.

Questions tumbled over and over in her brain. Why had Andreas been acting so strangely towards her? And, more worryingly still, why had she been having these sudden, unaccountable blackouts? Not just seconds or minutes, but hours lost at a time; and afterwards she remembered nothing of what had happened. She wondered why nobody had said anything about it.

Then there were the curious sexual urges, potent and equally sudden. Urges to touch herself, to fuck, to do things that even she had thought were beyond her imagination. Something very odd was happening to her, and she wanted desperately to know what it was.

Letting her gaze move down her body, Mara contemplated the ring passing through her left nipple. When did that happen? Focusing on it, she relived her last clear memory. She remembered that she and Andreas had been summoned to Docklands by the Master. Then Graveney's story about the little stone – and the stone itself, so needle-bright and sharp as the Master had stabbed it through her nipple. Then the weirdest sensation of all. The sensation of falling through time . . .

Followed by utter darkness.

The candle flames flared up like bars around her and a terrible drumming sound filled her ears.

'No. No!'

Fingers of meaningless, wordless dread were climbing her spine, tracing icy patterns on her skin. She shook, the sound growing louder, faster and more frantic, until it seemed to fill the whole world with a terrible, shrieking vibration.

She collapsed to the floor, unconscious; spilt candle wax dripping unheeded onto the back of her motionless hand.

It was perhaps minutes, perhaps only seconds, before her eyes opened. But they did not look like Mara Fleming's eyes, though they were the same shade of deep, luminous emerald.

Pushing herself up onto her haunches, Mara tossed back her long auburn hair and grinned. The effect was predatory and triumphant. Her moist lips parted and she whispered in a new and menacing voice.

'So. At last.'

She looked down at the clothes she was wearing: a floaty, semi-diaphanous skirt of thin Indian muslin and a cropped white tee-shirt through which her nipple ring showed like a tiny O. She sneered.

'This may be good enough for you, bitch, but then you never did have style.'

Her long fingernails clawed at the thin cotton, tearing it away, ripping it from her body. The pungent scents of sweat and sex rose up from her skin as she revealed her nakedness, stripping down her tiny white panties and dropping them to the ground.

Now she was naked, save for the nipple ring and a gold ankle bracelet. Laughing softly, she knelt up, closing her eyes and exploring her body with her hands.

'Beautiful,' she murmured. 'Every bit as beautiful as I remember. And far too beautiful to be wasted on a cheap slut like you, Mara Fleming.'

The flats of her hands moved smoothly and lightly over her sweat-streaked skin, discovering the generous contours of her heavy yet buoyant breasts, teasing the hard pink plugs of her nipples; making circular movements round and round those miniature pleasure centres until she growled with satisfaction.

Moving slowly down, she smoothed over the long, curving sweep of her back to the blossoming swell of her backside, its glorious curves emphasised by the tightness of her small waist.

'You *are* beautiful,' she repeated, her breathing slower and more laboured as desire overtook her. 'The most beautiful, potent, sensual creature in the universe. And soon, everyone will know your power.'

With a growl of lust, she reached out and plucked a candle from one of the overturned candelabra. It was eighteen inches long and more than two inches in diameter, smooth and divinely strokeable.

She ran her fingers along its length, smoothing it over her lips and cheeks. It was warm and fragrant, as sensual and desirable as a lover's dick.

'Come to Mistress Anastasia, my slave,' she whispered, kissing its tip. 'Pleasure me.'

Rocking back onto her haunches, she opened her legs, baring the dew-spangled triangle of her pubic curls and the wet-mouthed slit of her pussy.

'Want it, want it, want it,' she murmured. 'Got to have it, now, now, now.'

The thick tip of the candle stretched the lips of her sex, making her purr with gratification. Her luscious red lips framed more urgent demands, forcing the candle deeper and deeper into her womanhood.

'More! More, more. I want to take *all* of you.'

Throwing back her head, she spread her thighs wide and thrust the candle into the very heart of her sex.

'Yes! Ah yes. At last. At last . . . If only I had two dicks inside my pussy, another two in my arse, another in my mouth, another covering my belly with hot seed . . .'

She jerked and sighed as she brought herself to orgasm, sliding the candle out of her with infinite slowness. It glistened and dripped in the flickering candlelight. Thirstily, she raised it to her lips and let the droplets of honeydew fall onto her tongue.

Then she smiled to herself.

'Mara, you foolish little witch. Your enemy is me. Your enemy is *yourself*.'

The week-long Eiffel Tower celebrations were beginning to get Andreas down. Not only was he becoming very tired of the *Marseillaise* and warm champagne, he was also increasingly worried about Mara.

At the black-tie reception in the new wing of the Louvre, Andreas fidgeted uneasily, running his finger round and round the rim of his glass. It made an interesting squeaking noise, and people kept turning round and staring at him, but he scarcely noticed. Andreas Hunt was not a happy bunny.

Mara had gone off to the Ladies', to do whatever it was that girls did in the loo. He missed her. No, he missed having her the way she always used to be, the *normal* Mara. Well maybe not normal. Weird, yeah. Psychic, definitely. Hot sex-slut with attitude, woof, woof. But this new sex-'n'-shopping Mara, this unpredictably voracious and sometimes downright spooky Mara, well, he wasn't quite sure he could cope. You never knew what she was going to get up to next.

Still, at least whatever she was doing in the loo, she wasn't doing it out here, in front of five hundred hand-picked guests. He turned a shade paler as he remembered how Mara had started feeling up the wife of the French Foreign Minister during a garden party at the Elysée Palace. Just as well it had turned out that she *liked* that kind of thing.

He was just wondering what shit Mara might land them in next when a sweet, syrupy voice insinuated its way into his thoughts.

'Still, you never can tell what may happen. Isn't that so, Mr Hunt?'

He started. Looked up. Right into the face of the woman he'd seen watching him at the Eiffel Tower ceremony. Tall, black, beautiful, her tumbling hair piled high on her head and her enviable figure poured into an elegant evening gown that shimmered with every sinuous movement.

He gaped, running his finger around the inside of his wing collar, which had suddenly become very tight and constricting.

'I'm . . . sorry?'

The very tip of a rose-pink tongue flicked over the full lips, making the plum-coloured lipstick glisten wetly.

'No, please, I'm the one who should be apologising. I didn't mean to startle you.' She extended a slim, elegant hand on which rings sparkled. The designs were as exotic as the woman, the gems huge and very real. 'I'm Anjula.' The voice was accented; French but not quite French, sexy and very, very exotic.

He took her hand and – on an uncharacteristically romantic impulse – pressed it to his lips. It was silky-smooth and very cool.

'I . . . er . . . didn't I see you at the Eiffel Tower?' he asked. Hunt, he scolded himself, you're pathetic. A beautiful woman with a gorgeous body comes on to you, and you can't even think of an original chat-up line.

A faint smile flickered over the plum-glossed lips. Andreas wondered just how much Anjula had seen of his and Mara's command performance.

'Yes. Yes, I think you probably did.' She took a glass from a passing tray and nibbled the cherry from her champagne cocktail. 'I certainly noticed you. I hear you're with the British delegation.'

'Yes. I'm . . . er . . . deputising for Anthony LeMaître, he . . . couldn't make it.'

Anjula laughed. It was a deep, husky, dirty laugh, and it made Andreas pant with enthusiastic lust.

'You mean, he had something better to do than stand around listening to Johnny Halliday?'

'Something like that. And you?'

Anjula shrugged.

'I'm from Isla Venemo.'

'Where?'

'Don't worry, no one has ever heard of it. It's . . . a little French dependency . . . near the Bahamas.'

'Your English is excellent.'

It was the only thing Andreas could think of to say. His attention was more than taken up by the contemplation of Anjula's breathtaking body, moving like warm oil underneath that sequinned sheath dress. With every breath she took, her bra-less breasts rose and fell and her firm flesh quivered, so teasingly kissable that Andreas could hardly restrain himself from touching. He reminded the aching erection in his pants that it was rude to point, but it didn't take a blind bit of notice.

'You're very kind.'

'And you're very . . . attractive.'

Their eyes met. Andreas was pretty sure that Anjula knew exactly what he meant. What's more, she wasn't blind or stupid, and there was no way she'd have missed the

54

painfully huge bulge which had appeared at the front of his trousers. He shifted position slightly, hoping to make it less obvious, but the friction of his underpants on the head of his cock only made the agony of lust all the more intense.

'Do you like Paris?'

'In . . . small doses.'

Anjula took another sip of champagne.

'I've always found it a very sensual city. The sort of city where two perfect strangers might meet and make love on a sultry summer afternoon, then part and never see each other again . . .'

He couldn't take his eyes off her. As she moved away from the subject of sexual fantasy to talk about something and nothing, he half-listened, made all the right noises, but all the time his eyes were straining for glimpses of the so-alluring shape of her underneath that thin, skin-skimming gown.

' . . . don't you agree?'

'What? Oh. Oh yes . . . absolutely.'

Absolutely sensational, thought Andreas, saliva filling his mouth as though he were anticipating a juicy sirloin steak. Those thighs . . . just look how firm they were, how athletic underneath the clinging skirt. And when Anjula shifted her weight onto her left foot, that dazzling glimpse of shimmering, stockinged thigh, visible for just a few tantalising seconds through the side split in her gown.

' . . . do you like it?'

Like it? He loved it.

'Hmm?' he murmured.

'Jet-skiing. Do you like it? It's very popular in the Caribbean, the sea is so warm . . .'

But not as warm as the deep valley between those breasts, thought Andreas. Or the abundant juice whose fragrance he could almost believe filled his nostrils; the sweet ooze he imagined between those thighs. God, how he longed to lie between those thighs. Or maybe *under* those thighs. Oh yes, hell that was a horny thought. To be tied down, perfectly helpless, while Anjula knelt over him and pumped down on his aching, straining cock . . .

'You know, Mr Hunt, I would love you to visit my island.'

Andreas noticed how she emphasised the 'my', almost as if the whole island belonged to her.

'Well, I . . .'

'Take this. Please.'

'W-what?'

Forcing himself to snap out of the trance, Andreas looked down. Anjula was pressing something into his hand. A tiny piece of that funny greenish-grey stone. How bizarre. He was just about to ask her where she'd got it from when another voice cut in.

'Andreas! Andreas, is something wrong?'

He swung round, slipping the piece of stone into his pocket. Mara was standing behind him. She looked . . . worried.

'Wrong? Why should anything be wrong?'

'No special reason.' Mara kissed him on the cheek. 'Only you were staring into space. You looked miles away.'

Andreas half turned to one side, meaning to introduce Mara to Anjula. But Anjula was gone.

'I don't understand. A minute ago . . .'

Mara laid a hand on his arm.

'Andreas . . .'

He rounded on her, uncharacteristically edgy.

'For fuck's sake, don't call me that! Someone will hear. Call me Nick. You know . . . that's . . .'

He hesitated, brought up short by a sudden realisation.

'What?'

'You know that's who I'm supposed to be. Nicholas Weatherall MP.'

Hold on though, said a tiny voice in Andreas's head. To

the world you may be Nick Weatherall, but to Anjula . . .

His blood pressure rose ten points. Anjula had known who he really was. Anjula had called him Andreas Hunt.

Chapter 4

Mara pouted so prettily when she wanted something. They'd just spent two hours rolling around on the king-size hotel bed but, even so, that look on her face made Andreas horny all over again.

She knelt over him, her full breasts half in and half out of her pink satin bra cups.

'Do you *have* to go?'

Andreas pulled her down until she was close enough for her nipple ring to skim his bare chest. He took it into his mouth and teased it a little. He was tempted. Very tempted.

''Fraid so,' he said. 'There'll be trouble if I don't.'

'Trouble . . . from the Master?'

'Don't worry, Mara. It's just one of these boring evening meetings. I'll be fine.'

He avoided her gaze by burying his face in her cleavage and licking the foothills of her breasts. If he looked her in the eye, he was sure she'd know instantly that he was lying. He was a rotten liar, and knowing that Mara was psychic didn't help. The fact was, he'd invented the evening meeting as a means of getting away for a few hours. He needed an excuse – a way of finding out what Mara got up to when he wasn't there.

Andreas felt a bit guilty about the deception, but he couldn't think of any other way. He had to know what was wrong with Mara. Maybe the Master had done something to her, maybe she was ill, maybe . . . there were just too many maybes for his liking.

'Feels nice,' sighed Mara. She was her normal, delicious, irresistibly sexy self this evening, and Andreas began to have doubts about his own doubts. There was nothing wrong with Mara. She was perfect.

'You taste good,' he murmured, pulling down her bra straps and unhooking the catch at the back. The large, firm globes of her breasts spilled forward into his hands and he stroked and kneaded them, pushing them together and taking both nipples into his mouth. 'Good enough to eat.'

'Mmm. Yes. Taste me. Do it harder.' Mara wriggled delightedly as he squeezed and sucked her nipples, and the sweet, heavy fragrance rising from between her parted thighs was intoxicatingly seductive. Her discarded panties lay half underneath her on the rumpled bedsheet, a testimony to the urgency of their first coupling. Now Andreas wanted her madly, all over again.

'Tell me what you want me to do.'

'Bite me.'

'Like this?'

'Mmm, yes. But harder. And don't stop.'

As he was nibbling and sucking at her erect nipples, she lowered herself smoothly onto his dancing prick. It never took long for Mara to make him hard again, no matter how many times he'd come. And the sensations were just as exquisite, whether it was the first time or the tenth. And frankly, Andreas wasn't counting.

Once he was inside her, Andreas rolled over onto his side, taking Mara with him. They tumbled gleefully into a squirming, thrusting heap, Andreas bracing his back against the wall as Mara wrapped her legs around his hips and forced the pleasure out of him.

'How is it', he panted, 'that you always, *always* know what I want?'

Mara giggled and rubbed her glistening breasts over his chest. He felt her tighten her sex muscles, squeezing them into an exquisitely narrow sheath about his dick.

'Call it . . . intuition.'

And, reading his dirtiest thoughts yet again, Mara screwed her whole body round ninety degrees, so that she was fucking him at an angle, making him penetrate her even more deeply. It felt . . . bloody great.

'You're a witch, Mara Fleming.'

'I'll take that as a compliment.'

He slipped his hand round underneath her buttocks and allowed one finger to sneak into the dark, deep cleft between them.

'I know what *you* like, too,' he whispered in Mara's ear. And, wetting his finger at the eternal spring of her pussy juices, he darted it deep into the tight hole of her anus.

'Ah!' she squealed, not at the intrusion but at the delightful suddenness of it. Now she was dancing like a ballerina, grinding her pubis against the root of his dick, and all the time forcing herself up and down on the smaller spike of his intrepid finger.

Andreas held back for as long as he could. He hadn't meant to come at all – hadn't even thought he could – but Mara's sensual skills could resurrect the dead, and he wasn't quite that far gone. And when she sighed and moaned and he felt her pussy twitch about his dick, he knew he was done for. He collapsed on top of her in an untidy, sweat-soaked heap, floating in a pool of delicious stickiness.

Sleepy with pleasure, he glanced at the clock on the bedside table. He yawned and rolled over.

'Got to go,' he mumbled.

'No, stay.'

'Wish I could.' He gave her a last, lingering kiss, then padded reluctantly off to the bathroom for a much-needed shower. Mara called after him.

'Are you wearing that new Armani tonight?'

He stuck his head out through the bathroom door.

'Nah, too flashy. The grey chinos'll do.'

Mara slid off the bed, shaking her tousled hair back over her shoulders.

'Tell you what, Andreas . . .'

'Hmm?'

She winked.

'If you're a *very* good boy, I'll help you get dressed.'

It was way past eight when Andreas finally emerged from the Hôtel Georges V. Mara's idea of 'helping' him to dress had involved more taking off of clothes than putting them on, and frankly he felt less than enthusiastic about hanging around on street corners when he could be taking a shower with Mara. A long, luxurious, sticky one; and then another one to get clean.

He found a seedy street corner; as an ex-tabloid journo it came as second nature. Time passed. He spent it people-watching, half an eye out for Mara while the rest of his attention was taken up by the kind of street-life that crawled out of Parisian gutters when night fell.

The hooker on the opposite corner of the street winked at him and blew him a kiss. She was leaning against a lamppost, smoking a Gauloise and sticking out one plump hip. Her PVC miniskirt was more like a wide belt, a six-inch strip of scarlet which skimmed her hips and made no attempt to conceal the lacy tops of her fishnet stockings. High-heeled red ankle boots and a black sequinned bustier completed the effect: cheap, tarty and very, very tempting. Kind of fast food for the sexual appetite.

'*Tu veux, chéri?*' whispered a sexy voice in his ear. Andreas jumped. He hadn't noticed the other streetwalker, sidling up to him as he stared in the opposite direction.

He shook his head.

'Not tonight, darling.'

'Engleesh? You are Engleesh, *chéri? Ah, que j'adore les anglais, que j'aimerais bien te sucer les couilles . . .*'

Now, Andreas's French wasn't up to much, but he got

the gist all right. The girl with the honey-coloured eyes and the tiny black dress was cupping his balls in her long, strong fingers. Even drained by Mara's expert lips, they ached with a kind of wistful longing.

'Down boy,' muttered Andreas, gently but firmly pushing away the hooker's hand and adjusting himself into a more comfortable position.

'*Je m'en fous*,' snapped the hooker, and turned her back on him, grinding out her cigarette on the toe of his shoe.

People passed by. Andreas's tabloid mind hazarded a few shrewd guesses about some of their lives. Businessman . . . you could tell by the mobile phone and the Rolex. Rich but no taste. Never polishes his shoes, just buys a new pair. That girl . . . the one walking just in front of him . . . she's tasty, cheap too but no hooker. He smiled. You're his bit on the side, aren't you, darling? You're pretending you're not with each other, but you're going back to his place . . . or yours . . . for a bit of illicit slap and tickle . . . Wonder if there's a front-page headline in there somewhere.

The game amused him. He could have played it for hours if he hadn't spotted Mara coming down the hotel steps. He followed her, not without difficulty; the streets were seething with people and it wasn't easy to keep out of sight without losing her in the crowd.

Mind you, once you'd got sight of Mara it was hard not to keep looking at her. Tonight, she was dressed to kill.

He'd never seen her dressed this way before, well, not from choice. What the Master commanded them both to do was something else. But tonight, Mara was dressed for a party, no ordinary party either. Her body was encased in leopardskin Lycra, a brief, clingy sheath which hugged her breasts and dared him not to stare at the deep, dark line between her rounded buttocks. White patent knee boots and matching elbow-length gloves contrasted with the black ostrich boa she wore trailed provocatively over one bare shoulder.

She took the second turning on the left, and headed for the Metro. Andreas struggled to keep up. She was walking quickly, as though she was eager to reach her destination. He bought a ticket and just managed to leap on board the train before the doors closed.

The carriage was cramped and crammed. He glanced around him. Everything looked slightly unreal behind a blue haze of cigarette smoke. Nobody, but nobody, smiled. They were all here, all the scum of the earth: beggars, clubbers, hookers – and Andreas Hunt.

Just when he was least expecting it, he spotted Mara getting off the train.

'Oh fuck, no. '*Scusez-moi, comprenez*? Get the fuck out the way, will you?'

Pursued by curses and the ache of an elbow in the ribs, he managed to squeeze himself out onto the platform. Mara was already in the distance, stepping onto the escalator. He couldn't let her get away from him, he had his pride.

Gasping like a stranded cod, he ran up the escalator, two steps at a time, and followed her out into the street. Dusk had fallen over the city, clothing it in mystery. They were in some kind of nightclub quarter. Neon lights flashed above doorways: CLUB ZSA-ZSA, NITE-CLUB, CLUB MARQUIS, LE VICE ANGLAIS.

He was just in time to see Mara walk through the doorway of the Club Atlantis and down a flight of steps, out of his sight. He followed close behind, only to be brought up short by two tons of concrete in a tuxedo.

'*Carte d'identité, m'sieur*.' A square hand was thrust in Andreas's face.

'What?'

'*Carte d'identité. Vous êtes membre du club*?'

Bugger, thought Andreas. Membership, why didn't I think of that? He shrugged, feigning ignorance; it had worked once, at the Hippodrome in Leicester Square when the editor had sent him off to get an exposé on rubber fetishism. The doorman had dubbed his raincoat 'retro chic'.

'*Anglais*,' he hazarded. '*Ne comprends pas*.'

The concrete features did not soften one iota.

'Membership, m'sieur,' said the bouncer, in almost unaccented English. 'Your membership card.'

'I haven't got one.'

'Then you cannot come in. It is members only, very exclusive.'

'How do I join?'

'I have told you, M'sieur, it is very. . .'

Andreas forestalled any further arguments by taking his hand out of his jacket pocket. Three neatly folded hundred-franc notes just happened to have found their way into his hand, he couldn't think how. He waved them about a bit. Two minutes later he was a fully paid-up member of the Club Atlantis.

In truth, 'exclusive' wasn't quite the word for the Club Atlantis. It just wasn't the sort of place you'd take your Great-Aunt Maud for a cream tea.

State-of-the-art lighting had turned the basement club into a world beneath the sea. Blue, green, turquoise, shot through with flashes of orange, white and flame-red, swirled around and over the faces of the dancers. Not that most of them were dancing. They were standing and watching, one or two of them masturbating. Andreas couldn't blame them; it was one hell of an erotic cabaret.

A man beside him nudged his elbow, raising his voice to make himself heard over the mind-numbing trance music.

'You're English?'

'That's right. And you?'

'American. Buy you a drink?'

Andreas couldn't take his eyes off the figures at the centre of the dance floor. But he was here to watch, to learn, not to make a scene. He nodded. His mouth was dry, he could do with a stiff drink.

'Thanks. Scotch on the rocks.'

The American snapped his fingers.

'Make that a double.' He paid for the drinks then turned his back to the bar and stood beside Andreas, observing the impromptu floor show. 'Some show, huh?'

'You . . . could say.'

'Wanna screw her? You only gotta ask and wait your turn. She's insatiable.' He grinned. 'Me, I prefer to watch if you know what I mean.'

Andreas just kept on staring. He didn't know why it tore at his guts to see Mara getting it on with three strangers in a nightclub. It wasn't as if he hadn't seen her screw other men before – lots of other men. And he'd enjoyed his share of other women. But it was something about the way she was doing it, something about the expression on her face. It was cruel, triumphant, lascivious . . . and it wasn't Mara.

Something terrible was happening to her. He knew that for certain now. But what, that was the question that ate away at him.

He sipped his drink and forced himself to look. Mara was at the very centre of the dance floor, a pale green spotlight trained on her to give the other members the best possible view. It had started off as dancing, sure; well, a kind of dancing. An erotic rubbing of body against body and Mara had no shortage of willing partners. But now she had three partners all at once, and what they were doing wasn't dancing in anybody's language.

There was a big black guy, stripped to the waist and gleaming with oiled muscle. He moved in time to the music, but his dance was pure sex. Mara was moving with him, her body clinging to his as she slithered down, down, down to the polished dance floor. As she did so, his fingers caught the hem of her too-short skirt and rolled it up, exposing

66

the tops of pale stockings and an expanse of bare, smooth skin.

Andreas felt hot, cold, angry, turned-on. He drained his glass but his lips were still parched. He wanted her, he hated her, he adored her, he needed her lips around his dick.

'She's good, huh?' commented the American voice at his elbow. 'Some talent.'

'Yeah.' Andreas ordered another double. He needed it. 'Tabatha Cash eat your heart out.'

His eyes followed Mara's every movement, mesmerised by the lustre of her white flesh as sleek black hands peeled down tiny pink panties and flung them into the cheering crowd. She was down on the floor, kneeling up doggy-style, her leopardskin sheath concertinaed round her waist and her rump thrust out, shamelessly bare. Her head was up and she was laughing, her painted lips forming a provocatively large red circle. He heard her voice above the disco beat, 'I want you. I want to have you *all*. Come on. Take me, all of you. I want you to take me. Can't you see how hungry I am?'

Andreas shivered. He was caught somewhere between *Carry On* Heaven and *Hammer Horror* Hell. There could be few sights more stimulating than Mara Fleming on her knees, inviting anyone who wanted her to screw her there and then, while Andreas watched. On the other hand, Andreas had the disturbing impression that whoever it was he was looking at, however much she looked and tasted and smelt like Mara, it wasn't Mara Fleming who was pulling the strings. Even her voice sounded different. Not like Mara's at all. Deeper, huskier, more aggressive. More . . .

And then he remembered. Remembered who it was that Mara reminded him of when she acted this way. Anastasia. Anastasia Dubois.

But that was stupid. The Master might *think* that Mara

was really Anastasia, but Anastasia was very definitely dead; her evil vampire soul long since chased from her body in a tomb in the Valley of the Kings. Robbed of her own body, Mara had possessed Anastasia's ever since that day. The question was . . . and it nagged at Andreas like an itch he couldn't scratch . . . who was possessing Mara? Surely it couldn't be Anastasia Dubois . . .

The American had put down his drink and was watching the floor show with a smirk of satisfaction. Andreas knew his type. They didn't screw, they got off watching other people getting it on. What's more, he could feel the same guilty excitement flowing into him too. He couldn't watch what Mara was doing and not want a piece of the action.

The black guy was standing over her, knees bent, flies unzipped. She was going down on him, the red circle of her mouth tightening greedily about his shaft. As he slid his hips back, the gleaming black rod of his dick slowly emerged, to disappear again in a fast, hard dive into Mara's willing throat.

Hands swarmed over her body like crawling insects. A woman with cropped blonde hair was stripping naked, revealing a tattooed body with boyish breasts and a shaven pussy. Pushing Mara's dress right up until it was a narrow strip of fabric under her arms, she straddled Mara's bare back as though she were a skittish mare.

Mara's back rose up to meet her, and the other woman spread her thighs wide, rubbing the mound of her sex hard and fast against the ridge of Mara's spine. Hypnotised with horrified lust, Andreas saw the slick of wetness appear on Mara's skin, dripping from the blonde woman's thick, swollen labia; and the pendulous, quivering fruits of Mara's breasts, shaking and swaying beneath her as she shared in another woman's sexual frenzy.

His dick ached. He yearned to weigh right in there, to pull apart those glorious buttocks and slide his dick into the pleasure palace within; or simply to stand over her, dick in hand, wanking himself harder and harder until the hot, sticky rain of his semen spattered her hair, her skin, her upturned face . . .

Another man. Another. Some kid – he couldn't be more than nineteen – was running his slavering tongue over Mara's backside, and she was dancing with excitement, letting other fingers open her up like a ripening fruit and slide between her thighs, seeking out the white-hot button of her clitoris.

She rolled sideways, sprawling on the floor, her mouth wet with white trails of semen. The woman who had ridden her writhed underneath her, and Mara embraced her, pressing lips to lips, then leaving a trail of kisses all the way down her belly from throat to pubis. Andreas watched, breathless, as she began licking the blonde woman out, lapping at her with short, quick strokes which made her nameless lover twitch and gasp with pleasure, reaching up to scratch and stroke at Mara's breasts.

The kid came up behind Mara and pushed his dick into her, and the three of them rode together like some phantasmagorical sex engine, instinctively finding their own rhythm without ever exchanging a word.

'You just can't *buy* this kind of entertainment,' remarked the American, snapping his fingers for another whisky.

'No,' said Andreas. He didn't doubt it. Mara was a great performer and this was the best free show on earth; hell, didn't he know that better than anyone else?

'Not in Paris, not in Hamburg, not even Bangkok, and I've seen them all.' He grinned. 'That's why I came back again tonight, just on the off-chance that she'd be here again.'

A lightning bolt shot through Andreas's head. He almost dropped his drink.

'She's . . . been here before?'

'Sure. Every night this week.' The American clapped him jovially on the back. 'Hey, don't get so uptight. She's here every night, you'll get your turn.'

Which was the last thing occupying Andreas Hunt's mind right now. It was hard not to be carried away by the sight of Mara, taking two dicks into her mouth and another in each hand, but the old journo's instinct took over.

'Let me get this straight. This girl . . . she's been coming here every night for a week?'

'Like I said.'

So that's where you've been disappearing to whenever I'm away, thought Andreas. But why? A thought struck him.

'Any idea who she is?' he enquired with an effort at casualness.

'If you mean, do I have her phone number, then sorry but no. But I do know her name – or at least, what she's been calling herself.'

Andreas stiffened.

'Go on.'

'Anastasia. That's what she calls herself. Anastasia Dubois.'

Mara smiled and rolled onto her belly on the bed.

'Hungry? Dinner's arrived.'

'Yeah. Yeah, I suppose.' Andreas glanced at the trolley by the door, the array of silver lids and tureens.

'So how did the meeting go?'

Andreas tried very hard to act normally. He pulled off his tie and slung it over the door handle, then started unbuttoning his shirt.

'Oh, you know . . .'

'Let me do that.' Mara sprang off the bed and started peeling off his shirt. He flinched momentarily, at the memory of what he had seen in the Club Atlantis. 'Sorry, did I catch you with my fingernail?' She pouted. 'Let me kiss it better.'

Her lips were moist and cool on his skin and before he

knew it she had him growling with pleasure all over again. Could this really be the same Mara he had seen crawling about on a nightclub floor, practically naked and dripping with sex? It was almost impossible to believe. And yet, if he closed his eyes, he fancied he could just catch the faint, lingering scents on her freshly washed skin.

'Later.' He kissed her then pushed her gently away.

'Something wrong?'

'Just . . . hungry.' He took the lid from one of the plates. Fresh salmon, Béarnaise sauce. There was chilled watercress soup in a silver-plated tureen, and a huge pile of summer fruits and redcurrant sorbet in a glass bowl, trickled over with fresh blackcurrant coulis and a frosting of crushed ice.

'We should eat the fruit before the sorbet melts,' murmured Mara, coming up behind him and slipping her arms round his waist.

'You reckon so?' Andreas reached out and took a fresh strawberry from the platter, rolling it in the crushed ice and sorbet, then turning round and presenting it to Mara's lips. They parted prettily, with a gleam of white teeth and the tip of a moist pink tongue.

She took the strawberry into her mouth and they kissed, the cold soft flesh crushed into a sweet, sharp pulp. Andreas drew back, breathless, wiping his hand across his mouth.

'You taste good.'

'Good enough to eat?'

Andreas took that as an invitation. Scooping up a dessertspoonful of melting redcurrant sorbet, he raised it as though he was about to eat it then, at the last moment, pressed it against the bare skin of Mara's throat.

She shivered and giggled as the spoon tipped slowly sideways, spilling syrupy, berry-red liquid down into the deep valley between her breasts. In the electric light it looked for all the world like fresh blood, oozing from a puncture wound in her neck. And, perhaps for the first

71

time in his life, Andreas felt a definite urge to play the vampire.

His chin nuzzled into the crook of her neck and he whispered delicious obscenities into the auburn cloud of her hair.

'You darling slut. You darling, filthy-minded, big-titted witch . . . have you any idea what you do to me . . . ?'

And have you any idea that I was standing watching you at the Club Atlantis, he added in the silence of his thoughts, fervently hoping that Mara, or Anastasia, or whoever it was that he was making passionate love to, was not reading his mind. Have you any idea what it felt like to watch you giving yourself to a dozen nameless lovers?

Screw redcurrant sorbet; it tasted nice, but not nearly as nice as Mara Fleming's bare breasts. Andreas uncovered them, untying Mara's robe and letting it fall to the carpet.

'Beast,' she murmured, in that low, husky voice which wasn't really hers. Was she mocking him? 'If you're not *really* good, I won't give you what I've got for you.'

'Give me . . . what?'

'Later. First, you have to earn it.'

Her green eyes sparkled with mischief. Andreas cursed silently. He hated riddles.

'Mara!'

'*Earn it.*'

She dragged him across the bedroom to the rather sumptuous period dressing table, the one with the hinged triptych of gold-framed mirrors. As she lay across it and he straddled her, Andreas caught sight of the two of them together, their reflections multiplied dozens of times and all the reflected eyes looking right back at him. It was like having sex in the middle of Wembley Stadium on Cup Final day.

'Mara . . . if you don't tell me what you've got . . .'

'Later.'

'If you don't tell me, I won't let you come.'

She laughed. A wicked, sultry laugh.

'Oh yes you will.'

Taking his hand, she guided it between her legs, closing them tight upon it and using his fingers to give herself pleasure. He ought to have punished her by taking his hand away, but the tropical wetness oozing onto his fingertips drove him mad with the need for her.

'Bad girl. Bad, wicked girl.' Pulling apart her thighs, he slid into the warm, welcoming depths of her. Laughter overtook him, bubbling out of him with each short, bucking thrust. Maybe it was just hysteria. He couldn't help wondering if this was how a boy Black Widow spider felt when he went out on a date.

It was quite a session. They started out on the dressing table, but ended up under the shower, Mara's legs wrapped round his waist and his hands squeezing her firm, round buttocks as warm water crashed and steamed around them.

'Well . . . all right then,' laughed Mara, reaching out and turning off the water. She smoothed back the wet hair from her face.

'All right what?'

'All right, I'll give it to you. The envelope.'

She slithered wetly to the ground and padded into the bedroom, leaving a trail of footprints on the pale pink Axminster.

'What envelope?'

Mara slid her hand into the pocket of her robe and took out a white square.

'*This* envelope. It's from the Master, a messenger brought it earlier on, while you were out.'

Andreas's heart jumped, screaming, out of a fifteenth-storey window. The Master. That was all he needed. Hadn't he got enough to worry about, wondering what the fuck was happening to Mara?

He tore open the envelope. There was a single sheet of typescript inside.

'Graveney has traced the provenance of the stone. It was donated to the Geological Archive by a citizen of St Malo, during the Second World War, for reasons unknown. We have a name: Gaston Lebecq.

'You will act upon this information immediately.

'M.'

Mara looked over his shoulder.

'Bad news?'

'Only if you don't like the seaside. Pack your bucket and spade, the Master's sending us to St Malo.'

'Is it far?'

'About a day's drive. We'll get up early and go tomorrow.'

Mara gave him that wicked, knowing, irresistible smile.

'Best get to bed now then.'

'Did you just read my mind?'

And maybe she had at that, thought Andreas, running his fingernails down Mara's bare flank. The fact was that he couldn't be certain about anything any more, not even Mara Fleming.

You can dance with the devil, Hunt, he told himself; but you'd bloody well better watch your back . . .

Chapter 5

Dew moistened her bare, caramel-smooth body. It formed glassy beads on her skin; quivering as she drew in a long, slow breath, then bursting to form tiny rivulets which scurried down over her breasts and belly, soaking the luxuriant black tangle of her pubic hair.

It formed a glossy sheen on her lips, her ringed fingers, her painted toenails; dripped down her flanks and formed pendulous droplets on the fine gold chain which lay across her right thigh. The chain was slung between two rings, one of which disappeared into the juicy flesh beneath her wiry maidencurls, the other neatly piercing the tight ring of her perineum.

She was sitting cross-legged on the grass, at the centre of a small island in the Seine. Facing east into the approaching dawn, she picked up the stone phallus which lay at her feet. It was carved from a green-veined stone, smooth and cold as polished ice. A groan of effort escaped from her full, parted lips as she pushed it between her thighs.

Her breath came in rasping, shuddering gasps of air as she began to masturbate. This had nothing to do with pleasure, it was arduous and almost painful to push the stone phallus again and again into the heart of her sex. The chain slapped and jingled on her thigh as she clasped her hands over the end of the phallus and forced it a fraction deeper.

'No. Ah. No more . . . this is too much, I can't bear it, not much longer . . .'

Sweat mingled with the dew, running down her face, her breasts, her back; dampening the black fleece of her hair and plastering spidery strands to her tawny neck and cheeks. She closed her eyes, every muscle in her body tense with effort, her nipples hard, sharpened points on her small, apple-hard breasts.

'But I must. I must . . .'

Her juices were flowing, hot and sweet and abundant. They formed a fine sheen of wetness on the dark green stone as it emerged, triumphant, from the jewel casket of her sex.

'Come,' she gasped, drawing air into her lungs in painful gulps. 'Hurry, come, possess me, come into me, join with me . . .'

Her body seemed to crumple as she fell forward, utterly exhausted. The stone phallus slithered into her palm, fragrant and smooth with a slick of fresh honeydew.

She smiled.

The stone glans dripped a fine trail of never-ending wetness onto her upturned breasts, the rosy light of dawn picking out the curious patterns she was tracing with infinite care on her skin. Stars and snakes, whorls and arrows of wetness appeared on her face, her buttocks, her belly, her inner thighs; and other symbols too, more esoteric, their meaning known only to her.

As she traced the last symbol on her forehead, the patterns began to glow; not simply to reflect the sun's light but to absorb it and then generate their own radiance. A peculiar warm stillness covered the land around her and the grass rustled with the sounds of animals and birds, creeping out of their hiding places to form a circle of watchful eyes.

By her side lay a small bundle, wrapped in white cloth. Quickly but reverentially she unwrapped it, taking out a flattish object of polished grey-green stone. It was a mask, a huge convex disc like the face of the risen sun, edged with small, needle-like stone spikes. Two were missing, like broken teeth in an otherwise radiant smile.

Lifting the mask, she put it to her face. The sun dawned; and in that moment she was gone.

Suddenly afraid, the animals and birds dispersed with a flutter of wings and a scurrying of feet. All but one, which came forward to stare intently at the flattened grass where she had sat.

A tatty-looking, brownish-white pigeon.

Andreas looked up from the last of his packing.

'Ready to go?'

Mara stuck her head out of the bathroom door. She was pink-skinned from the shower and her hair was wet and tousled.

'Almost.' She let the towel slip just a fraction, giving Andreas a tantalising glimpse of the tops of her breasts. 'Unless of course you've got other ideas . . .'

He grinned.

'Don't tempt me.'

He rolled up a pair of boxer shorts and threw them into his overnight bag. Spare pants, shaving tackle and a six-pack: that was him packed and ready. Mara went back into the bathroom, and he heard her humming 'Steamy Windows' as she turned on the hair dryer.

As an afterthought, he stuffed a few more items into Mara's suitcase. Notebook, camera, pocket tape recorder (you never knew when you might need one) . . . He checked the dragon's-eye bracelet which he always wore, the one which Mara had turned into a talisman to protect his true identity from being discovered. He hoped to fuck it was still working. Trousers, shoes . . .

He bent down and scooped up his crumpled dress jacket, the one he'd worn to that horrible cocktail reception. It was a bit the worse for wear, he'd have to get it dry cleaned. What *was* that crispy white stain on the lapel?

Patting it to smooth out the creases, he noticed something hard in the inside pocket. Not just hard. Warm. Which was really odd, because he hadn't worn that jacket for two whole days. Intrigued and slightly apprehensive, Andreas peered inside – and saw the tiny little spike of greenish-grey stone he'd been given at the party. It was blood-warm, as if it had been sitting in the sun for hours.

Black Cher. The memory of the seriously exciting Anjula came bouncing back into his mind. Of course. She'd pressed the stone into his hand, and he'd slipped it into his pocket and forgotten all about it. He wondered . . .

'Something wrong?'

The sound of Mara's voice made him jump. Instinct told him he had to hide the stone, but how and where? He swung round, feigning horror.

'Oh God no!'

At the sight of his expression, Mara took a step back.

'What is it?'

Andreas took advantage of the moment to slip the stone into the side zip-pocket of his camera case.

'This is terrible!'

'What is?'

He grinned, put out his hands and grabbed Mara round the waist.

'It's nearly seven o'clock, and I *still* haven't fucked the arse off you.'

'OK, comfort stop,' announced Andreas, turning the car into a parking space and putting on the handbrake. His neck ached and he was busting for a piss. 'So where are we?'

Mara opened the car door and slid out onto hot cobblestones. There was a big white sign right ahead, on the other side of the car park.

'Alençon.' She suppressed a smile as she read the rest of the sign. 'Twinned with Basingstoke.'

78

'There you are, don't say I don't take you to all the best places.'

'You don't . . .'

'Oh shut up!'

Shoving the car keys into his pocket, Andreas stared gloomily around him. Twinned with Basingstoke? It might as well *be* Basingstoke, for all the excitement it offered.

'I'm going to find a bar or something,' he said. 'How about you?'

'I'll take a walk round . . . see you back here in half an hour?'

'OK, fine.'

Andreas felt kind of relieved to be on his own again. He was beginning to feel uncomfortable with Mara, never quite sure that she was who she was supposed to be, and forever watching his own back. He had a beer and a slash and felt a bit less paranoid. But when he stepped out again, onto the oven-hot street, he immediately felt it all over again. That funny feeling he just couldn't shake off, like being followed – only different.

No, not being followed. This was something else. Like . . . like being *waited* for, his every step known in advance. And that felt really, really freaky.

He was pretty sure he was imagining it, but it bugged him that he couldn't get rid of the feeling, no matter what he did. He tried sauntering down the main shopping street, playing the casual tourist, but he walked smack-bang into a statue of the grim reaper, and he could have sworn it was looking right at him. Hunt, he told himself sternly, you can't afford to crack up now; so get a grip on yourself.

It was market day. Stalls crowded into the shade of the ancient church, offering the usual Gallic mix of gourmet food and nylon pullovers. Whoever had said the French had great fashion sense had obviously never bought a tee-shirt in Alençon market. Andreas kicked around, bought a baguette, some marinaded olives and a lump of cheese, then glanced at his watch. Still ten minutes to go, if he wasn't driving he'd have another beer.

Then he spotted the one really interesting stall in the whole market. It was so different from all the others that it stood out like a spare prick at a wedding. Andreas walked over to it. Tie-dye scarves, Indian print frocks, incense, candles, Tarot cards and runes . . . Mara would love this little lot. Correction. She would have loved it before she went . . . peculiar.

The stallholder greeted Andreas with a friendly 'M'sieur'. He smiled back, and had the immediate impression that – although it made no sense – he *knew* the woman. And then it struck him: without the sunglasses, the beaded hair and the nose ring she looked quite a lot like Anjula. Can't be, he told himself; it's just coincidence.

Two trestle tables were spread with jewellery; ethnic-type stuff, silver and semi-precious stones, leather thongs and beads.

'*Vous cherchez quelque chose de spécial, m'sieur?*' Hidden eyes searched his face, cutting into his daydreaming.

'Er . . .' he began, trying to formulate something from his schoolboy French. But before he had a chance to say more, the stallholder was smiling and reading his thoughts.

'You are English, m'sieur? You are looking for a gift for a special friend?'

'Well . . . I might be,' he replied. He hadn't really thought about it.

'She would like this, m'sieur?' Slender fingers selected something from the tangle of beads and shimmering stones and lifted it up for his approval. It was simple but beautiful, a fine thong of plaited black leather, on which hung a pendant of three pale pink crystals, wound about with a skein of artfully twisted silver wire.

He took it, looked at it and handed it back.

'No. Thanks, but I don't think so.'

'You're sure, m'sieur? Really sure?'

Something in the woman's voice made him look again at the necklace. It was true, Mara had always loved this ethnic stuff, especially crystals of all sorts . . .

'*Combien?*'

'*Deux cents cinquante.*'

Two minutes later, it was in his pocket, and he was walking back towards the church, wondering if he had just been fleeced.

Mara was waiting for him in the car, an opened bottle of Vittel in her hand, pouring the water over her face in tiny rivulets that evaporated almost instantly in the noonday heat. She smiled.

'Fancy a drink?'

'Uh-huh.'

He reached out his hand for the bottle, but instead of handing it to him, she upturned it and emptied a whole litre and a half of *eau minérale naturelle* over herself. It coursed down over her throat, her breasts, her belly, sticking her short cotton dress to her body, moulding itself to the countours of nipples and thighs.

'Come and get it,' she teased. And slipping out of the car, she dodged away, laughing as she ran across the car park and down a flight of old stone steps.

'You little . . .'

'Come *on*! Or aren't you thirsty any more?'

He ran after her. It wasn't difficult to catch up to her. She was waiting for him in the shadows at the bottom of the steps, leaning back against a rusted iron railing, her wet dress clinging irresistibly to her body.

'Well?' There was a world of meaning in the word.

He took her head in his hands and kissed her, luxuriating in the coldness of her wet breasts as it seeped through his open-necked shirt.

'What – here?' His eyes flicked briefly sideways, through the railings into the sunlit marketplace, where hundreds of people were still milling about.

'Here. What's the matter – not afraid are you?'

'As a matter of fact . . .' His fingers unfastened the buttons on the front of Mara's dress. 'Yeah. Shitless.' He wasn't entirely joking, either. His heart was thumping like a guilty schoolboy's, in fear of being caught having a knee-trembler in the bus shelter.

'Of course,' purred Mara, 'We don't *have* to. If you want, we can just go back to the car . . .'

Andreas chuckled, deep in his throat.

'Oh no you don't. You don't get away from me that easily.'

'Who says I want to get away? It's you who's afraid, Andreas. Not me.'

Mara's dress was open to the waist and he felt an electric buzz of pleasure thrill through him as his hands cupped the cold, moist flesh of her bare breasts. It wasn't like the flesh of a real, live woman. Her nipples were hard as galvanised rubber.

His mind reeled. There were so many things he could do to her, and he wanted to do them all. He could push her to her knees and get her to suck him off, long and slow; or he could wrap her corpse-cold breasts about the shaft of his dick and watch his seed spurting all over her face. She could kneel like a bitch; or he could sit on the steps and dance her up and down on his dick, screwing her slowly round, rotating her whole body about the axis of his desire until they came together, in a red rage of passion.

Or he could do this.

'Turn your back to me.'

She licked her lips.

'So make me.'

The show of defiance was a complete sham. She submitted with only the feeblest struggle as he flipped her over like a pancake, grinding her bare breasts against the rough, shadowed stonework of the old church wall.

'Is *this* how you like it?' he asked her, pushing up her

dress and pulling down her panties. 'You want it rough?'

She answered with an animal growl, snarling with enraged pleasure as Andreas pulled apart her smooth bum cheeks. Her panties slid soundlessly down her thighs to her parted ankles and she was his, all his; her long, bare, sun-browned legs leading up to the creamy round pleasure palace he was about to take for his very own.

Her juices smoothed the path beautifully and her anus welcomed him with a kiss of delight, dilating willingly to accept the rod of his sex. It felt so good that he almost shouted out, but just above him and to his right, feet were moving back and forth, people shouting to each other across the marketplace. Got to take his pleasure in silence, got to control himself somehow . . . but it wasn't easy.

'*Fromages, fromages tout frais.*'

'Give it to me.' The whispered invocation of ecstasy. 'Mara, you bitch, give it to me . . .'

'*Bonne viande . . .*'

'*Saucisses cheval, charcuterie . . .*'

Heavy breathing, hoarse and gasping; rising to a crescendo. Limbs moving together, skin rubbing over sun-warmed skin, juices blending, fizzing, bubbling, erupting . . .

'*Venez, m'ssieurs-dames, venez vite, c'est presque fini . . .*'

As Mara's magnificent arse sucked out the very last drops of Andreas's semen, he stooped to kiss and lick the nape of her neck.

'I've got something for you,' he whispered.

Mara giggled.

'Let me guess. Is it long and hard . . . and hot?'

'No, really. I've got you a present. Do you want it now?'

'Darling, I *always* want it from you.' She rolled round to face him, and licked her lips wickedly.

'Close your eyes then.'

Drawing back, he reached into his pocket for the necklace.

'Can I look yet?'

'Not yet.' He reached up, slipped the crystal necklace round Mara's neck, and fastened it. 'OK, now.'

Mara's eyes flew wide open and her hand clawed at the necklace as though it were a red hot coal, burning into her skin.

'No! Nooo . . .'

Andreas took a step back.

'W-what's wrong? I mean, if you don't like it I'll take it back . . .'

But he knew in his bones that there was much more to it than that. Even as he looked into Mara's face, he saw the spark of fear in her eyes turn to a blank, empty stare.

'Mara!'

But she wasn't listening to him; there was no way for him to reach her. And a second later she collapsed, unconscious, into his arms.

Chapter 6

It was a warm, moist place. Dark too, with thunder that rolled and drummed inside Mara's head.

Where was she – and why? How long had she been here? All she knew was the darkness and the wet, exhausting heat, the menacing sound of the drums; and the danger. There was no one to help her here. She must fight to save herself.

'So you thought you could overcome me, little white witch.' The voice was mocking, smug and spiteful.

Mara swung round. Anastasia Dubois was standing before her, naked, her hands upraised and her fingers contracting into red-tipped cat's claws.

'You . . . but . . .'

Questions whirled inside Mara's head. Things were not as they should be. She should be inside Anastasia's body, Anastasia was dead; and yet the vampire slut was standing right in front of her, laughing at her, daring her to take back what had been hers.

Lightning forked through the darkness, and for a split second Mara caught sight of her face, reflected in the fractured mirrors that surrounded her like jagged teeth. *Her* face, not Anastasia's or Queen Sedet's, but Mara Fleming's. Mara as she had been before Sedet stole her body and forced her spirit to take refuge in Anastasia's evil frame.

'I have been waiting,' said Anastasia, her expression darkening. 'You have been taking too long to die, Mara. My patience is running out.'

'Bitch.' Mara spat out the word in a whisper of pure hatred. She understood now. Somehow, her soul had been transported to the astral plane, to do battle with Anastasia for possession of the one body they both craved. It was a cruel game, and Anastasia held all the aces.

Anastasia sprang at her like a she-leopard, her sharpened nails raking down Mara's flanks, her teeth sinking into the flesh of her right shoulder. Mara let out a shriek of pain and fury and fought back with all her strength, burying her fingers in Anastasia's auburn mane and twisting, tearing, forcing her to loosen her grip.

They tumbled over onto the rocky ground. Mara felt the slipperiness of blood on her skin and the moist abrasion of Anastasia's tongue, licking it from the deep grooves at the side of her breast. Sickened, she kicked out with her bare feet and managed to land a blow in Anastasia's belly, momentarily winding her and throwing her onto her back.

Quickly she pinned her to the ground, one knee on Anastasia's stomach while her hands held her down by her wrists.

'I will never submit to you. Never,' she hissed.

But Anastasia smiled up at her, the violet eyes sparkling with triumphant evil.

'What a child you are,' she purred. 'A weakling. The world will be well rid of you.'

With a sudden strength, she reared up, throwing Mara backwards. Their bodies locked, they rolled over and over, sharp stones piercing Mara's skin, dizziness weakening her, blurring her mind. Where was she? Who was she? She forced herself to remember, concentrating with all her might.

Mara. I am Mara. And if I weaken, I will die. Andreas, she cried out silently. Andreas, help me. But somehow she sensed that he could not hear her, that she was locked inside this cage of darkness, and only she could find the key.

She could hardly believe Anastasia's strength. It crushed

the breath from her, making the strength ebb away, and she knew that she was beginning to lose control. Her whole body shook with the effort of resisting; how much longer could this go on?

'Die, Mara. Die, you pathetic little creature. Die.'

Only blind hatred drove Mara on, clawing and biting in the darkness.

'Evil slut,' she spat. 'Evil, worthless slut. You know I will never submit to you.' She kicked out and her thigh slid between Anastasia's, gliding between oily limbs to make contact with the hot, hard mound of her pubis. Anastasia laughed as her fingernails dug deep into the softness of Mara's breasts.

'Good can never vanquish evil,' she whispered. 'That is the one lesson you must learn before I destroy you.'

As lightning flashed, Mara was up and running, chasing the fleeting shadow of Anastasia as she led her between the forest of broken mirrors. A hundred fractured reflections deceived her, made it impossible to know which direction to take. And all the time the mocking laughter goaded her and led her on, knowing that she must not give up.

All at once Anastasia was standing right in front of her, arms outspread.

'Come to me, my child,' she purred. 'Come to me and feel the warmth of my embrace.'

Mara turned to run, but it was too late. The face and form of Anastasia Dubois were melting, transforming, vapourising into a cloud of cold white mist which engulfed her. How could there be any escape from an unseen enemy?

Intangible fingers explored and invaded, searching out her most intimate places.

'How do you like *this*, Mara? And *this*?'

The fingers scratched and dug; took her by the nipples and twisted them, clawed at her belly and invaded the soft, sensitive flesh of her vulva.

'No!'

'Yes, Mara. Yes. You cannot fight me, you know now that I am the strong one. I shall invade you and possess you, and it will be as if you had never existed.'

Mara moaned softly, her whole body aching and trembling, her hands desperately scrabbling at the faceless shadows which tormented her. As the fog began to solidify and transform itself into a writhing skein of snakes, the torment became yet more intense. Hot, dry, scaly bodies tensed and constricted as they wound round and round her body, stimulating, exploring, possessing. She clawed at them with her fingers, trying to prise them away, but they were too strong for her. And every one of them wore the face of Anastasia Dubois, a double tongue flicking in and out of a red-lipped mouth.

She felt the last of her strength beginning to ebb away, the clarity and colour fading from her vision. Slowly, she began to sink to her knees on the ground. Even as she fell, she felt it grow cold and slippery beneath her, turning from hot, wet rock into iron-hard ice. Only moments more and it would be done. Anastasia would be the victor and that would be an end of it.

Stroboscopic images flashed before Mara's eyes: one moment Anastasia's face, then a rough stone wall; then Anastasia again; rusty iron railings; Anastasia; a flight of stone steps, half-glimpsed faces; then Anastasia . . .

Mara lay on her belly on the ice, its fiery cold soaking little by little into her soul, numbing her, robbing her of life. There was something sharp and spiky inside her, pushing its way into her backside, taking her, humiliating her, making her feel unwilling pleasure even at the moment of ultimate defeat. Hands, cruel sharp-nailed fingers, were exploring her sex, scratching and probing, forcing her tormented clitoris to swell and throb with the approach of a terrible, final climax.

'No. No, no, no . . .'

It was no use crying out, no one was listening. She was

done for. A few seconds more, a crashing, tearing orgasm and then . . . infinite darkness. The end.

A sudden, terrible scream brought Mara back to her senses. For a moment she thought it was the sound of her own terror; then she realised, with a surge of hope, that it was Anastasia's voice, not hers. The crushing pressure relaxed enough for her to force herself free of it and scramble to her hands and knees.

Anastasia was standing over her, her face skull-white in the flickering brightness of forked lightning. But the look of triumph had gone. Her eyes were round, filled with horror and hatred . . . and yes, with fear. Her fingers clawed at her throat, her body writhing, her voice a rattling scream of furious anger.

'No! Hunt, no, I will not . . . you cannot do this to me, Andreas Hunt, you are slime, you are nothing!'

Andreas? Mara's heart beat faster. Had Andreas found some way to help her? She sprang to her feet. Anastasia's eyes were half closed, her body shaking and jerking. Her voice tailed off.

'No. You are nothing . . . you are . . .'

Strength coursed through Mara's veins. Seizing Anastasia by the shoulders, she forced her to her knees. Her body seemed to crumple and deflate, falling to the earth like a broken doll. In seconds Mara was upon her, forcing her to submit, thrusting her curled fist into the hot, wet haven of Anastasia's sex.

Anastasia screamed; her voice rising to an unearthly, high-pitched wail.

And then, for some unaccountable reason, everything went black.

'Mara? Mara, for fuck's sake wake up!'
    '*Qu'est-ce qu'elle a?*'
    '*Elle est malade?*'
    '*On est allé chercher le médecin?*'

'*Elle se réveille! Laisse-la respirer un peu!*'

Mara awoke suddenly, to find herself sprawled inelegantly across cobbled ground at the bottom of a flight of stone steps. Faces were peering down at her from all sides. Among them, she spotted Andreas. He looked shit-scared.

'A-Andreas? W-where . . . ?' She tried sitting up, but felt so dizzy that Andreas had to catch her and stop her falling over again.

'Take it easy, Mara, you had a funny turn.' His eyes seemed to be searching her face, as though they were looking for something, some sign; she wondered what it could be.

'But . . .' she began.

A gendarme pushed his way through the crowd, a large handgun secured by a white cable to his belt.

'*Qu'est-ce qui se passe?*' he demanded, his moustache bristling with self-importance.

'It's all right, monsieur,' began Andreas, though he didn't look very all right, thought Mara. She wondered why. More to the point, she wondered what she was doing here and why everybody was speaking in French, and what was going on. She couldn't remember anything since . . . '*Tout va bien.*'

'She is ill? Your wife?'

'She fainted, that's all. The heat . . . *le soleil* . . . *comprenez-vous?*'

Old ladies proffered wet handkerchiefs and glasses of water. A stallholder presented Andreas with a bag of oranges and the offer of a lift in his van to the local hospital. Andreas declined them all, politely but firmly.

Mara struggled to her feet, feeling stronger now but distinctly peculiar.

'Andreas,' she began. 'What happened?'

Andreas smiled at her, in the way that said, 'Be quiet, don't ask questions, I'll sort it all out.' Putting his arm round her shoulders, he whispered into her ear, 'It's OK, you've had too much sun, just let me get you out of here, everything's going to be fine.' He looked nervous but – for some reason Mara couldn't quite fathom – pleased too.

Half the town walked them back to the car and waved them off. It wasn't until they were a good five miles out of Alençon that Andreas's hands relaxed around the steering wheel. He darted her a kind of cagey grin.

'You OK now? You gave me a real fright back there.'

'I did?' Mara drew her hand across her forehead. 'Why? What did I do?'

'You don't remember?'

'Only . . . a dream. I had this really weird dream.' She blinked in the sunshine pouring in through the side window. 'Andreas.'

'Hmm?'

'Where are we?'

'Same place we were half an hour ago, give or take a few miles.'

'Which is where?'

'France of course.'

'Oh.'

'Why, where did you think we were?'

'I dunno. It's just . . .' She watched a herd of Charolais cows drift by, placidly chewing the cud. 'It's just, the last thing I remember, we were in the Master's new palace in Docklands. I can't remember for the life of me how I got here.'

It wasn't the best of days to visit St Malo, not if you fancied a bit of peace and quiet. There was some kind of inter-Celtic festival going on, and what with all the Breton shenanigans and bagpipe bands all over the bloody place, you could hardly move for trippers.

They drove in along the harbour, along the seafront,

and finally managed to find a place to park.

'It's a bit like York,' commented Mara with a yawn as Andreas slid out of the driver's seat.

'More like Eastbourne with battlements. Tell you what, you wait here with the car and I'll just check that the hotel's OK. Knowing our luck they've probably double-booked us with the Dagenham Girl Pipers.' He peered at Mara, not quite believing that she was still there, in one piece and behaving . . . well . . . like Mara. 'Don't go anywhere, will you?'

'Why should I?'

'And don't take that necklace off.'

Mara's eyes travelled downwards to the pink crystal pendant, as if seeing it for the first time. Her fingers caressed it.

'That's pretty. How did it get there?'

'It doesn't matter, I'll explain later. Just don't take it off, OK?'

Mara shrugged.

'Whatever you say. But don't be long.'

Andreas put the car keys in his pocket and bounded up the hotel steps into reception.

Now *that* was what he called Gallic chic. Not the hotel, that was so anonymous it could have been anywhere from Swindon to Vladivostock. No, it was the receptionist he was looking at, a real gourmet dish if ever there was one. Glossy black hair, coiled into a sleek knot, olive skin, sloe eyes and a supermodel's body, gracefully understated in a designer écru two-piece.

Andreas unfastened the top button on his shirt and switched on a five-hundred-watt smile.

'*Bonjour,*' he began. Unfortunately that was more or less as far as his schoolboy French went. He hoped the object of his lust wouldn't hold his linguistic inadequacies against him. Just her body . . .

'*Bonjour, monsieur . . . ?*'

'Hu . . . Weatherall,' he corrected himself, just in time. 'Monsieur Weatherall.'

'Ah yes,' she smiled. 'A double room, *c'est ça*?'

Yeah, thought Andreas, assailed by thoughts that would make a condom salesman blush. A double room with a double bed. Fancy sharing it with me for half an hour? On second thoughts make that two hours, why rush things when you're having fun?

His hand wobbled as he signed the register. His palms were sweating so much that his fingers kept sliding down the biro. Hell but she was tasty. He was panting like a mongrel dog with asthma and he could hardly take his eyes off those legs . . . that arse . . . those pert and jiggling breasts.

'Steady on, Andreas.' Mara's hand came down on his shoulder and he almost jumped out of his skin. 'You'll go blind.'

He turned to look at her and she winked.

'You're a dirty old man, Andreas Hunt.'

'As long as you're a dirty old woman, who cares?'

They laughed and necked like kids, all the way up in the lift to the seventh floor. Andreas was feeling good. This was more like it. This was more like the Mara he knew. Somehow, by some accidental twist of fate, that necklace seemed to have brought her back to her usual playful self. Or was it accidental? At any rate, he was more than relieved to see that she was still wearing it.

Closing the door of the hotel room behind her, Andreas flung himself down on the bed.

'Join me?'

Mara snuggled down beside him, slipping her hand inside his shirt and gently stroking the fine brown hairs on his belly.

'Andreas . . . ?'

'Whatever it is, the answer's yes. But be gentle with me, OK?'

'Andreas . . . what's going on? One minute I'm in London, the next I'm in France. And I'm having this crazy dream . . .'

Andreas felt a cold chill raise the hairs on the back of his neck.

'Tell me,' he said. 'About the dream.'

'I was in a dark place, I don't know where. And I was in my old body, and Anastasia was there . . .'

Andreas stiffened.

'Go on.'

'We were fighting over this body. Anastasia wanted it back, we were struggling and she was much stronger than me. She said she was going to destroy me . . .'

Andreas felt Mara shiver. He slipped his arm around her, drawing her more tightly to him.

'It's all right,' he said. 'Nothing bad's going to happen.' Which – on past performance – probably wasn't true, but what the hell. 'Don't stop, tell me what happened.'

'I knew she was going to win, it was only a matter of seconds. And then she started clawing at her neck and cursing at you – then everything went black, and the next thing I know . . .'

'The next thing you know, you're waking up in a street in Alençon with a gendarme taking down your particulars?'

'Quite.' Mara unfastened the last of Andreas's shirt buttons and laid a trail of tiny butterfly kisses, all the way from his navel to his lips. 'This necklace has something to do with it, doesn't it?'

Andreas stroked the pink crystals. They were only rose-quartz for fuck's sake, at least that's what he thought they were; but he, more than anyone, had cause to respect the power of crystals. He thought of the Master's old body, still lying entombed in a flipping great block of the stuff, in the walled-up cellars at Winterbourne. Yeah. Crystal power. He'd never bad-mouth it ever again.

'I think so, yes. You see . . .' This wasn't easy. How did

94

you tell your lover that she'd been possessed by the former owner of her body? 'I think Anastasia Dubois really is trying to get her body back.'

'But how? Anastasia's dead.'

'Apparently not. I think you and she have been sharing a body, and now she's out to get sole possession. It was only me putting that crystal pendant round your neck that saved you.'

Mara stared at him, stunned. She fingered the pink crystals, cupping them in her hand.

'You really think that's true? That if I took off this necklace, I'd go back to being Anastasia Dubois?'

'The thing is, Mara, these last few weeks . . .'

Mara sat up.

'These last few weeks *what*? I don't remember anything. Not since the Master . . . and that little spiky bit of stone . . .'

'I know. Like I said, I think Anastasia's been in control. Some of the things you've been doing . . .'

'Like what!'

Andreas ran through them in his head. Embarrassing? Somewhat. Horny? Definitely. But more worrying than anything.

'Well, there was this incident at the Eiffel Tower.' He ran through the brief details. 'And you kept getting over-friendly at the cocktail party. And then you started disappearing . . .' He didn't tell her about the 'Paris Vampire' headline on Canal+ News. It would only frighten her, and he wasn't convinced it had anything to do with Mara anyway. 'And I followed you a couple of times.'

'Followed me? Where to?'

He swallowed.

'There's this nightclub. The Club Atlantis.'

'And?'

'And . . . you've been going there every night for a week, having all kinds of weird sex with the punters.'

Mara gaped at him.

95

'But . . . I can't have been. I don't remember. What kind of weird sex?'

'*Weird* weird.'

'I don't believe you. I wouldn't.'

'You would. You did.'

'I *didn't*!'

Andreas sighed. He'd hoped to avoid this. Sliding off the bed, he unzipped his camera case and took out a handful of Polaroids.

'Take a look for yourself.'

Mara took the photographs from him. He watched her leafing through them, her expression turning from disbelief to amazement.

'But . . . but this is me . . .'

'Plus one or two intimate friends, yeah.'

'I really . . . ?'

'Yep.' He paused. 'Well, not you exactly.'

'No,' said Mara quietly. 'Not me. Anastasia Dubois.'

They sat there in silence for a few minutes, Mara staring at a photograph of herself in the middle of the club dance floor, one lover astride her, another in her mouth, a third wrist-deep in her succulent pussy.

'Andreas,' she began.

'What?'

'Did you enjoy it – watching me at the club?'

He hesitated, torn between honesty and diplomacy. He'd never been much of a diplomat.

'Yes.'

'It turned you on.'

'Come on, Mara, what do *you* think?'

'I think you're a horny-minded bastard, Mister Hunt. I think watching me made you want to *do* things.' She pouted prettily, provocatively, in the way that only Mara Fleming could. 'Well, am I right?'

'Could be.'

'You're disgusting.'

'Guilty as charged.'

'In that case . . . why don't we do some of those things right now?'

The flaxen-haired slut slumped to the floor, her barely clad body scratched and blotched with bloody kisses.

The Master regarded her with a sneer of disgust, nudging her exhausted form with the toe of his highly polished shoe.

'Get up,' he snapped. The girl tried to raise herself on her arms, stretching out a shaking hand to paw at her Master's leg, but he kicked her away. 'Pathetic.'

Hunger gnawed at his belly. He snapped his fingers and the Ethiopian Ibrahim glided out of the shadows, bowing his head respectfully.

'Master?'

'Send the Queen to me.'

'At once, Master.'

The Master watched him leave the throne room, his tall, athletic physique magnificent in a livery that consisted of little more than a skein of silver links that rustled and chinked together with every movement of his oiled black limbs. Perhaps, the Master mused, he would have been better to sate his lust on Ibrahim than this worthless piece of flesh.

He waited. The girl at his feet lay motionless. Evidently he had gone a little too far – not that the girl was of any consequence. Irritation twitched the ringed fingers of his right hand, lust bugging him like an unreachable itch.

His queen arrived in a cloud of perfume, magnificent as ever, her violet eyes bright with a cold and hungry fire. She was power-dressed for the City, her generous breasts testing the buttons on her emerald silk jacket. Her lips were painted deep burgundy, revealing the flash of perfect teeth.

'My lord.'

There was not the faintest hint of subservience in her smile. A fact which alternately angered and stimulated the Master. There was no denying the fact that Sedet did Mara Fleming's body far more justice than the white witch had ever done. She had provided Winterbourne with a fine mistress, and when the Master's evil empire had spread out its arms to cover the whole world, she would be a worthy empress. Her soul crackled with an evil energy.

Nevertheless, she was not and never would be his equal; and he intended to make sure that she never forgot that salient fact.

'I dislike being kept waiting.'

'And I dislike being summoned from my work.'

'Work!' He laughed drily. 'What work is this? Watching pretty young men fuck each other? Training sluts to drink your pleasure?'

'Sluts must be found and trained, my lord. To do your work. *Our* work.'

'Then you must pay more attention to your duties. You have displeased me.'

He kicked the insensible bundle sprawled across his feet. Sedet laughed.

'You did not enjoy the slut I sent you? A delicious sixteen-year-old virgin? Surely you cannot have exhausted her possibilities already?'

'The bitch was inadequate to satisfy my needs.' The Master turned his sullen gaze upon his queen. Through her tailored silk trousers, he could clearly make out the plump contours of her swollen pussy lips. 'And so you shall satisfy them for me.'

Sedet's painted lip curled in defiance.

'And if I do not choose to . . . ?'

The Master seized her by the hair, twisting it and holding her fast.

'It is not your place to choose. It is your place to serve.'

She scratched him with her long fingernails and spat

her venom into his face, even as he was tearing the designer suit from her body.

'You will not treat me like one of your cheap sluts!'

'I will deal with you exactly as I please.' Pleasure was flooding through the Master's veins; and he knew instinctively that for all her pretended hatred of him, Sedet was enjoying it too. A savage passion united them, turning pleasure into violence and violence into pleasure. 'Suck my dick.'

Sedet squirmed and bit and scratched as he forced her to the ground. Standing over her, he unzipped his fly with his free hand and pushed the beautiful, marble-smooth rod of his dick against her lips. She snarled at him and turned her face away.

'Let. Me. Go!'

With a sudden, powerful wrench she tore herself free of his grasp, wriggling away from him. It was her turn to demand control, lunging at him and striking his face with her crystal-ringed fist. He caught her by the wrist and twisted it down, but this time she retaliated by kissing him.

'You are my lord, but you can never tame me.'

Her lips carried the fresh, salty tang of newly shed blood. The Master shuddered at the exquisite pleasure of Sedet's kiss, loosening his grip on her and allowing her to work upon him with her skilful fingers. Her nails scored deep grooves in his flesh, her teeth bit lovingly into the softness of his lips and tongue, and he felt the need in him grow stronger.

'Vixen. I shall have you. Now.'

Sedet laughed, soft and low, her voice full of sex. 'Me . . . and another. See what I have brought for you.'

In the centre of the Great Hall stood a dais, topped by a gilded throne which overlooked a pool filled with rose-scented water. The water lapped invitingly about the head and shoulders of a beautiful youth, his dark eyes circled with black kohl and his full lips glossed in strawberry pink.

'Tariq. Your Master wishes to inspect his new possession.'

As the Master turned to look at him, he stood up in the water, and he saw how delectable the young man really was. His head and body had been shaven to the smoothness of oiled silk; and such a body it was, thought the Master. Young, strong, full of the vitality which swelled the Master's cock and made lust fill his balls with aching heaviness.

The youth was perhaps seventeen or eighteen, but he was ageless. Were it not for the hugely swollen cock dancing between his slender thighs, he might also have been described as androgynous, for his features were fine and sensitive, his lips as full and luscious as a young girl's. He stood stock-still, his thighs slightly parted, runnels of fragrant water trickling and dripping over his tight arse cheeks and little wavelets lapping at his shaven balls.

Sedet answered the Master's thoughts.

'Is he not beautiful, my lord?'

'He is . . . tolerable.'

Sedet rose from her knees with a trail of kisses, beginning at the Master's dick and ending at his lips.

'He is my gift to you . . . no, to us both.'

'He is skilled?'

'In *all* the arts of lust. For he pleasures men and women with equal . . . enthusiasm.'

The Master could not deny that Tariq was a morsel to tempt even the most jaded appetite. He allowed Sedet to lead him down the steps and into the warm waters of the pool. Tariq did not speak, but sank to his knees in the pool, so that the waters rose to the level of his chest. He raised his eyes to the Master's, begging, pleading.

'Tariq is a mute,' explained Sedet. 'He speaks with his eyes and his dick.'

'He has been initiated?'

'I undertook that . . . onerous task myself.' Sedet ran lascivious fingers down Tariq's cheek, to the tiny double puncture scar, so very faint in the crook of his neck.

The Master felt a twinge of regret. He would have enjoyed the taste and spurt of this boy's blood, salty and strong on his tongue. But no matter. He would enjoy him still. His cock throbbed with the need to explore the tightness of Tariq's boyish backside.

Sedet snapped her fingers.

'Undress the Master. Pleasure him.' She smiled. 'Pleasure us both.'

Sedet purred with pleasure. Her gift had been accepted, and a very fine gift it was too; even now, her thighs were wrapped tightly around Tariq's adorable waist. The mingled elixir of his seed and the Master's oozed out of her, forming creamy-white feathers and swirls in the pink-tinged water. She leaned back against the side of the pool, letting Tariq fuck her just one more time, as a reward for having such a huge and delectable cock.

The Master's hands were cupped tightly around Tariq's balls, his dick deep in the mute's backside. It was a wonderfully receptive anus, elastic as a woman's sex but glove-tight. It seemed to suck the pleasure out of him, the boy slut's buttocks squeezing hard about his shaft with every new thrust.

A long, luxurious spurt brought the Master's recreation to a close. He amused himself one last time by digging his fingernails into Tariq's scrotum, so that the pain-loving youth lost control, spurting his last drops into Sedet's welcoming haven. Then he pushed Tariq away and climbed out of the pool, slipping his arms into a soft bathrobe handed to him by the ubiquitous Ibrahim.

'Something is troubling you, my lord?' Sedet curled her wet limbs at his feet, stroking his bare legs.

He looked down at her.

'Possibly.'

'Tell me, my lord.' She kissed his feet, stroking them with the wet strands of her hair.

'It is Weatherall.'

Sedet looked at him, puzzled.

'Weatherall, my lord? But if he and the Dubois slut succeed . . . if they are able to obtain supplies of the mineral . . .'

'Then I shall have untold power, I shall be sexually invincible and more . . . but . . .' His fingers clenched and unclenched. The thought nagged at him and kept on nagging.

'But you do not entirely trust Weatherall?'

'Quite.'

Not that it made any real sense. Anastasia Dubois was among the Master's most favoured sluts and Nick Weatherall had served him faithfully ever since his initiation. And yet there was something about him, something secretive, something that had defied his attempts to probe Weatherall's thoughts.

'Then the solution is simple,' smiled Sedet. 'You must send someone else. Someone who will follow them and report back to you on their actions.'

'Yes.' The Master stroked Sedet's hair as though she were a favourite hunting dog. 'Yes, my darling bitch. I do believe you may be right.'

Chapter 7

Andreas and Mara finished dinner about eleven-thirty. By the time they had drunk the last of the Muscadet, they were the only people left in the hotel restaurant.

Mara leaned over the table and popped the last sliver of fresh strawberry onto Andreas's tongue.

'They're waiting to clear up,' she giggled.

Andreas glanced across to the door. The maître d' was ostentatiously polishing cutlery and the two waitresses were throwing meaningful looks.

'Tell you what, let's order another bottle of wine and some more strawberries,' he suggested, only half joking.

'What! And have them giving us the evil eye all through dessert?'

'We don't have to have them here,' he pointed out. 'We could finish them off in bed.'

Mara pouted at him in mock disapproval.

'Don't you ever think about anything but sex?'

'Not often.'

'That's all right then.' She leaned forward to kiss him, and he got a splendid view of her breasts, nestling bare and unfettered beneath that filmy peasant-style blouse.

'Bed?' suggested Andreas hopefully.

'Not just yet. Let's go for a walk first.'

'It's late,' he protested feebly. He winked. 'And you know I'm scared of the dark.'

'Don't worry, I'll protect you. Come on, let's go.'

So Mara was back to normal, thought Andreas as he

followed her out of the restaurant, happy as a dog with two dicks (and that was pretty damn happy). Here, away from the prying eyes of the Master and his Winterbourne minions, she could even take the opportunity to dress like Mara, instead of Anastasia Dubois.

It was a strange night, hot and rather blustery, and Mara looked like some exotic gypsy princess in that gossamer-fine white blouse, which skimmed her nipples and hinted broadly at the contours of her breasts, traced in patterns of light and shade beneath the thin muslin. She had teamed the blouse with beaded sandals and an embroidered white skirt, very full and floaty, which blew against her legs in the onshore breeze, and moulded itself closely to her body.

'Let's go and take a look at the old town,' she suggested, setting off along the esplanade towards the casino.

'It's not really old,' said Andreas, still half hoping she'd change her mind and accompany him back to their cosy hotel room. 'Most of it got flattened in the war, they just rebuilt it to *look* old.'

'Ah, but the *vibrations* are still here. Can't you feel them?' Mara laid her hands flat on the rough sea wall and closed her eyes, letting the wind buffet her face. 'Wild corsairs, blood and sex and treasure . . .'

'You and your vibrations,' grunted Andreas, slipping his arm about her waist. 'Tell you what, why don't you feel mine?'

Laughing, she pulled away; and he chased her all the way down to the end of the promenade, where the old town rose up like some crusader citadel. Through arched gateways, lights shone and he could hear the faint sounds of music. He groaned.

'I thought all the folkies had gone beddy-byes. What with all that real ale, they ought to be comatose by now.'

They walked into the old town through a short passageway which led underneath the city walls and found themselves in a maze of cobbled streets. Some of the cafés

104

and restaurants had shut for the night, but the Café Surcouf was still doing a good trade, with more than half its tables still occupied and waiters buzzing about with trays of pastis and espresso.

In the square outside the café, a group of musicians in Breton dress were playing a slow, syncopated dance tune. Frankly, Andreas had an in-built dislike of anything that sounded like a cat being castrated, but there was something about this particular bunch of musical vivisectionists that set his unwilling foot a-tapping.

'They're good,' said Mara, humming and clapping along to the beat.

'Not bad I s'pose,' muttered Andreas, trying not to look as if he might be into folk music.

The tune came to an end and Mara cheered.

'Bravo! Encore!'

'*Si m'selle voudrait danser?*' suggested the leader of the band, a tall, swarthy-looking guy in a flat-brimmed hat.

'Yes, yes, I want to dance!' Mara turned to Andreas, her eyes sparkling. She tugged at his hand. 'Come on, dance with me. They're going to play something specially for us.'

Andreas cringed with embarrassment.

'Go on . . . I'll just stay here and watch.'

A small crowd had gathered. They loved Mara, and Andreas could see why. She looked tasty as a *galette au jambon* in that peasant gear, and as she spun and leaped in time to the music, she offered her audience appetising glimpses of her bare breasts and thighs.

The singer tapped out the rhythm with his foot.

'C'est dans dix ans je m'en irai,
La jument de Michao a passé dans le pré . . .'

The musicians whistled and yelped as Mara jumped and spun, her skirt billowing out around her hips and revealing the open secret of Mara's hatred of underwear. One of

105

the musicians seized her round the waist and threw her right up into the air and her hair fluttered out like tongues of flame.

> 'La jument de Michao et son petit poulain
> Ont passé dans le pré et mangé tout le foin.
> C'est dans neuf ans je m'en irai,
> J'entends la loup et le renard chanter . . .'

And so it went on, with Mara dancing and Andreas watching, sharing a lustful kinship with every other red-blooded male in the lamplit square, every single one of them wondering what it would be like to throw her down on the cobblestones and have her. The difference was, Andreas Hunt actually *knew*.

It wasn't a sight you'd willingly tear yourself away from, but something caught Andreas's eye. Not something, someone. An old guy, smartly dressed, standing at the other side of the square and watching intently. It was the way he was staring that made Andreas notice him; he was staring almost unblinkingly at Mara. Dirty old man, thought Andreas. Well you can't have her, she's mine.

Their eyes met. It was only for the briefest of moments, but Andreas felt a cold shiver pass right through him, as though he'd swallowed a bucketful of ice cubes.

The music grew faster, more furious, as the dance reached its crescendo. Mara was dancing alone, so lightly and quickly that she hardly seemed to be touching the ground at all. She had kicked off her sandals and was leaping barefoot on the cold cobblestones. As the final chorus ended with yells and shrieks, she leapt into Andreas's arms, laughing and panting as she sank down, laying her head in his lap.

'Was I good?'

He shook his head.

'Bad. *Exceptionally* bad. Especially the bit where you

showed everyone you're not wearing any knickers.'

'You're complaining?'

'Actually that was my favourite bit.'

His eyes lingered long and lovingly on Mara's wonderful cleavage, most of it laid bare by the untied drawstring at the neck of her blouse. When Andreas looked up, the old man was gone. Still, who cared?

Mara took his fingers and began licking them, one by one, taking them deep into her mouth then letting them escape with breathtaking slowness.

'Dancing always gives me an appetite,' she said.

'But we've already eaten.'

Mara's tongue-tip circled the inner surface of his palm. 'Who's talking about food?'

The ribbed sand was wet and cold underneath Andreas's back, but he couldn't have cared less if he was lying on quicksand. He was naked in the surf at the edge of a wild sea, and Mara was astride him, her hot thighs squeezing tight about his hips.

A full moon was spilling its light onto them out of a tumbling night sky, turning everything an unreal shade of silver. But there was nothing unreal about the pumping pleasure of being screwed by Mara Fleming. She was hot and firm, hungry and vital, her strong thighs dancing still as though they could go on dancing for ever. Dancing on his oh-so-grateful prick.

Cold sea spray showered their bodies, but the danger of the incoming tide only added to the excitement. Andreas found himself imagining that they were strangers; two holidaymakers who'd just met, who didn't even know each other's names. Who wanted each other so badly that they couldn't even wait long enough to get back to the hotel. They had to have each other right here and right now.

Rolling over and over at the margin of the sea, they rediscovered the raw thrill of the very first time. That time on the beach in Whitby, when neither of them had trusted the other, but their desire had been stronger than both of them.

And tonight was bigger even than that, thought Andreas. His wet fingers, gritty with sand, grappled hungrily for the hand-hold of Mara's deep bum cleft. Two beautiful handfuls of firm bum flesh, more than two hands could hold. He jerked his hands towards him and she came too, her whole body bumping against the root of his dick.

'Steady,' gasped Mara. 'You'll make me come too soon.'

'So I'll make you come again.'

'Andreas!'

'And again.'

He did it again, squeezing his fingers tight, holding her firm in his two hands and pulling her so close and so hard that pubic bone jolted against pubic bone. It was almost painful. And it was bloody fantastic.

There was sand everywhere, wet and gritty, abrasive and uncomfortable. It was between his thighs, his buttocks, smeared over his belly and chest and nipples. There were even grains of sand on his dick, tiny but needle-sharp; sliding in and out of Mara with every new thrust. And the weird thing was, the discomfort only served to make the pleasure more intense.

'This. Is. The best,' he gasped, rolling over so that it was Mara who was on her back, her hair floating about her head like a seaweed halo. 'The best it's ever been.'

'Don't stop. Don't let it finish,' pleaded Mara, her eyes turned to metallic discs by the silvery moonlight. Andreas caught his reflection in them, looming closer then receding with each new thrust of his pelvis into Mara's ready warmth.

He held on. It wasn't easy. He wanted to make those last few strokes and gush into her, take the easy route to pleasure. But this was too good to waste. He had to make it last.

Withdrawing from her was the only thing he could do.

To stay inside her would push him over the edge of self-control. The cold water swirled about his knees as he knelt over Mara, kissing her thighs as he pushed them apart.

'Let me in,' he murmured. And he bent to lay a trail of salty kisses all the way from her knees to her dark-fringed pussy lips.

'Ah. Ah yeees,' she moaned, twisting and bucking her hips as his lips and tongue came closer to the heart of her sex. He knew she was on the edge, her clitoris swollen to the point of explosion. But Andreas wasn't going to spoil it all by making her come.

He took a tuft of her maidenhair into his mouth and pulled it with his teeth. Mara groaned.

'Harder.'

It was amazing how much more pleasure you could make a lover feel, without actually making her come. Andreas's tongue explored the crease between pussy lips and thigh, the frilled inner lips of Mara's sex, the concentric petals which protected the fragile flower stalk which throbbed with lustful need.

When at last he entered her again, he knew that it would take one thrust, no more, to bring them both to the apex of pleasure. But it was worth it. Coloured lights burst inside his head as they came together, hugging each other tight as though by doing so they could share each other's orgasm.

There was only one fly in the ointment – and it wasn't much of a fly, thought Andreas. But it did haunt him as he lay panting on top of Mara, savouring the final waves of pleasure. And that was a curious, twisted sense of *déjà vu*. The weird feeling that whatever he might do tonight, sooner or later he would have done it all before . . .

Graveney drove into St Malo just as the last lights were going out in the hotel rooms. Her favourite time of day. She licked her lips. Darkness, strangers, a warm night; it all added up to good hunting.

She parked the car in front of the hotel – the best in town, naturally – took her luggage out of the boot and went to check in. A smile played about the corners of her mouth. All in all, she was feeling rather pleased with herself; her status among the Winterbourne elite had really skyrocketed since she'd found that little grey-green stone. The fact that the Master had chosen her for this special task proved that beyond any doubt.

An amusing thought wandered into her mind. Perhaps, rather than just monitoring the activities of Weatherall and his flame-haired slut, she should actually seek out the origins of the stone herself? Success in locating an inexhaustible supply would be sure to place her above all the other sluts in the Master's entourage. Perhaps even above Queen Sedet herself . . .

The night porter was slouching behind the desk, reading some girlie magazine or other. Spotting Graveney walking into reception, he hastily thrust it into the waste paper basket. He was appetisingly young and quite good-looking, she thought; appealing in a puppyish kind of way.

'Good evening.' She smiled, laying her passport on the desk. She didn't bother making any attempt at French. They all understood English if you spoke it loudly enough. She let her gaze wander casually down to the scrunched-up magazine in the waste bin. A pouting mouth, a huge and crumpled breast and a peroxide tuft of pubic wire blazed out of the open page.

The night porter coughed. When she looked at him again, she saw that he had blushed to the roots of his hair.

'Madame?'

'You have a room for me. A double, en-suite, with a sea view.'

She let his eyes linger on her. Why not? What was the point of dressing to kill if you didn't attract any prey? Graveney knew she looked good, even better than usual. Her red halter-necked top more than did justice to her glossy black hair and tanned skin, and hugged her small breasts with a lover's caress. It stopped just short of the waistband of her red and black sarong, revealing the glittering crystal set into her pierced navel.

'I . . . er . . . *oui, madame* . . .'

He looked around, confused, rifling through papers and drawers of keys.

'You're not going to keep me waiting, are you?' Graveney's voice was smooth but icy cool. 'I hate being kept waiting.'

'I . . . here it is, room seventy-seven.' He handed over the key. Graveney couldn't help noticing the way his tongue-tip kept flicking out, moistening his lips. The dear boy was a bundle of nerves. 'M-may I carry your bags for you, madame?'

An apple for the teacher, thought Graveney. Well, well. And after all, I am hungry. It's so long since I . . . fed.

'If you like,' she said, airily. 'But mind you don't damage them. One scratch on that leather . . .'

'*Oui, madame.*'

She watched with pleasure as he struggled into the lift with her cases. The doors closed behind them. In the few moments it took for the lift to reach the seventh floor, she amused herself by watching the young porter, teasing him by trying to get him to look her in the eye.

'Here we are, madame. Room seventy-seven.' The key slid into the lock and the door swung open. '*Zut alors, mais non! Vas-y, vas-y, sale bête!*'

Graveney followed him into the room and saw the cause of his sudden outburst. The window was ajar, and sitting in the middle of the dressing table was . . . a pigeon. A sort of piebald brown and white thing, rather tatty and disreputable-looking. It seemed to look straight at her for a few seconds, almost as if it was weighing her up; then the porter ran towards it waving his arms around, and the pigeon fluttered out through the window, into the night.

'Oh madame, madame, I am so sorry! I will get you another room.'

Graveney smiled.

'That will not be necessary.'

'But, madame . . .'

She beckoned him towards her. He came hesitantly, like the half-trained boy he was.

'What is your name?'

His chocolate-brown eyes returned her questioning gaze. They were very round, the pupils hugely dilated. Graveney heard his breathing quicken, could smell the light tang of his sweat as his adolescent hormones screamed for release.

'J-Jean-Marie.'

She took his face between her hands and kissed him, very softly, on the lips. They were trembling.

'And how old are you, Jean-Marie?'

'Seventeen, madame. Please . . . madame, *je vous en prie, c'est interdit de . . .*'

'I don't care if it is forbidden,' smiled Graveney. 'You want to please your guests, don't you?'

'Of course, but . . .'

'And you'd like me to please you? You'd enjoy that, wouldn't you, Jean-Marie? Having a real woman, instead of some picture in a sleazy magazine?'

He didn't reply, but closed his eyes and let out a low moan as Graveney's fingers travelled lightly over his body, stroking him through his shirt, finding their way with a sensual inevitability to the guilty throb of his manhood.

'Mmm,' purred Graveney. 'You're all hard. Are you hard for *me*, Jean-Marie, or for some picture in a magazine?'

Her fingers curled about the long, hard stem of his dick and squeezed it through his uniform pants.

'*Mon Dieu, madame, je vous en prie . . .*'

There were tears at the corners of his eyes. How sweet, thought Graveney. How adorably childlike you are, Jean-Marie.

'I want you, Jean-Marie,' she whispered, unbuttoning his shirt and easing it over his shoulders. 'I want to teach you to do all those things you've read about in your magazines. I want you to do them to me. Isn't that what you want too?'

The whisper of silk made his eyes flutter open. He stood and gaped like a schoolboy as Graveney untied her halter top and let it fall down to her waist, exposing her breasts.

'Go on,' she smiled. 'You can touch them if you like.'

'I can . . . ?'

'Touch them, Jean-Marie. I'm *ordering* you to touch them.'

A sob of need escaped from him as he buried his face between her breasts, pressing his lips to her flesh, exploring her nakedness with a child's wonderment. She stroked his bare back, breathing in his scent. He smelt delicious, young and juicy and full of an erotic energy she longed to taste.

Her hands slid down and unfastened her sarong, letting it fall to the ground. Gently, she pushed him away.

'Do you like what you see?'

'Oh yes! Oh yes, madame.'

It was all Graveney could do not to laugh at the boy's naivety. The chocolate-brown eyes were round as saucers, fixed on this unbelievable manifestation of an adolescent boy's wet dream. A beautiful woman was standing right in front of him, wearing nothing but tiny red briefs, a matching suspender belt with sheer stockings, and high-heeled shoes. A moment later, even the panties were gone.

'Undress for me, Jean-Marie. I want to see your dick.'

She enunciated the word 'dick' with a lasciviousness which she knew would shock her little protégé, yet thrill him to new heights of sexual desire. She knew the feelings that must be coursing through him, the unbearable throb of his dick, the terrible need to ejaculate into the warm softness of her flesh; and she fed on those feelings, delighting in his agony as she took him to the edge of endurance.

His fingers shook as he unbuckled his belt, then unbuttoned and unzipped his trousers. He was so nervous that he almost tripped and fell as he was stepping out of them.

'Now the underpants. And the shoes and socks. I want you naked, Jean-Marie, you can't have any secrets from me.'

His coyness delighted her. The way he turned away, presenting his smooth, slender back to her as he peeled down his white underpants, so that the first she saw of his nakedness was the kissable smoothness of his perfect backside.

'Turn and face me.'

Slowly, he complied. Graveney shuddered with pleasure at the sight of Jean-Marie's eager cock, arcing up out of a forest of soft black curls. It was not the longest she had ever seen, nor the thickest, but it was certainly one of the prettiest. Its glass-smooth head dripped with wetness, simply begging to be tasted.

'Have you ever licked a woman out, Jean-Marie?'

He stared at her, his head moving slowly from side to side.

'Then it's about time you learned. Come here and get down on your knees.'

He was slow in complying, so she took him by the gold chain round his neck and twisted it, forcing him to his knees. The discomfort slightly impeded his breathing, but a look of utter devotion filled his eyes.

'Put your hands between my thighs and open me up. *Gently* now, that's it. What do you see?'

'A . . . a pink rose. Soft petals. They smell so sweet. And a flower stalk . . .'

'Take it on your tongue. Lick it and suck it. If you are a good boy I will let you drink my come.'

She sighed with pleasure as he began his first, clumsy attempts. She would teach him well, and when he had learned his lesson she would show him how good it felt to have a woman's lips around his dick. And how much better still to feel her teeth in his flesh, her lips drinking greedily at the warm, luxuriant gush of his blood.

Chapter 8

Andreas had always been a beach bum at heart. And there couldn't be many things more satisfying than necking on a topless beach with Mara Fleming, six cans of ice-cold lager and a cumulus cloud of pink candyfloss.

'I suppose,' began Mara drowsily, rolling over onto her back, 'we should really be *doing* something, not lazing about on the beach.'

'Like what?'

'Like finding this bit of magic rock the Master wants, before he starts nosing about himself and finds out a few home truths about us.'

'This bloke . . . what's his name . . . ?'

'Lebecq. Gaston Lebecq.'

'Lebecq, that's the one.' Andreas pulled off a big clump of candyfloss and dangled it over Mara's lips. 'How exactly are we supposed to track him down? All we've got is a name.'

'The phone book?'

'I looked. There are about two hundred Lebecqs.'

'Then I guess we'll have to phone them all.'

'And say what? "Hello, you don't know me but I'd love to get my hands on your rocks"? They'll have us carted off to the cells.'

Mara wound a strand of candyfloss about her tongue. It made her lips all pink and sticky and Andreas felt compelled to spend the next couple of minutes licking all the stickiness off.

'You'll think of something,' said Mara. 'You always do.'

'There must be some sort of public record office round here,' mused Andreas, screwing his eyes up to get a better look at a pair of exceptionally well-developed tits, bouncing up and down on the chest of a nearby volleyball player. 'And I suppose the local churches would have records of births and breasts . . . I mean deaths, and so on.'

'We might get somewhere,' observed Mara with dry humour, 'if you could concentrate on the job in hand.'

Andreas's gaze lingered wistfully on the large, well-oiled breasts. They seemed to have an independent life of their own. Now *there* were a couple of things he'd really like to have in hand.

Putting thought into action, he rolled over and laid a sticky hand on Mara's breast. Laughing, she wriggled away.

'Not here! Someone will see.'

'Bollocks to the lot of 'em,' replied Andreas, and promptly bent over to take her nipple into his mouth.

Somewhere in France, a woman with black hair and caramel skin was standing beside an ornamental pool, gazing down into the water. The pool itself was nothing out of the ordinary, just a hole in the ground edged with a few stones, part of a display at an out-of-town garden centre. There were many more interesting things to look at, but Anjula was transfixed by what she saw.

Beneath the surface of the gently lapping water, she could make out the images of two people: a man and a woman. Nick Weatherall and Anastasia Dubois. They were lying side by side on a beach, laughing and kissing like young lovers as they shared a stick of candyfloss. Damn them. She cursed them under her breath. Why did they have to end up in St Malo, of all places? And what was that they were saying . . . ?

'Madame? Can I help you, madame? You wish perhaps to make a purchase . . . ?'

People were coming towards her. With a scowl of annoyance, Anjula waved her hands across the surface of the water and dispersed the images. She turned towards the elderly male assistant with a look of contempt.

'All I want is for you to get out of my way.'

Andreas and Mara had talked through all the possibilities. Unfortunately Mara was right. If they were going to track down Gaston Lebecq, they would have to do more than laze about in the sunshine. So they agreed to split up for the rest of the day and begin their investigations separately. Which was why Andreas was about to make his first visit to a museum since – aged eleven – he'd been thrown out for sticking plasticine willies on the dinosaurs.

He wasn't particularly looking forward to it. Still, you never could tell; maybe museums weren't boring any more. And, more to the point, maybe Lebecq would turn out to have been famous, with his own gallery of magic rocks or something.

He paid his forty-five francs (daylight robbery) and wandered through a couple of rooms filled with bones and bits of menhir. The most interesting thing in there was the attendant, who looked mildly naughty in her too-tight navy blue uniform, with the top button that wouldn't quite do up.

It was when he turned right instead of left at the model fishing boats that Andreas walked into trouble. For some reason, he just couldn't seem to find his way out. And what kind of museum was this, anyway? No signs, no display cases, no exhibits – just a maze of gloomy corridors. Forty-five francs, and not so much as a window to climb out of.

He was starting to feel tense. Bloody museums, he'd never liked them. Left. Right. Straight on. Was he going round in circles? The corridor seemed to be sloping down slightly, but he guessed that was just his imagination. Knowing his luck, he'd probably wandered into the basement, the bit where they kept the corpses of all the tourists who'd never found their way out. Momentarily he thought of the cellars at Winterbourne, and the Master's discarded body, trapped insect-like inside its crystal prison. Where was the bloody way out?

Hang on though, there was a light at the end of this particular tunnel; a yellowish haze of electricity. As he got closer, he saw that he was approaching some kind of observation window. He breathed a sigh of relief. At last he was getting somewhere. This had better be worth the wait.

He found himself peering through glass into a room. Inside, waxwork figures had been arranged into a World War II tableau – good waxworks, too, so lifelike you'd have sworn they were real if they weren't frozen into impossible postures.

Mind you, it was all a bit tasteless. A bloke tied to a chair, bare chested and staring up in terror at a man in an SS uniform. A man with shiny boots, black breeches and a very big whip.

Andreas felt faintly queasy. It didn't help that the guy on the chair looked vaguely like himself. Ouch. He was glad it was only a waxwork exhibit. Now, where to next?

It was just as he was turning away that the unthinkable happened. The waxworks *moved*. But . . .

'*Schweinhund!*'

The officer's hand fell and so did the whip, slicing across his captive's chest. Blood sprang up in crimson beads as the plaited leather seared his flesh; and . . . and the captive threw back his head and screamed in pain.

Bloody realistic waxworks. *Bloody* realistic. Only they weren't waxworks, were they? Andreas assimilated the truth with a shock that kept him rooted to the spot, his mouth hanging open and his eyes staring. They were very horribly real.

And worse than that, much worse still; he was a part of it all.

* * *

While Andreas checked out the museum, Mara was doing what she did best: investigating the local vibrations. She had decided to make a tour of the old town, seeking out all the places where the stone might have been kept, in the hope of picking up its trail . . . or at least some clue as to the fate of its former owner.

As she walked through the narrow streets of the old town, the rose-coloured crystals bounced gently on the end of their leather thong, teasing the bare swell of her cleavage. She stroked the necklace thoughtfully. It seemed so trivial, so unimportant; and its resonances were interfering with her psychic sight, making it much more difficult to pick up thoughts and images from the stones which surrounded her. Perhaps . . .

A softly whispered voice inside her head seemed to be urging her: go on, take it off, what harm can it do? Her fingers hovered momentarily over the stones, then drew back, as though they had touched hot coals. She recalled what Andreas had told her about those 'lost' days, the things she had done . . . and the dream of her struggle with Anastasia Dubois.

Or had it been a dream? There was no way of knowing. Best not to take any chances. For the time being at least, the crystal pendant would stay where it was.

The authorities had made a good job of rebuilding St Malo. You couldn't distinguish the genuinely old bits from the parts which had been restored or completely rebuilt – at least, not by sight. Mara felt the pulse of history all around her, but the sounds and images were jumbled up and fragmented, like the old stones which had been salvaged and reused.

It was frustrating work, but she knew she had to persevere. Realistically, her powers were probably their best chance of success. She paused on a crowded corner, dizzy with sound and colour, leant back against the wall of a café and closed her eyes.

Concentrate.

"*Scusez-moi.*"

'*Que fais-tu là, tu es folle?*'

She tried to block the voices and the jostling elbows out of her mind and focus on the scrappy, incomprehensible messages she was getting from the cool stones under her hands. Nothing. Or at least, nothing of any significance. Disappointed, she opened her eyes. People were staring at her. She stared right back and pushed her way through them, ignoring the large, male hand which took the opportunity to grope her backside through her tight white shorts.

Turning left into a narrow alleyway, she found the peace and quiet she needed to think. She skimmed her hands over the stones, walked through into a deserted courtyard and drank in the atmosphere. But there was nothing *but* atmosphere. No communication with the spirits of the past, no surge of sudden psychic electricity as she plugged into history. Perhaps rebuilding had wiped the history from St Malo after all, perhaps there was nothing left to find.

Once more round the town, then she would give up and go and find Andreas. The Public Record Office was beginning to look like a better and better option. It wasn't until she passed the funny little house with the turrets that Mara realised, no matter which direction she took, no matter where else she might go, she kept coming back to this place. But why?

She walked to the end of the stone-flagged alleyway. The tall, narrow, turreted house rose up in front of her like an anorexic fairytale chateau, the whole thing squeezed into a tiny space as if the buildings on either side were trying to crowd it out. A wooden balcony decorated with weird and wonderful carvings overhung the street and she stepped a little closer. Perhaps if she climbed on to the top of that wall, and stretched out her arms, she'd be able to touch those carvings . . .

And then she saw it. This really weird thing, like a cloud of heat haze emerging from the mouth of a carved eagle. As she stared at it it got larger and started moving straight towards her. It all happened so quickly that there was no time to get out of the way.

Something struck her on the side of the cheek, hard enough to make her flinch and screw up her eyes. When she reopened them . . .

What . . . what was going on? She knew where she was, she was still standing in the very same place, in front of the turreted house; but *when* was she? Her skin prickled with psychic energy and she knew, even before she saw the two figures standing beside her, that she had somehow travelled back in time.

The woman with the caramel skin and tumbling black hair was lavishly dressed, in a high-waisted gown of silk brocade, cut low in the bodice to display her small, well-formed breasts to best advantage. The second blow from her ringed hand caught Mara on the shoulder and she stumbled, falling forward onto her knees on the smooth flagstones.

'Impudent girl,' sneered the dark-haired woman. Mara opened her mouth to reply, but a swipe from an ivory-handled riding crop drove the breath from her body. 'You *dare* defy your mistress?'

Mara remained silent, her bare arm smarting from the swish of the crop. Her mind whirled. Where . . . what . . . who . . . ? Looking down at herself, she saw that she was dressed not in finery but in a cheap cotton print and a soiled white apron. In front of her, on the flagstones, lay the shattered remnants of a broken wine jug.

'My lord Roberto,' continued the dark-haired woman. 'This clumsy servant girl is nothing but a good-for-nothing slattern.'

'Indeed?'

A man walked forward, nudging Mara's silent form with

the toe of his boot. She kept her eyes cast down and saw only polished riding boots, buckskin breeches and an engraved scabbard. She let out a curse of pain as his gauntleted hand seized her by the hair and forced her to look up at him. A cruelly handsome, sun-bronzed face leered down at her, delighting in her discomfiture.

'Do you like what you see, slut?'

'Let go! Let go of me!'

He laughed and pushed her away from him.

'A spirited little vixen – more . . . stimulating than the usual run of servant girls. You intend to punish her of course?'

'Of course.' The lady contemplated Mara for a few seconds. 'You have rendered me good service, my lord Roberto. In payment for that service, I have decided to give the slut to you. You may deal with her as you see fit.'

Roberto's dark eyes narrowed with satisfaction.

'My lady is a generous mistress. I am most . . . gratified by your gift.'

'Then use it well.'

'Have no fear, I will teach the slut better manners.'

With a sweep of scented muslin, the dark-haired lady melted into the shadows, leaving only Mara and her tormentor. There were others nearby – she could hear their voices, could even make out the vague shapes of their peering faces, but no one seemed to be taking the slightest bit of notice of her. It would have been almost like a dream, if it hadn't felt so disturbingly real.

'So,' said Roberto, regarding his prize. 'You are a disobedient jade, a clumsy slattern. And you shall begin by begging me for forgiveness.'

Mara answered him by spitting in his face and scrambling away. But she did not get far. Roberto's muscular hands seized her by the collar of her dress and, throwing her to the ground, ripped it from her back.

'No. No, I will not! I will not . . .' She was not so much

124

afraid as enraged. However darkly attractive Roberto might be, he was an arrogant son of a bitch and she would not let him humiliate her like this.

Kicking and spitting, she succeeded in rolling onto her side and fetching Roberto a blow in the solar plexus with her high-heeled shoe. But this seemed only to increase Roberto's ardour. The knife glittered in his hand and, as Mara caught her breath, convinced that he was about to pierce her flesh, he slashed the torn dress from her breasts.

'Bastard,' she hissed between clenched teeth. She criss-crossed her hands over her breasts, but Roberto stood over her and grabbed her wrists, forcing them apart.

Underneath the torn shift her breasts were bare, the nipples adrenaline-hard, shamelessly stimulated by the violence of the encounter. At this moment, Mara hated herself more than she hated Roberto; her body had escaped from her control, an arrogant stranger was stripping her in the street and all she could feel was the insistent throb of sexual need between her thighs.

'Try to hide yourself from me, would you? 'Tis no use playing the prude with me, young miss. You're hot for me and before I've done you'll take every inch of me into that pretty quim.'

'Never! I'll not submit to you.'

'So you're game to fight me! I like a maid with spirit.' He laughed. 'Though by your reputation you're no maid . . .'

He cut the last of the dress from her body, and Mara felt the sun's dry, unforgiving heat on her bare belly, her thighs, her mossy mound. There was something mesmeric about the dazzle of the hot sun, the warm smoothness of the flagstones beneath her back and Roberto's cruel eyes, glittering in that wild, wind-tanned face. And for some reason she didn't understand, Mara found that she couldn't move; could only lie there beneath him, gazing up at her tormentor as he threw down the knife and began to undress.

Beneath his blue soldier's jacket and fine linen shirt,

Roberto's nut-brown torso was massively muscular, with curls of coarse black hair which disappeared tantalisingly under his belt. He stripped off his shirt and let it fall, unbuckling his belt with a kind of slow-burning hunger which left Mara hating him yet silently pleading for more.

'It is high time someone taught you the proper way to behave.' The belt curled tight about his fist, the leather flexing as he raised his hand.

Mara scrambled to one side just as the belt came swishing down and it flicked against the stones at her elbow, but she could not long escape Roberto's thirst for vengeance. The second swipe of the belt caught her across the breasts, with a calculated savagery which sent the very tip licking and flicking at her nipples.

As it came down a third time, Mara caught hold of the belt and tried to wrench it out of Roberto's hands. But he was ready for her, and so strong that as he jerked the belt it pulled Mara into his arms.

'Slut,' he murmured, his voice syrupy with anticipation. His rough hands roamed over her shoulders, scratching the smoothness of her skin, awakening desires she did not even want to admit to.

'Let me go. Let. Me . . .' Mara's voice tailed off into a low sob of longing. Roberto's fingers had found their way down her back to the swell of her arse and they were exploring the secret tightness within.

'Let you go?' He chuckled. 'Darling slut, that is the very last thing you wish me to do. What you desire is for me to throw you down upon the ground and take you. Is that not so?' He took her chin in his hand, forcing her to look at him. 'You will answer me.'

'N-no. No.'

Roberto stifled her protests with a proprietorial kiss, his mouth covering hers, one hand filled with the yielding softness of her buttock, the other probing between her thighs, opening her up, triumphantly smearing her with her own sweet oozings.

'Yes, little slut. Yes.'

She was helpless in his arms, all the strength gone from her limbs. Only his hands prevented her from falling. At the very moment of her complete surrender, Roberto pushed her from him, hurling her to the ground. Her juices glistened on his leather-gloved fingers.

'Where is all your modesty now, gypsy whore? Filthy gypsy whore, I will teach you to take pleasure in your punishment.'

Her face ground into the dirt, she felt his weight upon her back, and then the sudden, hot hardness as he sliced into her. His breath was a hoarse rasping, in time to the rough thrust of his body against hers. She scrabbled at the ground with her fingernails, but it was a half-hearted resistance.

Between her thighs she was wet with the juice of a too-willing submission. Her sex felt like wet velvet, slippery-smooth and so sensitive that every movement sent aches and shivers of excitement through her entire body. Instinctively she clenched her sex muscles, delighting in the thick hardness which filled her so completely. This was her enemy, her tormentor; she should be afraid, and in a way she was but, if anything, fear added an edge of intensity to the sensations which coursed through her.

There on the ground, as she squirmed beneath Roberto, Mara wondered what strange power had brought her to this; and how punishment could bring so much pleasure.

Sometimes, thought Andreas, there was only one thing for it: run like fuck.

He took his own advice and raced hell-for-leather away from the window and the sight which still filled his thoughts. Corridors stretched out in all directions; which one was he supposed to take? He couldn't remember how the hell he'd got here, and Mister Panic was firmly in the driving seat.

What's more, it didn't matter how fast he tried to run; his legs were moving in slow motion, and everything around him was strobing lazily like a faulty disco light. He couldn't tell where the light was coming from, but it was dazzling him; it flashed and he put his hand up to cover his eyes. When he blinked them open, he realised that something very odd had happened to him. Very odd indeed.

He was dressed like a Nazi stormtrooper.

Now hang on a minute, said the voice in his head. This isn't happening. It can't be. Oh yes it is, said the polished jackboots as he ran on down the corridor, fighting breathlessly to make any headway, like somebody swimming in warm treacle.

The light pulsed again. This time when he looked down at himself, he was wearing some kind of old-fashioned lounge suit. The end of the corridor was almost in sight. Again. Ugh. Breton folk costume this time, big pants, clogs, the full monty. God, he hoped he wasn't going to stay like this, he must look a right dick.

Again. Again. Almost there. Again.

By the time he emerged through a side door into blazing sunlight, Andreas was dressed like a fancy-dress pirate, complete with cutlass and gunpowder pouch. Normally he'd have stopped to admire himself in a shop window, but all he could think about was getting away from this place before the weirdness closed in on him for ever, sucking him back into its belly like a squid's dinner.

He was running faster now, his legs moving more easily; he could almost breathe freely and hardly cared about the bare feet or the pistol banging against his hip. He could feel the pull lessening, the power dissipating.

Then the sun seemed to switch off for a fraction of a second. When it switched back on, Andreas could hardly move at all for the full set of chain mail suddenly weighting his body to the ground. Ha bleeding ha. He dragged his leaden feet over the cobblestones. Very funny I'm sure, we've all enjoyed the joke, now how the fuck do I get out of this?

As Andreas twisted and turned, trying to wriggle his way out of the suit of armour, he saw something which turned fear and annoyance into full-blooded crimson rage. Some bloke, some bastard bloke in poncey breeches and shiny boots, had Mara – *his* Mara – pinned to the ground and was grinding his dick into her while she spat and snarled and scratched helplessly at the ground, unable to free herself.

Suddenly he didn't care about the weight of the armour, all he cared about was Mara – and smashing his chain-mailed fist into that bastard's smug features. He half ran, half lumbered towards him, shouting his head off, screaming obscenities he didn't even realise he knew.

And now the bloke was facing him, grinning, daring him. Come on, come and get me, think you're hard do you? Well come and have a go then. The bloke wasn't a soldier any more, he was a peasant – and so was Andreas, clattering across the flagstones in a pair of huge wooden clogs. The light was fading in and out, brightening, darkening, and with each blaze of sunlight came another change.

They were moving back through history, Andreas and this nameless bloke. God alone knew why, but that's what was happening. They were evolving *backwards*. Knights in armour, peasants, Vikings, Romans in little white tunics and leather sandals that laced to the knees. Much more of this and they'd be tadpoles in the primeval soup.

By the time they were eyeball to eyeball, all three of them were dressed in furs – if you could call it dressed, seeing as Mara was wearing nothing but a tiny strip of something striped and furry across her gorgeous backside, and as for Andreas and the bloke, they had huge droopy moustaches and were wearing more blue body paint than anything else. Asterix the Gaul, that's what I look like, thought Andreas. A sodding kids' cartoon.

However, the iron-headed battleaxe in his right hand definitely wasn't a cartoon, which was something of a comfort, and Andreas ran full-tilt at the bloke with the express intention of burying it between his shoulder blades.

'Get your fucking filthy hands off her!'

He'd picked a fine time to turn macho. This bloke was twice his size, evil as hell and looked like the axe blade would just bounce off the top of his head. Ah well, too late to turn back now, even though Mara was screaming at him to keep away, not to be so bloody stupid. Mara ought to know by now, bloody stupid was what Andreas Hunt did best.

The funny thing was, he never got to find out which was harder, the axe blade or the bloke's head. As the two made contact, it was almost as if Andreas had completed an electrical circuit. No, more like pissing into the mains. A huge rush of heart-stopping energy zapped through him, paralysing him in mid-lunge and, for a split second, he was frozen in mid-air, both feet off the floor and every single hair on his body standing to attention.

Then there was a bang, somewhere in the distance. Not a loud one, not a very impressive bang at all, more of a damp squib. But a circuit breaker had tripped somewhere in the universal fuse box and – not for the first time in his life – Andreas Hunt couldn't tell if he was on his arse or his elbow.

Chapter 9

Jean-Marie was only dead for a few hours. But by the time he woke up, Graveney was more than ready for fun.

'*Chéri*,' she purred. 'It's almost dark. Why don't you show me some of the places where the young, beautiful people go?'

Jean-Marie returned her kiss with a renewed, more knowing ardour. She allowed herself to sink back onto the bed and luxuriated in the refreshing sensual hunger of the brand-new vampire which she, and she alone, had just created.

'I want . . .' he murmured, his lips exploring the crook of her neck, the swell of her breast. 'I want . . .'

She stroked his silky hair and whispered softly to him, as a mother might reassure a child.

'You want to satisfy your needs, Jean-Marie?'

'Yes. My needs.' He spoke the words wonderingly, struggling to understand the meaning of this new and very different life. 'This . . . hunger.'

'It will pass,' smiled Graveney. 'But first it must be fed. You understand that, don't you, Jean-Marie?'

Jean-Marie growled low in his throat. She knew that understanding was dawning in him. He was like her now, no longer a feeble mortal but gloriously undead, a vampire creature who would derive his strength from the sexual energy of his prey. Together they would grow stronger than ever. She was sure that he would prove not only diverting, but a very useful ally.

His hands roamed over her body, pushing open the robe and insinuating themselves into the embroidered silk teddy she was wearing.

'Hunger,' he repeated. 'I want . . .'

'Not now,' she said. 'Later.'

'But Diana . . .'

She stroked his young and beautiful penis lightly, teasing the impudent hunger within him.

'You have a lot to learn, Jean-Marie. But I will teach you.'

Her nails curled about the hard, smooth shaft and dug into it with sudden force. Jean-Marie let out a soft whimper of satisfied pain and spurted into her hand.

'Oh. Oh, Mistress . . .'

'See, little one, I know everything about you, how to give you pleasure, how to make you suffer. Tonight we are going to share the most exquisite pleasure.'

He raised himself on his elbow and looked at her questioningly, with those soft brown eyes.

'Mistress Diana?'

'Tonight we are going out hunting.'

At the height of the summer season, the town of St Malo was chic and teeming with tourists. If you closed your eyes and breathed in deeply, you could smell freshly minted money. But more than that, thought Graveney, you could breathe in the irresistible aromas of blood and youth and sex. A potent cocktail, and one of which she intended to drink until she could drink no more.

The casino overlooked the seafront. At this time of night it was teeming with life, live music thundering out of its open doors and punters spilling out onto the esplanade.

'Here, Maîtresse Diana?'

She shook her head.

'Not tonight. Take me to the place you told me about. The bar.'

132

The Bar Justine was several streets back from the seafront, on a corner in a very ordinary part of town. Outwardly, it was just a run-down café, an American-style joint where kids met to drink Coca-Cola and play the pinball machines. Anonymous kids, just passing through St Malo on their way to somewhere more exciting. No one would miss one or two if they just kind of . . . disappeared.

Graveney stopped to take a look at her reflection in the window of an *épicerie*. She looked understated but terrific in black Levi's, a black vest-top and silver jewellery, with her dark hair gelled and pinned into a sleek Fifties' ponytail. And Jean-Marie was pretty and succulent as spring lamb in collarless shirt and waistcoat, worn over denim shorts. The perfect bait to ensnare unwary prey.

'This is the place, Mistress Diana.'

She kissed him, her caresses subtly reminding his dick how well it would be rewarded if he pleased her tonight.

'Good. It seems perfect.' She licked her lips. 'Which of them do you crave, little one?'

His eyes roamed over the young people talking and laughing in the café. It was obvious, thought Graveney with amusement; he wanted them all, each and every one.

'The blonde girl is very . . .'

'Yes.' Graveney's gaze settled on the girl and approved of Jean-Marie's taste. A scant eighteen, the girl managed to combine fragility and sensuality in that petite frame, those huge dark eyes and those pouting, bee-stung lips. 'Yes, she is isn't she? And the dark-haired one opposite her?'

'A little skinny?'

'Perhaps. But look at that generous mouth, little one. Think of those lips sucking the juice out of your dick.'

She heard him let out a faint sigh.

'*Ah oui, Maîtresse Diana.*'

Graveney touched his arm, sliding her fingers down to

his then lifting his hand to her mouth and kissing it.

'What about the boys, Jean-Marie? Which of them do you find most attractive?'

Jean-Marie looked at her quizzically. She knew what he was thinking: should he tell the truth?

'For you, madame?'

'For us both, Jean-Marie. Surely you have desired other men?'

'I have never . . . thought of it, Mistress Diana.'

'Then think of it now. Why deny yourself the pleasure of another man's dick in your mouth, or his tongue sliding between your thighs, lapping at your balls?' She scanned the bar, looking for exactly the right prey. 'Which one, Jean-Marie?'

He swallowed.

'The . . . the blond . . . by the counter.'

'Ah yes.' She murmured her agreement. 'He *is* rather beautiful, isn't he?'

Sixteen, maybe seventeen, it was so difficult to tell. The youth was sitting at the bar, trying to look grown-up and managing to look like exactly what he was: a delicious morsel of adolescent manhood, bursting with sensual vitality.

'Would you like to fuck him, Jean-Marie? Would you like to slide your dick between those tight little bum cheeks and hear him squeal for mercy as you take that last, prudish virginity?'

Poor dear Jean-Marie. Even after his initiation, the old inhibitions lingered on. She heard him hesitate before forcing out the truth.

'Y-yes, Madame Diana.'

'And have him fuck you?'

'*Peut-être.* And . . .'

'Go on.' Her lips pressed lightly into the crook of his neck. 'Tell me. Everything.'

'I would like to watch him and you . . . together. I would like to see you masturbating over his face . . . and I would like to see you make him lick you out, and . . .'

'Enough, little one.' Graveney let her fingers slip down until they were resting on the swollen rod of Jean-Marie's young, eager cock. 'Soon all your fantasies will be turned to reality. Go into the bar, Jean-Marie.'

'Alone?'

'To begin with. I will follow shortly, but I wish to observe. I want you to pick up the blond boy, Jean-Marie.'

'But what if . . . ?'

'You will bewitch him. Seduce him, then we shall enjoy him together. I will give you the sign.'

She watched through the window as Jean-Marie walked into the bar. Heads turned, but that was small wonder. He was a very beautiful boy. Raw and sensual, yet curiously innocent. Young and untouched – and now that she had initiated him into the realm of the undead, he would stay that way, for ever. Graveney anticipated enjoying the fruits of his gratitude for many a long and delicious night.

He went up to the counter.

'*Tu veux?*'

'*Un Coca.*'

'*Quatre cinquante.*'

Money changed hands. Graveney saw how the girl behind the bar let her fingers linger as she counted the five francs and fifty centimes into his palm. But Jean-Marie wasn't paying her any attention. He had turned his back to the bar and was slowly sipping his iced cola, his eyes fixed on a point in the middle distance.

Well, not a point exactly. A boy. The luscious blond playing the video machine, studiedly grungy with his cut-off denims and that washed-out tee-shirt with the rip at the shoulder, revealing sleek golden skin. Graveney licked her lips. Perfect.

Jean-Marie finished his drink and set the empty glass down on the counter. He had made eye contact with the object of his desire and his gaze never left him as he licked the last drops of cola from his lips and began walking across the café towards the bank of game machines.

'*Tu veux boire?*'

The blond boy nodded.

'*Orangina.*' His voice was low-pitched and gruff, but it was still a boy's voice.

'*On va jouer?*'

'*Si tu veux.*' He was trying to look casual, but his voice was shaking. It was obvious to Graveney that he was as excited by Jean-Marie as Jean-Marie was by him. Two pretty virgin boys, terrified by the force of their own sexuality. A thrill of expectation sent tingles down her belly, and she rubbed her thighs together, making the centre seam of her jeans tease the swollen nub of her clitoris.

The drink arrived and was set on top of the machine. It stayed there untouched. The game was in full swing, but Jean-Marie was paying it less than full attention. His left hand strayed from the joystick to the blond youth's waist and slid down until it was resting on his backside. Graveney held her breath, waiting for the brush-off; but it didn't come. She'd been right – Jean-Marie was a natural seducer and his prey was clearly aching to be taught a few lessons in lust.

The blond boy won the game. Laughing, he turned to face Jean-Marie and Graveney saw that the crotch of his denim shorts was stretched tight across a long, hard swelling, his tee-shirt too brief to cover it. Jean-Marie's gaze travelled down over his body, until it rested on the secret of the boy's desire. Instantly he blushed scarlet to the roots of his hair and tried to cover himself up; but Jean-Marie caught his hand and laid it on his own dick, making him feel the force of his need.

Jean-Marie cast a look towards the door of the café, and saw Graveney walking in. She smiled and nodded, then turned and walked towards a corner table, pretending not to know him.

The boy pulled away from Jean-Marie's caress in sudden, embarrassed realisation. His gaze darted around the café. Had anyone seen? Were any of his friends here? Had they guessed what was going on between him and the young hotel porter?

For a moment, Graveney thought Jean-Marie had blown it, but she had underestimated his powers of seduction. He nodded towards the sign behind the bar: it read TOILETTES. The implication was clear. I'm going in there, and you can follow if you want. Nobody's forcing you, but you know you want to. Don't you, pretty boy?

He turned and walked quickly away, pushing open the door which led to the washrooms and disappearing from sight. It glided shut behind him, tantalising as a slowly closing mouth.

Graveney ordered a cold beer and watched. The blond youth was still standing by the games machine, his fingers tapping distractedly on the top, his eyes fixed on the door. She knew exactly what was going through his mind. Should he? Dare he?

It was only a matter of time.

A few moments later, she saw him drain the bottle of Orangina and set it back on the top of the machine. Then he pushed his way across the bar. He hesitated for a few moments, then opened the washroom door and went inside.

Graveney almost purred with satisfaction. A few more moments, no more, and she would follow where Jean-Marie had led. A little minor tampering with the lock would ensure that the three of them were not disturbed. Ignoring the lecherous gaze of a twenty-something Algerian who kept trying to offer her hashish, she sipped her beer and watched the seconds tick round.

Leaving her glass on the table, she got up and went into the toilets, securing the door behind her. At first she could hear nothing, then she caught a faint moaning coming from the men's washroom. She opened the door very quietly, after all she didn't want to disturb anything interesting – and she wasn't disappointed.

The blond youth was on hands and knees on the cold tiled floor, his shorts stripped down to his ankles, bare arsed and completely delectable. His head was hanging down, his face almost obscured by the cascade of silky, corn-gold hair, and he was panting and moaning like a soul in agony.

'*Ah non, non! C'en est trop, je n'en puis plus!*'

Poor dear boy, smiled Graveney, slipping into the washroom and watching, unseen by Jean-Marie's pretty prey. How adorably naive you are. You are so afraid of what my darling Jean-Marie is going to do to your tight little arse, when what you should truly fear is the bite of my teeth in your sweet young flesh.

She blew Jean-Marie a kiss, and he smiled; understanding for the first time what a wonderful gift she had given him in making him a vampire. An eternity of dark pleasure. Who could ask for more than that? When he cradled his dick in his hands and slipped it between those tight young arse cheeks, she knew that his every act was a tribute of gratitude to her and she shared the exquisite violence of his pleasure.

'*Non! Non, aie!*'

A high, tearing cry shook the young, tanned body as Jean-Marie possessed it in the most intimate way he knew. Ah, such sweet pain, mused Graveney, and her clitoris swelled so hard that she knew she must satisfy her craving.

Her Levi's unbuttoned, she stepped out of them and slid down her g-string. Naked from the waist down, save for a pair of red stilettos, she walked slowly across the washroom.

Jean-Marie was thrusting rhythmically in and out of the dear blond boy's backside. The youth was making such a terrible fuss, weeping and wailing and sighing, that he did not even notice her until she was standing right in front of him, her red shoes practically under his nose.

Grabbing him by the hair, she jerked up his head. Her smile was a glittering snare, luring him to his downfall.

'Pretty one,' she purred. 'My sweet pretty boy.'

'Please,' he gasped, sweat and tears running down his cheeks. 'Please . . . no more, *je vous en prie*.'

'No more?' She affected a look of puzzlement. 'But, my dear one, your pretty cock is straining with juice, and your darling backside is begging for Jean-Marie to fill it with his come. Don't lie to me, sweet boy, I know all your desires. *All* of them. And I can make your dreams come true.'

Taking his head in both hands, she forced it hard between her thighs.

'Lick me out,' she directed him. 'I *know* that's what you want.'

The dear, sweet boy was clumsy in the extreme. It was obvious that he had never had his tongue between a woman's pussy lips before, but in a way his rough, inexpert enthusiasm added to Graveney's pleasure. She came three times in rapid succession before he howled and writhed and ejaculated in a pearly stream all over the toes of her red stilettos.

He lay in a heap on the floor, barely conscious, begging them to leave him be, but that was not a part of Graveney's plan. Her subtle hands soon had him ramrod stiff, and when she bent over him, taking the whole of his shaft into her capacious mouth, he was so lost in lust that he was begging her to take him and never, never stop.

Of course it would have to stop, but not until the dear boy had come once more – it was the least she could do for him before her teeth pierced the flesh of his groin and she and Jean-Marie shared the velvet-smooth elixir of his lifeblood.

Somehow, Andreas knew it must be a dream. How else could he find himself swimming in a tropical ocean, surrounded by a shoal of naked women?

Still, he might as well enjoy it. The water was warm and he was hot, touching willing flesh wherever he reached out his hands. Hey, this was his idea of a wet dream.

The only problem was the noise. No matter what he did, it wouldn't go away, and he knew it wanted something. Him.

Oh bugger off and let me be, he groaned, but there was a light as well as a voice now, and a force like triple-strength magnets was making him stare up at it. All of a sudden, he felt himself rushing up through the water towards the dazzling light, popping up into warm air like a champagne cork.

'Lebecq.'

What?

'Lebecq, wake up!'

Lebecq? Andreas blinked. What the fuck was going on? Wasn't Lebecq that guy he and Mara were supposed to be looking for? He felt dizzy and disorientated. Opening his eyes, he found himself lying in the middle of the street, with two faces staring down at him. One was Mara's, the other the face of that old guy he'd seen watching when Mara danced in the square.

'Who the . . . ?' he stuttered. The old man had him by the shoulders and was shaking him.

'It is I, Henri, do you not recognise me, Lebecq?'

'But I'm not . . .' Andreas began. He looked across at Mara. 'What's going on?' He sat up.

The old man saw him looking at Mara.

'Camille is fine, she is fine now. You must try to think, Lebecq. Is it time?'

'Time?' Andreas was beginning to feel distinctly uncomfortable. He got unsteadily to his feet, shaking his head to clear it. Time to find the six-lane freeway out of loonyland.

'Lebecq,' repeated the old man, seizing Andreas by the shoulders. 'Is it *time*?'

140

Andreas shook him off like a dose of measles. Who *was* this nutter? It was probably safest to humour him.

'No,' he said, as soothingly as he could manage. 'It's not time yet. Just . . . wait. All right?'

And taking Mara by the hand, Andreas legged it out of the alleyway. He didn't stop running until he reached the sea.

'It has been a long time since Winterbourne hosted such a spectacular orgy,' commented Heimdal, the Master's trusted henchman and self-styled Lord of Winterbourne.

'Too long.' Queen Sedet stood beside him in the long gallery, looking down at the Great Hall through one of the observation windows. 'Winterbourne must have its sensual feasts. The faithful must feed. And a queen,' she purred, running her fingernails down the sleeve of Heimdal's tuxedo, 'must satisfy her appetites.'

'Indeed, Mistress.' Heimdal's ice-blue eyes were bright with a slow-burning fire. He took her hand and pressed it to his lips. 'And I am sworn to serve her in all things.'

Sedet tossed her dark, wavy hair over her shoulders. They were smooth and bare, their creamy skin highlighted by her strapless, figure-hugging gown of wine-coloured velvet. With each breath she took, her generous breasts rose and fell, quivering like timorous creatures which longed to be kissed and caressed. She knew how she mesmerised Heimdal, but then Heimdal was just one of the many who were completely unable to resist her overwhelming sexual power. Principal among them, of course, was the Master.

She gazed down through the observation window at the scene in the hall below. Tonight's theme was one of schoolgirls and schoolmasters, and the guests were throwing themselves wholeheartedly into the spirit of it, blissfully unaware of the fate which awaited them before dawn rose over Winterbourne.

Sluts in short skirts and knee-length socks, gymslips

and ties askew, straw boaters and navy-blue knickers, dishevelled white shirts straining to button over balloon-like breasts . . . the Great Hall was awash with a great tide of giggling, running flesh. And after the girls came their pursuers, middle-aged men chasing them round and round the sunken pool, catching them and throwing them to the ground. The sound of spanked buttocks and indignant squeals mingled with the groans of pleasure that were almost too intense to bear.

'You find the festivities satisfactory, Mistress?' enquired Heimdal. Outwardly respectful, he was edging closer to her, his lips almost brushing the back of her neck.

'Quite satisfactory.' Sedet paused. 'Except for one thing.'

'Mistress?'

'The Master. Where is the Master? Why is he not here?'

'I am sorry, Mistress Sedet, I do not know. But surely . . .'

He bent to kiss her and slip his hands round to cup her breasts, but she pushed him aside.

'You are beginning to irritate me, Heimdal.'

'Yes, Mistress.'

Sedet stalked down the grand curving staircase, in search of the Master. It was too bad. She had gone to all the trouble of arranging this very special orgy, with the express purpose of initiating certain influential oil and mineral magnates, and the Master could not even be bothered to attend. She bristled with righteous indignation. Here she was, going to all this trouble to find him his precious little bit of grey-green stone, and where was he?

As she expected, she found him in his study. She did not bother knocking, but simply walked straight in. The Master was sitting in the dark, curtains drawn, one fist clenching and unclenching on the desk before him. His eyes glittered as they snapped up to meet her gaze.

'I did not summon you.'

She ignored his hostile tone.

'All the guests have arrived. They are expecting you.'

'Do not bother me with these trivialities.'

She draped her body around his shoulders and stroked his cheek with a vampish delight.

'They are asking after you, my lord. Come with me, take part in the initiation . . .'

He dashed her hand away.

'Leave me.'

'But, my lord, come with me, feed with me, taste young flesh . . .'

All at once, the Master's rage exploded like a fireball. A huge blast of mindforce hit Sedet like a miniature thunderbolt, lifting her off her feet and holding her there, flailing and thrashing above his head.

'Aah! Put me down, put me down!' She kicked and squealed, but to no avail. She was powerless to resist. 'Master! Master, why are you doing this? Who has angered you . . . ?'

The Master got to his feet, cold in his slow-burning rage.

'I have been betrayed,' he said, very quietly. 'Betrayed.'

As the word left his lips, Sedet felt a terrible energy enter her body, shaking and tossing it like a puppet.

'Master!'

He seized the paperknife from the desk. It was razor-sharp and tapered to a keen point. In a single slash, he cut Sedet's gown from hem to throat and it fell away, baring breasts and sex and round, white backside, succulent above black-stockinged thighs.

'Betrayed, do you hear? And I *will* have satisfaction. Because you, my dear Queen, are going to provide it.'

Trudie was just nineteen, American and game for anything. In fact, it was her love of adventure which had brought her to St Malo, the first stop on her backpacking tour of Europe.

She giggled to herself as she walked along in the twilight.

Streetlamps hung like yellow blossoms in the navy-blue sky, and she felt good, good, good. And, maybe, just a little drunk. French beer was so cheap and she wasn't used to drinking. That was probably how she'd come to be lost in this strange town, with no money in her pocket and nowhere to spend the night. Still, who cared? She was young and drunk and having fun.

Turning the corner, she saw a young man standing under a lamppost. He was tall and silky-haired, dressed in white shirt and waistcoat, and denim shorts, his long, straight back leaning against the lamppost and his arms folded. He was looking right at her.

She didn't stop to think. She wasn't afraid at all, even though he was a complete stranger. When he held out his hand to her she took it gladly, laughing with pleasure and excitement at the warmth and strength of his clasp.

'Come.'

It was the only word that passed between them. They didn't need words. Trudie went with the stranger gladly, her whole body on fire for him, knowing instinctively that the two of them were fated to make passionate love.

They passed through an archway and up a narrow flight of stone steps which led to the city walls. As she emerged onto the battlements, Trudie saw a dark-haired woman in black Levi's, standing by the edge, her lips curving into a crimson smile.

'You have done well, Jean-Marie,' said the woman, stepping out of the shadows into the moonlight. 'Tie her and strip her. We shall enjoy her now.'

Chapter 10

Winterbourne Hall prided itself on being able to cater for *every* sexual taste, no matter how bizarre. And so it was that Heimdal had created dozens of 'suites', each with its own erotic theme: 'Imperial Rome', 'Truckers', 'Cowboy Dreams', 'Cleopatra', even 'Deep Space', they were all here.

In 'Swinging Sixties', nothing could be heard but the soft purrs and moans of ultimate satisfaction. It was a triumph of period design, a pastiche of a Sixties' nightclub, complete with zebra-striped sofas in orange and shocking pink, basket chairs hanging on chains and – dangling from the mirrored ceiling – a series of golden cages, very popular with those guests who enjoyed a little bondage.

On this particular afternoon, the suite contained an unusual guest. One of the golden cages had been removed and, hanging in its place from one slender ankle, was Sedet.

Long, ragged scratches and reddening welts covered her naked body; spent juices dried to a semi-opaque crust on her skin. She scarcely breathed as she hung from the chain, her body slowly turning round and round like some bizarre ceiling fan. Sedet was utterly defeated. And utterly satisfied.

'My lord . . .' she whispered, raising her head to steal a glance at him.

The Master was immaculately dressed in a Steed-style suit with a velvet collar, and was sitting on a tangle of naked slaves. They lay perfectly still and silent beneath him, knowing better than to revive the Master's anger.

'Oh my lord . . . such exquisite pain.' Sedet's tongue flicked over parched, cracked lips. Her nipples stiffened at the memory of her torment.

'Yes.' The Master amused himself by grinding the heel of his shoe into a slave's outspread fingers. The fingers tensed momentarily at the pain, but the slave did not cry out. He was well trained. Perhaps too well trained to afford very much pleasure.

Disappointed by the Master's monosyllabic response, Sedet spoke again.

'I am indeed fortunate to be my Master's plaything. To be the object of your anger.'

'Soon I shall begin again. I shall refine my anger.' But the Master was not looking at Sedet, he was staring straight through her as though whatever it was that had distracted him was taunting him from the opposite wall.

'My lord?'

'No word from Weatherall. No word from Dubois, nothing even from Graveney. Do you understand what that means, my beautiful, empty-headed Queen?' There was more than a hint of contempt in his voice. 'Are you remotely capable of comprehending?'

Sedet's lithe body wriggled at the end of the chain as she attempted, without success, to right herself.

'Master . . . you are angry with me, Master?'

The Master let out his breath in an irritable snort.

'Let me explain it to you. Weatherall, Dubois and Graveney have failed me.'

'Perhaps . . . perhaps something has happened . . .'

'No earthly power could have claimed all three of them. Only their own defiance.' Taking a snake-thin whip from the open torture cupboard, he twisted its fine, cruel tip about his fingers. 'Well, my Queen, if they choose to plot against me I shall meet them with hellfire.'

Lightning crackled from his fingertips as he hurled the whip into the air above his head. And in that moment it was transformed from an inanimate coil of black plaited leather into a living serpent, a deadly mamba with ruby eyes and razor-sharp fangs.

He watched it with grim satisfaction as it flexed and spat, its forked tongue stinging Sedet's flesh again and again, making her cry out as she writhed in a helpless ecstasy of total surrender.

'Master! My lord, enough . . .'

'Enough is when I choose, Sedet, it is not of your choosing. Remember that.'

With a flick of his hand, he summoned the serpent from its prey and it sprang back into his hand, once more a thing of silver and supple leather.

'If the children of night defy me,' he said softly, 'oblivion shall be their reward.'

In the gaming room at the casino, all eyes were on the spin of the roulette wheel.

'*Rouge impair.*'

No winner this time – except the bank. Expressions of wistfulness, regret, resentment and grim determination showed on the faces of the gamblers as they watched the croupier raking in a multicoloured pile of chips.

Some were professionals, habitual gamblers who came regularly to play the tables, in the expectation of a modest profit and the hope of a king's ransom. Then there were the amateurs, the tourists, the kids; and the few desperate souls who had come to stake their last thousand francs, who had sunk so low that they had nothing left to lose.

Fortunes were won and lost here, every night. To those who played the tables, the roulette wheel was a magical thing, a maker and breaker of futures. But those who worked here had seen it all before; perhaps that was why their faces were expressionless, devoid of any emotion.

The croupier – a fabulous brunette with rhinestones in her hair and a black, strapless gown over flawless, milky skin – looked only at the table as she called in the next round of bets. Chips were placed on numbers, black or red, odd or even.

'*Faites vos jeux.*'

The hushed murmur of conversation stilled almost to nothingness as the croupier called a halt.

'*Rien ne va plus.*'

Breath caught in the throat; time seemed to stand still and then the wheel was spinning, the tiny white ball rattling round and round. In a moment it would come to rest on a number, but whose number? Who would be chosen? Eyes followed it, spellbound, willing fortune to be kind.

Suddenly, as if from nowhere, a slender brown hand reached across the table and stopped the wheel. Faces froze, eyes stared in incomprehension. For a split second, nothing and nobody moved.

Then they looked up. The croupier was gone. And in her place stood a tall, caramel-skinned beauty with tumbling black curls and plum-glossed lips. Anjula. Deliciously, formidably naked.

'W-what . . . ?'

'Who . . . ?'

Anjula did not speak. She simply turned round and walked away from the table, leaving the little white ball sitting at the centre of the wheel, motionless. Dead.

'What I want to know,' said Andreas as he and Mara left the hotel, 'is what the Gordon Bennett is going on.'

Mara smiled and kissed him on the end of the nose.

'So what's new? I mean, when was the last time you really *did* know what was going on?'

'True.' Andreas cast his mind back over the last few years. From tabloid hack to vampire MP, it was quite some career. Sometimes, when he woke up, he had to think very hard indeed about who he was pretending to be today. To the world he was Nick Weatherall MP, but if he was a stick of seaside rock he'd have 'Andreas Hunt' all the way through. 'Still, one day I'll write some great memoirs.'

'Ah, but whose memoirs will they be? Yours or Nick Weatherall's?'

'Whichever one gets the bigger advance.'

Side by side, they walked onto the promenade and strolled towards the old town. The tide was out and golden sand stretched out like fresh-baked shortbread in the afternoon sunshine. Andreas slipped his arm about Mara's waist.

'Fancy a paddle?'

'I've not brought my swimsuit.'

Andreas winked.

'Even better.' He teased the pink crystals hanging round Mara's neck. 'Go on, walk onto that beach and take off all your clothes, I can't wait to see their faces.'

'Or mine, when the police come and arrest me.'

'Bet you could persuade them not to. You could persuade me to do *anything*.'

'Sounds like fun. But it's time we started to get answers to a few questions. Like why I might stop being Mara Fleming if I take this necklace off.'

'And who Gaston Lebecq is.'

'And why some complete stranger would call *you* Lebecq.'

'Do you reckon it was a dream, or what?'

'If it was a dream, Andreas, we were both having it. Does that sound normal to you?'

Andreas let out a low chuckle.

'What?'

He winked and pointed towards the beach.

'Now that's what I call normal. Doing what comes naturally.'

There were two figures on the beach, a young blond man and a petite, dark-haired woman, half naked and quite obviously making love in the lee of the sea wall. You could

149

only get a proper look at them if you bent right over the wall and looked in exactly the right direction. Mara laughed.

'Trust you to spot them.'

'It's my journalist's nose.'

'More like your journalist's dick. If there's any humping within half a mile, you'll home in on it.'

'Hey, don't knock it, it's a natural talent.'

'Some talent. Most people prefer playing the piano.'

'More fool them.'

They walked on together, Andreas's hand in the back pocket of Mara's very short shorts; sauntering past the courting couple and the doughnut seller, the fat old lady with the ginger poodle and the squabbling crocodile of children from the local *colonie de vacances*.

It was several minutes later when the petite, dark-haired woman rolled off her lover onto the hot sand, pulling up her bikini top. There was a sparkling gold-dust of sand all over her skin and her young lover set about smoothing it away with subtle strokes of his caressing fingers.

'One moment, Jean-Marie.'

'But, Mistress Diana, I want to do it again . . .'

'And in a moment you shall. But first you must receive your instructions. If you wish to enjoy pleasure, you must earn it. Isn't that so, my little one?'

'*Oui*, Mistress Diana,' he sighed. His fingers continued to roam over the sleek contours of her barely-clad body, unable to control the hunger within him, swelling his dick and weighing down his balls even when he thought he could desire her no more.

'Weatherall and the Dubois slut. You have seen them?'

Jean-Marie nodded.

'The tall Englishman and the red-haired girl. She is very . . . well formed . . .'

Graveney laughed, but there was a faint sparkle of jealousy in her dark eyes.

'Perhaps,' she conceded. 'But your task is not to sniff

after her like some undisciplined puppy. They are to be watched, do you understand? You will watch them carefully and report every detail back to me. Is that quite clear?'

'*Parfaitement*, Mistress Diana.'

Chapter 11

Andreas was feeling moderately pissed off.

No matter how much you tried to sort it out, life just seemed to get more and more complicated. First the Master sending him and Mara on a wild-goose chase, then Mara behaving like a born-again bride of Dracula; and before you know it, something funny happens to time and you haven't a clue what day of the week it is.

A small but growing corner of him hankered after the days when he was one more hack with an eye to the main chance. No matter how rabid, news editors tended not to sink their fangs into your neck. Still, pretending to be the vampire servant of an undead sorcerer did have its compensations – and the main one was by his side as he walked up the side-street in quest of a cold beer. She touched his arm.

'How about this one?'

He gave the bar the once-over. A bit poncey but it would do.

'Yeah. Why not?'

He followed Mara to a pavement table and sat down, his knees touching hers under the table. Phwoar. Kicking off his deck shoe, he ran his bare foot up her calf. She pouted at him. Naughty, naughty. He did it some more – it was only fair. Mara Fleming did things to him all the time. She didn't even have to try. All she had to do was look at him, or run the tip of her tongue over those moist pink lips, and Andreas Hunt was instantly thinking bedtime thoughts.

A beer and a *citron pressé* arrived. As Mara sprinkled sugar into her drink, Andreas thought out loud.

'By now we must know every inch of this flaming town.'

'Probably.' Mara licked sticky white sugar grains from the tips of her fingers.

'You should let me do that.'

'I will – next time I have a spare two hours.' She winked. 'I know how you like to do things properly.'

Andreas drank half his beer and slumped back in his chair. Swallows were chasing each other over the rooftops, making that shrieking noise that made them sound like they were taking the piss.

'We've looked everywhere. And still no sign of Lebecq.'

'There was that . . . incident. When the old bloke called you Lebecq. We could try looking for him.'

'We already did. He's disappeared off the face of the earth. If he ever existed. You know what we need?'

'What?'

'Max. Max Trevidian, psychic investigator. He'd know what to do.'

Mara sighed. Reaching across the table, she patted Andreas's hand.

'Max is dead, Andreas. The Master vapourised him, remember?'

'I'd hardly forget a thing like that.'

'Then what's the point . . . ?'

'Look, being dead didn't stop Max helping us before. We know he's out there somewhere. He could help us now if he wanted to.'

'Yeah, well, maybe. But I think we're going to have to sort this one out on our own.'

Andreas stared disconsolately into the bottom of his empty beer glass. His lower lip jutted like a sulky schoolboy's.

'I suppose.'

'So what next?'

154

'We go down the local over-eighties' club with a rubber hose and a bright light? I've a few searching questions I'd like answered.'

'Andreas, I'm serious. Do you think we should contact the Master and tell him we've drawn a blank?'

Andreas laughed humourlessly.

'Why not? I've always wanted to die horribly.'

'Andreas . . .'

'In fact, while we're at it we might as well tell him who we really are. Kill two birds with one stone.'

'Shut *up*, Andreas!'

Her exasperated voice brought him up short, like a busty schoolmistress with a plunge neckline and a springy new cane.

'What?'

Mara was bright-eyed with excitement. Andreas was excited too, or at least something in his pants was. That was a very, very tight swimsuit and she filled it to injection-moulded perfection.

'I've seen something, Andreas. Look. Over there.'

He followed her pointing finger. On the other side of the street, set into the wall about fifteen feet off the ground, was a circular blue plaque. The sort that might say, 'Somebody you've never heard of lived here a long time ago, twenty years before he did anything interesting.'

'So what? It's one of those blue plaque thingies.'

'Is your eyesight failing? Look closer. Can't you see what it says?'

'Hardly, it's bloody miles away.'

'Look at the capital letters – there, on the second line down.'

Andreas squinted up into the sun, trying to make out the faraway lettering. There was just one word on the second line down, printed larger than all the other words on the plaque. A name. LEBECQ.

'Flaming hell, why didn't we notice that before?'

'I've got a weird feeling it wasn't *there* before.'

But Andreas didn't stop to listen. He was up and out of the café-bar in record time, slamming a fifty-franc note down on the table and legging it across the street with Mara in hot pursuit.

'Oh bugger, it's in French.'

'What did you expect – Sanskrit?'

'What does it say?'

Mara skimmed the text.

'I can't make it all out. Something about heroes and the war.'

Andreas felt agreeably impressed. If he was going to be mistaken for somebody, it might as well be a war hero.

'So our friend Lebecq's a big hero, eh?'

'Maybe, but . . .'

As they stood looking up at the plaque, a funny-looking piebald pigeon fluttered down from the roof and dive-bombed Andreas's head. He waved it away with his sun hat, vaguely aware that he'd seen it somewhere before. Undeterred, it came back on a second sweep, almost slicing the end off his nose. He ducked, muttering curses about Mad Pigeon Disease.

'Look, there's a door over there. I'm going in.'

Mara looked dubiously at the faded sign over the door: 'Bar Colombie'. Andreas already had his hand on the handle, turning it, opening the door, but she hesitated. Something wasn't right.

'Andreas . . .'

'Come on.'

'Andreas, I've just made out one of the other words. Andreas . . . !'

The door opened and Andreas slipped inside.

'Andreas . . . it says "traitor"!'

Mara followed Andreas through the door. Inside, the bar was like the entertainments lounge on the *Marie Celeste*.

Chairs stood round empty tables, one or two glasses were scattered over the top of a battered upright piano. A thin film of dust lay over everything.

Andreas sneezed.

'I don't think they've hoovered in here since 1945.'

Mara tugged at Andreas's sleeve.

'There's nobody here. Let's go.' A creeping uneasiness was stealing over her body like a cold shiver.

'In a minute. There might be something here . . .'

A voice from the far side of the bar made them both start and swivel round.

'Good evening.'

A woman was standing behind the bar. She hadn't been there when they came in, Mara was sure of that. An exotically beautiful woman, with coffee-coloured skin and thick, black hair tumbling over bare shoulders.

Andreas walked straight up to the bar, a stupid grin all over his face.

'Anjula!'

The woman smiled. Smiled like the cat who'd got the cream, thought Mara. She followed Andreas to the bar, feeling uncharacteristically possessive.

'Aren't you going to introduce me?'

Not that he needed to, she realised with a jolt. For Mara had seen this woman once before – in that weird flashback through time, when she had been given to Lord Roberto by a fine, dark-haired lady . . .

'My name is Anjula.' Dark eyes flashed with an enigmatic fire, but betrayed no glimmer of recognition. As she came out from behind the bar, her body moved beneath her red sequinned dress like molten metal, smooth and hot and dangerous. She reminded Mara of a venomous snake, beautiful and deadly. 'And yours is Mara Fleming.'

Mara glanced uneasily at Andreas. He seemed mesmerised, a grinning idiot schoolboy who couldn't take his eyes off the two firm, fluid breasts that quivered and bounced beneath the thin, shimmering fabric.

'My name is Anastasia Dubois.'

Anjula pursed her full, glossed lips.

'That dark spirit is within you, it is true. Even now it struggles for supremacy. But you are the white witch, Mara Fleming. And your companion's name is Andreas Hunt.'

How could she know? Mara's head was spinning. This man-eating seductress, seemed to know all the secrets she and Andreas had hidden for so long.

'Who are you? What are you doing here?'

Anjula took Mara's hand and carried it to her lips, planting the softest of kisses on her fingertips.

'Why am I here? To answer all your questions.'

Andreas was naked. As he knelt and Mara crouched over him, thighs wide-spread, the tip of his dick only just touched the blossoming petals of Mara's sex.

It was hot in the deserted bar. Tropical hot, making perspiration bead and trickle over bare skin, over muscles that screamed with tension as they strained to hold their precise, body-stretching positions.

'You must not move before the moment of empower-ment,' Anjula instructed them, her voice curiously commanding even though it was no more than a soft whisper. 'Complete self-control is essential. Anything less, and you will break the power of the Tantra.'

Andreas groaned, but it was a silent groan. Somehow he knew that if he spoke he would ruin everything. He yearned to thrust those few, tantalising inches into the warm heart of Mara's sex, and yet with each new second of agony the pleasure seemed to increase tenfold. If this was agony, he wanted it to go on forever.

Mara rocked gently back and forth on the balls of her feet, letting the very tip of Andreas's dick tease the clipped auburn hairs which curled tightly over her pudenda. The sensations flooding through her were intense and incredible.

With each tiny movement, Andreas's fingertips brushed very lightly across her nipples, sparking electric shocks of yearning that made her whole body tingle and flame. It was like being plunged alternately into fire and ice.

Sweet, fragrant liquid trickled from between her wide-spread thighs, dripping soft and slow onto the tiled floor. Through half-closed eyelids, Mara watched Anjula weaving circles around them, strewing flowers and drawing mystical patterns in white sand. Mara was surprised by the savagery of her emotions. There was something about Anjula that she hated, loathed, feared . . . and perhaps, most terrible of all, desired.

So Anjula was a witch. Andreas had seemed surprised by this revelation, but Mara had known it from the moment she set eyes on the woman. A witch, yes; but black or white, good or evil? That was the question Mara found impossible to answer.

According to Anjula, she had sensed that something strange was going on the first time she saw Mara and Andreas at the embassy reception. Not that Mara remembered anything about that night, only the little Andreas had chosen to tell her. For Anastasia had been in control, Anastasia the dark spirit trying to steal back her body. And if Mara's suspicions were correct, only the crystal necklace was preventing her from slipping back into Anastasia's greedy clutches.

No time now to question or to fear. The need for pleasure was becoming all-consuming. As a dreamy, otherworldly excitement began to overwhelm her, Mara recalled what Anjula had told them.

'I was curious about you. I followed you, tracking you by means of a fragment of stone which I gave to Andreas. Place that stone in my hand and I shall use it as the focus for a simple Tantric ceremony. Through it all power shall be channelled, and you shall gain knowledge and sight of past events.'

The question was, had Anjula spoken the truth; and even if she had, why should she choose to help them?

As Anjula began to chant, Andreas felt his balls grow tighter and heavier. A kind of reverse gravity was pulling him upwards, defying the ache in his overstretched muscles, urging him to make the one, delicious thrust that would take him into the silken sheath of Mara's sex.

But it wasn't time yet. He had to resist. It wasn't quite time . . .

He kissed Mara's throat, his hungry lips devouring her sweet flesh, his tongue lapping the drops of sweat from her skin. And all the time his fingertips were skimming her so-hard nipples, itching and aching to take them between finger and thumb and squeeze and pinch and bite them until she squealed with the pain of pleasure.

Now.

It was now, instinctively they both knew. Anjula was raising her hands, throwing back her head, her voice rising to a screech that seemed to shake the walls of the room. And suddenly Andreas and Mara were not two bodies, but one squirming creature of pure hunger. Their hands clawed at each other as they slid together, skin on skin, lips and tongues and teeth devouring as Mara's tight wet sex closed like a silk-gloved hand about the shaft of Andreas's dick.

At first, they wriggled and scrabbled in their greedy quest for gratification. They were like kids having sex for the first time, knowing what they wanted but not the right way to do it. Gradually they relaxed into the symphony of sensations, finding their natural rhythm, moving together – at first slowly, then faster and faster as the need to climax drew them on.

It was paradise. There could be no other word for it. An earthly paradise of perfect sex. Andreas couldn't begin to understand why it felt so good, but hell, who cared? A dozen pairs of soft, smooth hands were invisibly caressing his body, a dozen mouths kissing his every intimate place. Fiery tongues were flicking between his buttocks, icy fingers licking down the curve of his spine, lapping up the cool trickle of his sweat.

Mara moaned softly. The ultimate in pleasure was so close. She had lost the ability to understand where her own body ended and Andreas's began. Together, they made one flawless, seamless sex machine, the perfect engine of pleasure.

As orgasm approached, Andreas became gradually aware of something very odd going on around him. Not that he particularly cared; he'd gone well beyond the point of rational thought. But slowly the colour was leaching out of everything, turning the room around them to a kind of indigo monochrome.

They were in the ocean, two rutting sea creatures tumbling over and over in the cool, heavy slowness of the deep, deep waters. Mara let out a slow, luxurious gasp as she felt Andreas twitching inside her. It was dizzying, enchanting . . . and all at once it was explosive and exhilarating, and they were sliding down a waterfall of pleasure; down, down, falling and falling and falling, and . . .

What the . . . ?

Andreas and Mara blinked at each other. They were lying semi-naked on the floor, not on cold tiles but on dozens and dozens of pearls, scattered all over a polished wooden floor.

'Mara?'

She sat up slowly, trying to cover her breasts with her tiny white silk blouse.

'Andreas . . . where are we?'

Not the Bar Colombie, that was for sure, thought Andreas. In fact this didn't look much like a bar at all. If it looked like anything it was a jeweller's shop. An untidy one, to judge from the pearls rolling all over the floor.

The sound of shouts and heavy footsteps outside made Andreas's mind up for him. At the first sound of something heavy splintering the door, he damn near wet himself.

'I don't know, but I think we ought to get out right now.'

And they would have done, if events hadn't been one step ahead of them. At that moment the door gave way and burst open. Now, Andreas was no militaria nut but even he knew jackboots and SS uniforms when he saw them.

And when the man in the leather trenchcoat said, '*Kommen Sie mit mir*,' Andreas Hunt wasn't the man to argue with him.

Chapter 12

Anjula contemplated Andreas and Mara's bodies, slumped shapelessly across the dusty tiles, their souls lost in time; agents of her old enemy the Master. Ah well, they would be easily dealt with now.

The white witch might have been a problem, but the crystal necklace she had hypnotised Hunt into buying had done the trick. Not only had it quietened Mara Fleming's psychic powers, it had also bound the dark and unruly spirit of Anastasia Dubois.

Anjula relaxed, spent after the considerable effort of the Tantric ritual. She could afford to relax; she was safe now. Without Mara and Andreas, the Master would never find the source of the magical rock; and if he could not find that, he would never master time and so find and conquer Isla Venemo.

How strange. A moment ago it had been steamily hot in here, yet now... Anjula shivered. It was becoming curiously cold in the deserted bar.

And then she saw it, her beautiful features distorting with horrified realisation. As she looked down she saw that an icy white mist was rolling in through the open door to fill every corner of the Bar Colombie. Nothing but a cloud of white mist, yet she felt its power even before it touched her; insubstantial, unseen hands pawing and clawing at her skin, making her flinch and spin round, only to see... nothing. Nothing but mist.

Then she heard it, the mocking laughter. At first it was

curiously distant and distorted, like interference on a radio. Then, as though a signal were being tuned in, it became clearer, sharper, more cruelly distinct.

As she turned to face the sound she saw that she was no longer alone. Diana Graveney was standing in front of her, flanked by her devoted acolytes, Trudie and Jean-Marie.

'Whatever is the matter, Anjula?' The painted lips curled into the prettiest of sneers. 'Aren't you pleased to see me?'

Anjula tried to speak, but the words dried to a soundless gasp in her throat. She tried desperately to move, but found she was paralysed, frozen to the spot, utterly at Graveney's mercy.

Graveney took a step forward and reached out her arms. Her fingers took Anjula by the hair and pulled her down to her knees. Bending forward, she kissed Anjula on the face and neck. Long, lingering, triumphant kisses that delighted in the look of impotent rage in Anjula's dark eyes.

'Mine,' she whispered. 'You're all mine now.'

'Mistress,' said Jean-Marie hesitantly.

Not without regret, Graveney turned her attentions to Jean-Marie.

'What is it now, little one?'

'Forgive me, Mistress. But Weatherall and the Dubois slut.' He nodded at the two unconscious bodies sprawled on the floor at his feet. 'What shall we do with them?'

'With *them*?' Graveney spared them a brief, dismissive glance. 'Throw them into the sea, with the rest of the rubbish.'

Anjula hung face-down from the ceiling like a trussed fly in a spider's web. Criss-crossed with leather straps buckled tight around her nakedness, she was suspended from iron rings by chains attached to her wrists and ankles. These pulled her arms and legs taut, bending her supple body into an ox-bow of appetising flesh.

She was hanging at shoulder height, a helpless prey for Diana Graveney's pack of young predators. Countless eager tongues and fingers explored Anjula's body, probing the most secret creases and dimples, sharp little teeth nipping playfully at the hard, pendulous fruit of the witch's breasts. Her nipples were like hazelnuts, hard and juicy, made for biting and sucking.

Anjula's body flexed like a snake's, whipping this way and that, desperately trying to free itself from the chains; and from the torment which forced it to pleasure even at the moment of its greatest humiliation.

'Bitch,' she seethed. 'Bitch, I curse you.'

Graveney laughed.

'To Hell perhaps? My dear Anjula, I can think of nowhere more perfectly suited to my disposition.' Pushing aside the pawing, fawning bodies of her acolytes, she stepped right up to Anjula and jerked her head back. 'You will tell me what I want to know.'

Anjula snarled and spat, a dribble of white saliva spattering Graveney's face.

Apparently undisturbed by this outrage, Graveney simply wiped her hand across her face and snapped her fingers.

'Jean-Marie.'

He was at her side instantly, her beautiful blond boy. The first and favourite of all her vampires.

'Mistress?'

'Tighter.'

Jean-Marie turned a handle on the wall and the chains tightened a fraction, stretching Anjula's body so that her bones were visible beneath the cappucino skin. Anjula moaned softly but did not speak.

'You may increase the stimulation.'

A rippling sigh of pleasure passed through her night-children as they surged forward, hands and tongues and teeth their favoured instruments of torture. They were so devoted, so eager, so fresh and new. For them, the realm of the undead was only just opening up its sinister black blossoms, and Graveney fed on the sensual energy of their exhilaration, growing ever stronger and more invincible.

'Tell me, witch. Tell me who you are and why you are here.'

Silence. A nod from Graveney, and gulls' feathers ran their tapering tips over Anjula's skin, their soft lightness even more unbearable than the bite of hungry teeth.

'You *will* tell me. Why have you been following Weatherall and Dubois? What secrets have you discovered? *Tell me.*'

Still Anjula resisted, her lips clenched tight shut, her body tense and squirming under the torture of terrible pleasure. Graveney watched with irritation, mingled with a certain dark satisfaction. There was something to be said for resistance in a captive; it allowed her to experiment and observe, a most stimulating experience.

Jean-Marie was between the witch's legs, his hands on her thighs, holding open the ripe red fruit of her sex. It was an attractive sight; folds of ruby flesh running with sweet juice, the impudent stalk of a large, swollen clitoris, so unwillingly roused to iron hardness. The tight hole of her vagina showed as a dark line, surrounded by the soft, wet flesh of her inner lips, succulent and so biteable. And now the darling boy was tasting her, biting and lapping at her, taking her clitoris onto his tongue and teasing it with the sharp points of his teeth.

Graveney felt the warmth of sexual need between her thighs. Later, when the bitch had been subdued, she would have her. Teach her what it meant to be Mistress Graveney's plaything.

A pretty vampire slut with eyes as green and slanted as a cat's was bolder still. A wine bottle was in her hand and she was pushing the neck between Anjula's buttocks, laughing as the witch wriggled and fought, only to impale herself more perfectly upon the cold, slippery glass.

My darling children, thought Graveney. My darling,

166

obedient, inventive children of night. How I shall reward you for your loyalty.

Again she rapped out a question.

'What were you doing here? Answer me.'

No answer came. She would almost have been disappointed if it had. At a sign from Graveney, fingers forced open Anjula's mouth and not one but two fat dicks were thrust into her, half choking her in their haste to have her.

'Well, well, my dear bitch,' purred Graveney, her clitoris throbbing most agreeably underneath her catsuit of tailored leather. 'If you will not talk to me willingly, we shall just have to make things even more . . . pleasurable for you.'

And, taking up the whip, she contemplated a dozen different ways of adding to Anjula's delicious torment.

Things were looking bad for Andreas and Mara. The men in jackboots were disturbingly real and had driven them in a German army lorry through streets which sported swastikas and guard posts. Either this was the most convincing film set in Hollywood history, or somehow they really had slipped back through time.

And now they were tied up in some stinking cellar, with the officer in the leather trenchcoat, two guards with fixed bayonets and a one-eyed shaved gorilla, stripped to the waist with a bullwhip in his hand.

'Answer me,' rapped out the officer.

Mara gazed back at him, dumb with shock.

'I . . . I don't know . . .'

Andreas wriggled on his chair, spitting out the gag.

'Leave her alone.' He made an impotent attempt to kick the officer in the nuts.

'Shut up.'

'Ow.' He should have known the Sir Galahad routine was a mistake. The butt-end of a pistol came down thwack on the back of his neck. The next thing he knew, the gag was back in his mouth and the gorilla was standing over

Mara, the bullwhip quivering with anticipation in his raised hand. And there was not one bloody thing Andreas could do about it.

'Where is it? Answer me!' repeated the officer, one gloved fist pounding into the palm of his other hand.

'I don't know, I don't know!'

'Very well. I can see we shall have to persuade you to be more cooperative.'

Mara squealed as she was hauled out of the chair and thrown forward over the back of it.

'Tie her securely.'

Andreas strained at the ropes tying him down, but all he succeeded in doing was making the legs of the chair jiggle on the uneven floor. Rough hands were tying Mara's wrists and ankles to the legs of her chair, so that she was bent almost double, her hair cascading down over her face and her back arched.

A gloved hand seized the neck of her white blouse and tore it down, bursting the buttons. A quick flick of a bayonet cut through her bra and slashed open her skirt, baring the tanned flesh beneath.

Naked from waist to knee, Mara shivered. Cold, damp air seemed to crawl over her skin like teeming insects. All she could see of her tormentor now was his feet, the polished toes of his jackboots moving impatiently back and forth in front of her as he barked out questions.

'Who are you?'

'Dubois. Anastasia Dubois . . .'

'You lie! Who are you?'

'Mara. Mara Fleming.'

'If you continue to lie to me, you shall suffer.'

'My name is . . . Mara. Mara Fleming.'

'Why are you here?'

'I don't know.'

'Where have you hidden it?'

'Hidden what? I don't understand . . .'

The first swish of the whip caught her across the buttocks, the flexible tip flicking into the deep cleft between her arse cheeks like a hornet-sting. She cried out, tears springing to her eyes.

'Please! Please don't . . .'

'Tell me what I want to know.'

'I . . . can't. I don't know what you're talking about.'

The second whip stroke was directed with demonic skill, the main force of the lash striking her back but the tip curling underneath her to the hypersensitive bud of her nipple. She squirmed and writhed, pleading with her tormentor to let her go; but there was no escape.

She felt the slight rush of air as the whip was raised for a third stroke. But something happened; a kind of judder in time, as though for a few brief seconds the needle had jumped and the whole world stuttered, stuck in a groove in the middle of nowhere.

When the colours came back and everything was still, something had changed. Something small, but significant. Mara wondered what it was. She waited, but nothing happened. Slowly, she raised her head.

There were no jackboots. Standing in front of her was a petite woman in a purple leather catsuit trimmed with fur, a bullwhip in her raised right hand. As Mara's eyes travelled slowly upward, she saw that the woman's face was concealed by a strange mask of greyish-green polished stone, radiating spokes like the rays of a noonday sun.

'My dear Dubois,' said a soft, syrupy voice from behind the mask. 'And so I have you at last.'

The mask slid away from the face, but Mara had already guessed the woman's identity.

'Graveney.'

'Yes, my dear slut.' The smile became a sneer. 'Shall I tell you something, Dubois? A few home truths? You've had this coming to you for a long, long time.'

The whip came slashing down across Mara's arching

back, cutting into her flesh with a searing heat.

'And now I'm going to make you beg for more.'

'Ah. Aaah *yes*. Yes, yes, yes.'

Graveney's sweat-soaked body rose and fell on the never-tiring apex of Jean-Marie's beautiful cock. He was lying beneath her on the floor of the Bar Colombie, his adorably youthful body fragrant and slippery with the juices that had oozed and spurted from their joining. He was her unquestioning partner in the joys of evil, his cock obediently hard at all times.

This was pleasure indeed, perhaps the ultimate in gratification. Behind the stone mask, Graveney's eyes were closed and her mouth open. She panted and moaned as the last of a thousand orgasms crashed through her body, making her muscles shudder and tense. And at last she slumped forward, her body for a few moments weak and vulnerable as she lay trembling on Jean-Marie's chest.

Recovering her composure, she sat up and removed the mask. Her face was radiant with triumph as she reached behind her to stroke sensual fingernails down Jean-Marie's belly. Her fingers closed about his balls, nails digging hard into the delicate flesh with a delicious sadism.

Jean-Marie screamed his ecstasy, every atom of his being crying out for more and greater torments. Only his mistress, his beloved mistress, could teach him the arcane pleasures of pain.

'Ah. Ah, *Maîtresse Diana* . . .'

'Anything,' hissed Graveney, ignoring the stickiness of Jean-Marie's semen trickling over her fingers. 'I can go anywhere, any time. I can do *anything*. Can you understand that, my little one?'

'Mistress?'

'Ah, little one, how can you understand? Such greatness is beyond your powers of comprehension.'

Setting the mask aside, Graveney slid down onto Jean-

Marie's belly, skin slithering over skin, her still-hot sex welcoming the slippery shaft of his dick. As she began to fuck him, moving slowly back and forth, she took his head between her hands, her nails piercing his flesh until crimson blood beaded on his temples.

'Listen to your mistress, little one.'

Jean-Marie's eyes gazed up into hers, filled with the absolute devotion of a beloved pet spaniel.

'*Oui, Maitresse?*'

'Dear, sweet boy; darling Jean-Marie, you would willingly *die* for me, wouldn't you?' She laughed, pleased by her own joke. 'But of course, you already have . . .'

She governed the pace and the rhythm, fucking him with long, slow strokes which allowed him almost to escape, only to recapture him and swallow him so deep that the wiry hair on his balls was pushed into the soft, sodden flesh of her vulva.

'Sweet boy, listen to me,' she whispered, crooning her own dark love song as she drove down upon him, tightening her muscles to drive him to the very edge of ecstasy. 'The Master is nothing. The witch Anjula cannot harm us. Weatherall and Dubois have been swept away like so much worthless dust, their bodies cast to the waves and their souls awash in a timeless limbo.

'But I, sweet Jean-Marie, possess a source of ultimate power. Soon, I shall cast my shadow across the whole world and bring darkness and eternal night to it all.'

She smiled, gouging her nails down Jean-Marie's tanned throat. He whimpered, like a pet puppy begging for another chocolate drop.

'And then I shall be its Queen. The Queen of Night.'

Chapter 13

'I tell you I didn't see anything,' protested Andreas in an aggrieved whisper, punctuated by the plink-plink of water dripping from the ceiling onto the floor of the old wine cellar.

'But he turned into Graveney,' insisted Mara. 'She was wearing a stone mask and then she took it off and laughed at me. She said she was going to punish me and make me beg for more.'

'Wishful thinking?' suggested Andreas, shaking his left foot to get rid of some of the water. If this was prison, where was the colour telly and the games room?

'Listen to me!'

'I *am* listening. I'm just saying I didn't see anything. No one but that gorilla with the bullwhip. Are you all right?'

'The undead regenerate almost instantly, remember? There are one or two advantages to living in a vampire's body.'

'Look, we have to do something. Get out of here.'

'Got any suggestions?'

'I don't suppose you could turn yourself into a bat, squeeze under the door and unlock it from the outside?'

'And I don't suppose you could talk sense for once?'

'It was only an idea.'

It was cold and dingy in the cellar, the only light coming from the moon, shining in from the street through a series of high slit-shaped windows. Mara shivered and huddled closer to Andreas, his chained wrist draped over her shoulder and his fingers idly stroking her breast.

'Cold?'

'Freezing.'

'I can think of a way of keeping warm.' His fingers flicked open the top button of Mara's blouse, but all of a sudden her whole body became rigid and she pushed his hand aside.

'Don't.'

'What's up?'

'Footsteps, can't you hear them? Somebody's coming.'

Before the words were out of her mouth, Andreas caught the sound of footsteps coming down a flight of stone steps. Not the sound of jackbooted feet, but the light tap-tap of a woman's high-heeled shoes.

'Quick. Pretend you're asleep. Maybe we'll have a chance to escape.'

Curled up together, eyes tight shut, they lay very still, hardly daring to breathe. Keys turned in the lock and the door swung open, letting in a flood of light which showed red through closed eyelids. A woman's voice spoke in heavily accented French.

'*Vous pouvez partir. Je m'occuperai des prisonniers.*'

Then a man's voice, gruff and subservient.

'*Mais, madame . . .*'

The woman's voice again, more insistent now, tinged with menace.

'*Partez, imbécile. Vous commencez à me taquiner.*'

This seemed to do the trick, as the cellar door swung shut again and the light muted back to a pale grey. Mara tried opening her eyes just a fraction, enough to see the silhouette of a tall, strongly built woman, sleekly groomed in a sable-trimmed fitted coat, silk stockings and black patent leather shoes with tall spiked heels. Her plaited and coiled blonde hair was topped by a small hat with a fur trim and a black polka-dotted veil which left half her face in shadow. Only the lips were clearly visible, a full-blown blossom of peony red.

'*Vous dormez? Ah non, je ne pense pas.*'

The woman laughed and nudged Mara's prone body with the toe of her shoe. The contact was sudden and painful, and Mara let out a gasp, rolling over onto her back. Andreas leapt to her defence, only to receive the spiked heel of the woman's right shoe in his solar plexus, no more than a painful inch away from his balls.

'You bitch! Who the hell . . . !'

She laughed in his face, amusing herself by pressing the heel a little harder into Andreas's flesh and watching the changing expressions on his face.

'So. You and your companion are English.' Mara recognised the accent now. It was German.

'What if we are?'

The woman shrugged.

'I had expected a Frenchman called Lebecq. But it matters little. I am bored. I need amusement. And I have heard that the English have a taste for the more piquant pleasures of love.'

Andreas didn't like the sound of this.

'Who the hell are you anyway?'

'I? I am Marthe von Kleewort, wife of the garrison commander of this pitiful town.' She dropped her cigarette on the wet floor and ground it out under her shoe. 'And who might *you* be?'

'Find out for yourself.'

Mara nudged Andreas's elbow.

'There's no point in antagonising her.'

'Very sensible, my dear.' Marthe von Kleewort smiled. 'I have a certain influence in this town and, believe me, you would not wish to incur my displeasure.'

Mara thought for a moment. In this place, who was she? Mara or Anastasia? How was it possible to be anybody in a time before you were born?

'My name is Anastasia. And this is Nicholas.'

'How charming.' Marthe placed the toe of her shoe on

175

Andreas's chin, then ran it slowly and dangerously down his chest and belly until it was resting right over his groin. With his wrists chained, it was hard to do anything but wince and wait for the worst to happen. 'Well, I shall enjoy tonight's little entertainment. I am sure you are going to be very cooperative.'

'Don't count on it,' snapped Andreas. Normally he'd have welcomed the chance of free kinky sex, but something about this German drama queen really teed him off.

'My dear arrogant little Englishman,' scoffed Marthe. 'Surely you don't believe *you* are the one I want?'

This shut Andreas up, at least for the moment. In any case, Marthe's attentions were fully taken up with Mara, her eyes devouring the large, firm breasts under the wet blouse, the torn remnants of the skirt clinging so avariciously to bare, slim thighs and rounded arse cheeks.

'You have a talent, Anastasia.'

Mara stared up at Marthe.

'I . . . ?'

'A talent for pain. I was watching earlier, when Günther was teaching you a valuable lesson. The way you responded to the whip, as though it were a lover's kiss . . .'

Mara trembled at the touch of Marthe's satin-gloved fingers, cupping her chin. How much more did this woman know about her secret desires? She felt helpless in her hands.

'I found it most stimulating, Anastasia. So much so that I have come back to see you again. And this time you are not only going to arouse my lust, you are going to satisfy it.'

Opening her handbag, Marthe took out a length of silky cord. She threw it onto the ground at Mara's feet.

'Expose your breasts. Then bind them with this. *Tightly*.'

Mara stared down at the cord. She shook her head silently.

'Do it.'

'No.'

A satin-gloved hand seized her torn blouse and ripped it from her, exposing the pink-tipped crest of one breast. Moments later those same smooth fingers had seized her nipple and were pinching it, twisting it round and round, so relentlessly that Mara felt certain the flesh would tear.

'No, please!'

Her whole body was shuddering, transported by the sweet and subtle pain that only a loving torturess can give.

'Yes, Anastasia. Yes please. In your heart of hearts, you are begging me to do this to you and never stop. Your pussy is running with juice, I can smell it.'

'No!'

'Yes. To you, pain is pleasure. And your pain is my ecstasy, Anastasia.' At last she released Mara from her grasp and she slumped to her knees on the wet flagstones. 'Now bind your breasts as I commanded you.'

Mara whimpered as she gathered up the silk cord. She could hardly bear to admit, even to herself, how much it excited her to think of the delicious discomfort of the cord biting into her flesh, squeezing out her breasts into blue-veined globes which stood out on her chest, seemingly disconnected from the rest of her body.

'Under your arms. That is right. Now, criss-cross the cord over and between your breasts. Again. Good girl. You have a talent for obedience. Now draw the cord tight.'

'Please . . .'

'Tighter. I want to see you weep with ecstasy.'

The cord pulled tighter, millimetre by millimetre, squeezing the breath out of Mara's body as her breasts turned to crimson-stalked apples, flooded with juice.

'Very well. Enough.'

Mara sobbed as Marthe tied and secured the cord, not from an excess of pain but from the dreadful humiliation of her own pleasure. How could she allow herself to feel like this, to respond to the depraved demands of this

Teutonic torturess? How could she bear the scent of her own yearnings, strong and sweet and musky as it crept out from between the damask petals of her sex?

Marthe walked up and down the rows of wine bottles, stacked on their sides on wooden racks.

'An excellent selection of wines. But then, my dear Anastasia, you are worthy of the finest vintage.'

She selected a bottle from the rack and blew off the dust.

'A Mouton-Rothschild thirty-one. Perfect.'

Turning back to Anastasia, she held the bottle for a moment, then deliberately dashed it at her feet. Blood-red wine gushed and splashed everywhere, over the ground, over the walls, even over Marthe's shoes and stockings. Mara stared up at her, dumbfounded, wondering what would come next.

'Lick it up. Every drop.'

'But . . .'

'Every drop.'

Andreas watched in silence, half furious and half excited by what he was seeing. Mara, his Mara, was on her hands and knees on the cellar floor, chains clanking at her wrists, her rump half bared by her tattered skirt and her breasts bound so tight that they seemed swollen to twice their normal size. And here she was, her auburn hair trailing in the wetness as she pressed her lips to the ground and lapped thirstily at the spilt wine.

Marthe watched her for a while, occasionally barking out instructions.

'Faster. Bad girl, you are leaving more than you are drinking. To your right, bend lower, I want your nipples to rake along the ground. Good girl, good Anastasia . . .'

Then she jerked the chains which held Mara's wrists.

'Lick my boots. And my stockings.'

Mara began lapping the wine from Marthe's shoes, with little flicking movements of her tongue. Marthe stroked her hair as though she were a pet dog.

'Make sure they are spotless. I don't want to have to punish you.'

The long pink tongue moved slowly upwards, from Marthe's gleaming shoes to her ankles, lapping up over her calves, sliding over the fine silk stockings. Andreas gaped. Where would this game end?

Almost as the question was forming in his head, Marthe was unbuttoning her coat. One button, two, three. And then untying the belt. As she opened the coat and let it slide to the ground, Andreas's eyes almost popped out of his head. Underneath, Marthe von Kleewort was completely naked, if you didn't count the silk stockings with the embroidered tops, held up by simple white garters.

'All the way up,' purred Marthe.

'But there is no more wine . . .'

'All the way up. There is wetness in my pussy and you shall lick up every drop.'

The scent of her was so strong and intoxicatingly sweet that Andreas could smell it, breathing it in greedily like Chanel perfume. He almost came in his pants at the sight of Mara's tongue climbing up Marthe's thighs, lingering fleetingly at the crease between thigh and shaven pussy, then darting like a lizard's into the tropical paradise within.

Marthe's face betrayed not a trace of emotion as Mara licked her out, but her hands were on Mara's head, pushing her face right into the warm delta of her sex, making her taste and breathe and live the fragrance of her pleasure.

It lasted long enough to drive Andreas to distraction. He hated her, he wanted her, he hardly knew who he wanted: Mara or Marthe or both. He just knew that his dick was on fire and only the coolness of a woman's lips could extinguish the flames.

When she had done, Marthe picked up her coat and slipped it back on, doing up the buttons perfectly casually, as though nothing untoward had happened. She hadn't even taken her hat off. Mara lay on the ground at her feet, motionless, uncomplaining, only her heaving shoulders bearing witness to the spasms of excitement which had taken over her body.

Marthe turned to walk towards the door, but stopped a few steps in front of Andreas. She smiled.

'Poor boy. Are you feeling neglected?'

Andreas didn't answer. Marthe stood by him and leant back against one of the wine racks.

'I am not a cruel woman, Nicholas. In fact I can be quite merciful.'

She slipped off her shoe and Andreas felt her toes burrowing into his crotch, feeling for the telltale hardness of his prick beneath his sodden trousers. He could have protested, but only a brainless idiot would complain that a beautiful woman was masturbating him with her silk-stockinged foot.

And so, like the true-born Englishman that he was, Andreas put up with it manfully until she brought him to a shuddering climax.

Afterwards, she slipped on her shoe and picked up her handbag.

'*Gute Nacht, liebchen.*'

And blowing them a playful kiss, she was gone.

The Master's mind might be on other things, but he was still Anthony LeMaître, leader of His Majesty's Opposition, and there was no ignoring the fact that a general election was not too many months away. His duties could not be neglected indefinitely. One way or another, the Master was determined to add to his already considerable power. And that meant currying favour with all the right people.

Ibrahim arrived promptly at seven-thirty with the limousine and the Master's party headed towards the theatre. It was the premiere of a new ballet, *Antony and*

Cleopatra, starring some pretty nymphette that Sedet had taken as her latest protégée.

Frankly the production mattered little to the Master. It was far more important to entertain the six influential businessmen and media personalities who had accepted his innocent invitation to the ballet. Little did they realise that, before the night was out, one or more of them might have been selected for a very special invitation to Winterbourne – and induction into the Master's dark empire of the undead.

The Master walked into the theatre to the accompaniment of a few press flashbulbs. He smiled and offered a few quoteable sound bites.

'Are you looking forward to an early election, Mr LeMaître?'

'The Nationalist Party welcomes any opportunity to rid this country of the present corrupt and incompetent administration.'

'And have you any words for the Prime Minister?'

The Master smiled.

'He's welcome to call me, I have the name of an excellent removal firm. Now, gentlemen, if you'll just allow me and my guests to get through, we're looking forward to an evening of first-class British entertainment.'

The party swept through into the lobby and were escorted into the auditorium by a flunkey in a red and gold uniform. As the Master had planned, they were five minutes late and the production had already started: he had judged this an excellent way to get noticed as they walked down the centre aisle to their reserved seats on the front row.

As he walked into the auditorium, something unexpected happened. The entire audience stood up, turned round to face him and started to applaud. Well, well, how very gratifying. He felt compelled to push his guests aside and walk slowly down the centre aisle, basking in adulation.

Once he reached the front, the audience had turned once again to face him and were applauding as loudly as possible. Naturally he didn't want to disappoint them, so he climbed up onto the stage. It seemed like the natural thing to do.

Even more natural was the fact that when he looked down at himself, he saw that he was dressed as a Roman general. Cleopatra was waiting for him on the stage . . . only it was Graveney. She was wearing a magnificent headdress and necklace, made of the grey-green stone he had been seeking for so long.

'Come. Come to me.'

Some force that was greater than himself compelled him to walk towards her smiling face and open arms, to slip between her thighs and begin to fuck her. All around, the audience were cheering, screaming, roaring with hysterical adoration.

And then it occurred to him. This was not right, not right at all. Nor was it real. Somebody was playing games with his mind.

He had to do something, take control of the situation before it overwhelmed him. As the anger within him grew, so did his being. He grew, swelled, expanded; but Graveney grew too. He flowed into her, she into him, until their melded entities became like some colossal Yin-Yang, caught in an eternal balance from which neither could escape.

But Graveney continued to grow, the vast malevolence of her swelling and spreading and proliferating until the Master felt the first touch of real fear. Any huger, any more powerful, and she would surely consume him. A vast pink mouth, wet with juice, pulsated with the need to suck him in.

'No!'

Almost at the moment of no return, rage overwhelmed the Master, cutting through his inertia. Lightning crackled from his fingers as he reached out, grappling with the force

182

that dared to imagine itself greater than the Master.

As he touched her, everything seemed to become two-dimensional and flat. Seizing the vision before him, he twisted his fingers about it and tore it as if it were a poster, ripping it to shreds and dropping them to the ground.

In the next breath he found himself sitting in his theatre seat, calmly watching the ballet. On stage, the corps de ballet were hailing Cleopatra, Queen of the Nile . . .

Priestess of Night.

'Lebecq.'

Andreas awoke from a fitful sleep, blinking in the sepulchral darkness of the wine cellar. He knew that voice . . .

'W-what?'

'It is I, Lebecq. Henri.'

Henri? Lebecq! Andreas shot upright. He squinted into the darkness, but all he could make out was a black silhouette. The voice was unmistakeable, though: it was the voice of the old man they'd seen watching them in the square.

Mara jolted awake.

'Who . . . ?'

'Henri. I came with a delivery of wine and managed to get the guard drunk. I stole his keys.' Andreas heard them jingle as he hunted for the locks on the manacles. 'There, I have freed you – but hurry, there is not much time.'

The three figures slipped silently out of the cellar and up the unlit flight of steps. It was pitch-black, the only way you could move was to feel your way along the wall.

'This way. Hold onto me, it is very foggy tonight.'

Cold, dank night air hit their faces as they slid out of a side door. Foggy? It was a real peasouper, so dense you couldn't even see your own feet, let alone anybody else's. It was like breathing cold custard, sickly yellow swirls that clogged your lungs and made you cough.

Somewhere to the right, Andreas made out a few blurred patches of light, and heard the muffled sound of an engine. Seconds later, distant sirens wailed.

'German patrols!' hissed Henri.

'Damn,' cursed Andreas. 'They must be looking for us.'

'In here, quickly.'

They squeezed into a narrow alleyway and the sound of jeeps grew closer then rolled gradually away.

'We are in the old town now, it is safe for a few moments' rest.'

In the faint, filtering light from a café doorway, Andreas saw Henri's face. Bloody hell. This was no old man, he couldn't have been more than thirteen or fourteen. Just a boy. Yet the features were unmistakeable: the hook nose, the bright button eyes. This *was* Henri all right; but Henri in the past . . .

'What do we do now?' asked Mara.

'We must get away from here. I will come with you.'

'No.' Andreas laid his hand on the boy's arm. 'You've done enough already.'

'But it is dangerous . . .'

'And that's precisely why you're not coming any further. Tell us what to do.'

'You must make for the harbour. For my uncle's fishing boat, it is waiting for you. But I . . .'

'You will get yourself somewhere safe. And listen, Henri.' Andreas seized him by the shoulders, hoping to goodness that the boy *was* listening, because this might just turn out to be bloody important. 'Meet me here.'

'But when, Lebecq?'

Andreas swallowed hard.

'In fifty years' time. Understand?'

Mystified, the boy nodded.

'A-as you wish. But hurry, or the patrols will find you. You are certain you can find the way?'

'Certain. Now go.'

Mara watched Henri disappear into the fog.

'What was that all about?'

'I'm not sure. But look, it's obvious I must have told him something, because we know it happens . . . happened . . . oh, whatever. Now let's find this fishing boat.'

'You know how to get to the harbour?'

'Of course I do. How many times have I walked round this flipping town? I could do it with a bag over my head.'

Five minutes later, they were completely lost.

'Oh Andreas, you're hopeless!'

Andreas shrugged sheepishly.

'When they rebuilt this place, they must have had the plans upside down.'

'Just as well I've got a good sense of smell.'

'Why?'

Mara dotted a kiss on his hopeless chin.

'Salt, Andreas. Where there's salt there's sea water. We'll just follow my nose, OK?'

Mara's nose led them through featureless, foggy, empty streets towards a gateway in the town wall.

'This is it, the harbour. I can hear the water lapping against the quayside.'

If Andreas tried very hard, he could hear it too, though everything sounded muffled in the fog. Naturally there wasn't a single light to stop an unwary journalist from plummeting over the edge into freezing-cold sea water. He shuffled along uncertainly, feeling his way until he made out the fuzzy outline of a jetty and a tall-masted ship berthed at its far end.

'That must be it,' whispered Mara. 'Henri's uncle's fishing boat.'

'It doesn't look much like . . .' began Andreas, but then again he was hardly a world expert on ships. He shut up and followed Mara along the jetty, jumping down onto the deck then reaching up to help her down.

'Hello?'

185

'Hello, is there anyone here?'

No one answered. The decks creaked beneath their feet. Somewhere behind them, they heard the clink and swish of mooring ropes being cast off; and suddenly the ship was moving away from the jetty, out of the harbour and into the open sea.

Andreas wasn't sure whether to be relieved or worried. He looked around him. The moon had emerged and was shining bilious yellow through the fog, offering just enough light to raise severe doubts in his mind. This was a really old ship, *really* old, rot and rags everywhere, the decks mouldering and the sails hanging in tatters. And not a fishing net in sight.

'Mara . . .' he hazarded.

'Mmm?'

'This isn't a Breton fishing boat, is it?'

'Indeed she is not,' replied a voice that definitely wasn't Mara's.

Mara and Andreas swung round to face the direction of the voice. The figure of a man, tall and broad-shouldered, stepped forward out of the swirling fog.

'This vessel is the *Plaisir de Mort*, and I am her captain.'

Chapter 14

'Well it's . . . quiet,' remarked Andreas, desperate to think of something – anything – good to say about the *Plaisir de Mort*.

Mara pursed her lips and lay back on the worn velvet coverlet, spread across the straw palliasse on the bunk bed. She gazed up at the painted ceiling of the cabin. It must have looked quite impressive once, about five hundred years ago. But now the painted cherubs had peeling faces and limbs missing, making them look like celestial amputees.

'Quiet as the grave.' Thoughtfully, she stroked Andreas's thigh. 'The question is, why are we here?'

'Not to catch fish,' volunteered Andreas.

'I think time is playing tricks with us again.'

'But why? And where are all the other passengers and crew? So far all we've seen is the captain, and he gives me the creeps.'

Mary Shelley herself couldn't have created a more authentically gothic character than the captain. Tall and thin, with deep-set eyes and a sweep of black hair scraped into a ponytail, he had the kind of good looks best described as cadaverous. His tattered black frock coat was of black and gold brocade, faded but retaining some of its ancient splendour. Heavy gold sovereign rings glowed on his long fingers and a cutlass swung against the leg of his buckskin breeches. He might have been thirty-five or five hundred and thirty-five.

'I don't think there *is* anybody else on the ship. Before

we came down to the cabin, I saw the wheel. There was no helmsman there. It seemed to be steering itself.'

'The *Flying Dutchman*,' murmured Andreas thoughtfully. His gaze wandered idly around the cabin, resting on a few of its more curious contents: a brass-bound chest, its lid flung open to reveal a pile of silver and gold chains; walls hung with leather harness that had never been meant for any horse; a collection of whips, crops and leather paddles that filled the cabin with the compelling scents of sweat, sex, stale piss and linseed oil. 'Or an SM playroom.' His eyes glinted. 'Is it playtime yet?'

Mara chuckled deep in her throat and rolled onto her back. That period gown really suited her, thought Andreas: the whalebone corset and the low, square-cut neck made her breasts not so much impressive as overwhelming, thrusting forward above a tiny waist and flaring hips. What's more, every tiny movement she made was accompanied by the seductive swish of mulberry satin and antique lace.

'It might be.' She seized him by his starched linen shirt frills and pulled his face down to hers. 'That rather depends on what sort of game you had in mind.'

'How about I'm the pirate king and you're the gorgeous damsel I've just kidnapped for an enormous ransom?'

He ran a line of light, dancing kisses all the way down from Mara's mouth and chin to her throat and buried his lips between her breasts.

'Sexist! How about *I'm* the pirate queen and you're my helpless slave? I could chain you up naked and force you to pleasure me.'

Andreas grinned.

'Yep. That works for me. Only don't lose the key, OK? Walking the plank is difficult enough without leg irons.'

He grabbed hold of her and they tumbled onto the bunk together, his hands scrunching up her skirts and petticoats (how many were there? It felt like two dozen). Her stockings ended just above the knee and – joy of joys – she wasn't wearing bloomers. Nothing. Just smooth, velvety skin that enticed his fingers higher and higher until they met the tight auburn curls that fringed her pussy.

Mara slid her thighs a little way apart and the sap-filled petals of her sex blossomed, opening to let his fingers slide inside. She let out a soft sigh and wriggled her hips, pushing herself against his fingertips so that they slipped into her tight, well-lubricated tunnel of love.

'You hussy,' he murmured into the perfumed nest of her cleavage. 'It's like the Angel Falls in here.'

And much too good to waste. With so much warm wetness, it was easy as pie to slip one finger, then two, three, his whole hand inside her, filling and stretching her, delighting in the tight muscle which pulsated around him, trying to suck him in deeper.

His curled fist plunged in to the wrist, moving with the long, slow pulses of her vagina. She was a rainforest of desire, deluging him with her sweetness at each deep, rhythmic thrust. He felt so hyped-up that he could simply have replaced his fist with his dick and brought himself to a climax in a few seconds; but that wasn't the name of the game. Far more powerful, far more erotically stimulating, was the thought of Mara helpless on his fist, Mara coming again and again all over his curled fingers. And all that pleasure without even the slightest brush of his tongue across the tip of her swollen clitoris.

The thought seemed to communicate itself to Mara, because Andreas felt her sex muscles ripple and tense. He stopped thrusting and lay still between her thighs for a few seconds, not wanting to bring her off too quickly.

'Andreas . . .' she whimpered.

'Soon.'

With his free hand, Andreas reached into her bodice and scooped out her right breast. Its bone-hard nipple offered itself like a mother's to a child, and he took it into his mouth, suckling with all the passion of an infant Oedipus.

He sucked while Mara writhed and sighed, and a fine mist of perspiration broke out on her skin as her body twisted and turned on the rumpled coverlet.

Andreas waited his moment. When neither of them could bear it a second longer, he started thrusting again, harder this time, pumping and twisting into her with his screwed-up fingers, boring into her like a fat drill bit.

Mara clutched at him as she came, her head arching backwards and her bottom lifting off the bunk as she tensed, quivered, then drenched him with wetness; her pleasure rising to a peak then tumbling down, like ice-cold meltwater cascading down a mountainside.

'Nice?' he whispered, snuggling up against her on the bunk. Beneath them the ship was creaking and rocking. He hadn't the faintest idea where they were headed, or even if the old rotbucket was seaworthy, and frankly at this precise moment he didn't much care. It was probably all a dream anyway.

'You're a wicked boy. Just you wait until I chain you up and make you my slave.'

'Can't wait.'

But he had to. Because a sound made him look round; the sound of seaboots on seasoned oak timbers.

'Good evening,' said the captain, observing them from the doorway of the cabin. 'I trust you are . . . refreshed.'

Andreas sprang up in guilty embarrassment. Mara reacted more languidly, slowly easing down her skirts – and not until the captain had had ample opportunity to admire her bare thighs and dew-spangled maidenhair, thought Andreas with a touch of unwonted jealousy.

'Where are we headed?' demanded Andreas. The captain shrugged.

'Who can say? Dinner will be in my cabin at eight bells.' Turning, he left the cabin, leaving the door creaking on its rusted hinges.

At the sound of eight bells, Andreas and Mara found

themselves descending a rickety companionway to the captain's cabin. As they entered, the ship made a sudden roll to port, and Mara was thrown into Andreas's arms, making both of them stumble down the last two steps.

'We are in treacherous waters,' observed the captain, pouring dark red wine from a cobwebbed bottle.

'Where . . . ?' began Mara, but it was obvious the captain had his own agenda.

'Welcome. Please take your seats, eat, drink.'

The captain indicated silver dishes spread out on a mahogany dining table; Andreas made out a whole salmon in aspic, some kind of chicken dish, a roast rib of beef and trays of fruit and sweetmeats, all things that Andreas and Mara liked eating. Something else worried Andreas about all this. Where the hell did you get this kind of fresh food in the middle of nowhere?

All the same, waste not want not. Andreas slid into his chair and helped himself to a poached fillet of salmon and a chicken leg.

The captain, meanwhile, was paying a great deal of attention to Mara. Andreas couldn't help noticing the way he just sort of *accidentally* stroked her arm as he leaned over to place the choicest morsel of salmon on her plate, or the lingering glances directed down Mara's admittedly irresistible cleavage. He might be the soul of politeness but there was something extremely predatory about the captain, Andreas decided. It was like watching the Grim Reaper helping your granny down a very steep flight of stairs.

'Where are we headed?' Andreas decided that bloody-minded repetition was his best chance of getting an answer.

The captain tore his eyes off Mara for a few seconds, to turn his dark and glittering gaze on Andreas.

'That would depend,' he replied.

'Upon what?' asked Mara.

'Upon the nature of the duty which the Master wishes me to perform.'

Andreas choked on a salmon bone and had to be thumped on the back.

'The . . . Master?'

The captain smiled.

'You have concealed your true identities with skill. However, it is clear to me that you are the Master's kindred.' He licked his lips as his gaze strayed back to Mara. 'Only the very beautiful are admitted to the realm of the undead. And you are most assuredly very beautiful, my lady.'

'I . . . yes.' Mara did her best to bear the captain's covetous gaze. 'You honour me.'

'I give voice only to the evidence of my eyes. And so you see, I deduce that the Master has sent you to me to fulfil some task . . .'

Andreas flashed Mara a look. A look that said, 'Go along with it, it's almost true anyway.'

'Actually . . . the Master has sent us to recover . . . the stone.'

'At last. It was as though the weight of centuries dropped from the captain's shoulders. His eyes burned with an exultant, fanatical light. 'After so long, the Master honours me with a task! It has sometimes seemed to me that my voyage has no end, that it has lasted for centuries . . .'

It probably has, thought Andreas, judging from the state of your socks. But he knew when to keep his mouth shut.

'You will help us?' Mara had a wonderful way of looking vulnerable and potent at the same time. Her full lips fairly shimmered with tremulous, kissable dew.

The captain took Mara's hand and pressed it to his lips.

'I am bound to the Master, to serve him in whatever path he chooses. And therefore I am bound also to serve you.'

'Very grateful, I'm sure,' said Andreas lamely. He was suffering from a foolishly macho urge to punch the captain's lights out and defend his woman. 'But we're very tired. If we could just . . .'

192

The captain wasn't listening to a word he was babbling. He still had Mara's hand in his and he was gazing deep into her eyes.

'I have one boon to ask of you,' he whispered.

Mara trembled as she answered him. 'Name it.'

Don't you dare, thought Andreas. He bit his lip and aimed murderous thoughts at the captain, but they just bounced off.

'It has been so long, my lady. So long since I tasted a woman's sweet flesh. Permit me to taste your flesh tonight.'

'It wasn't that bad,' said Mara soothingly, pouring Andreas a nice vintage brandy in the privacy of their cabin.

'Really?'

'Really.'

'You pervert. Since when have you been into necrophilia?'

'Charming! I'll remember that, next time we're in a life-or-death situation and *you* have to shag someone you don't fancy.'

'All right, all right, pax. But we'd better dream up a way of getting off this flaming ship, before the captain thinks of any other boons he wants granting.'

Mara went over to the porthole and peered out into the grey light of dawn.

'The question is, *which* ship are we trying to get off?'

'It's not still there, is it?'

'Sure is. Take a look for yourself.'

Andreas padded over to the porthole and looked out. Instead of the deck of the *Plaisir de Mort*, he found himself looking straight into the first-class cocktail lounge on the *Titanic*, complete with several dozen passengers and a full dance band.

'Which one is it this time?' asked Mara, peeking over his shoulder.

'The *Titanic*.'

A couple of seconds later, the scene became fuzzy, then

time turned itself inside out again and they were looking at galley slaves on a Greek trireme. Wait a little longer, and the cosmic slide show would move on to the flickering quarterdeck of an East Indiaman, the *Fame*. Then back to the *Plaisir de Mort* and the *Titanic* again.

'None of this makes sense,' said Andreas. He liked to state the obvious as often as possible, it made him feel more secure.

'Nothing ever makes sense on its own, we have to make sense of it. Look, time's gone a bit crazy, agreed?'

'Like in St Malo, when it was nineteen-forty-something, and people kept calling me Lebecq?'

'Precisely. Only it's even worse here, it can't stay still for five minutes. Something very powerful is at work here, Andreas. And I bet I know what it is.'

'The stone?'

'The stone. Lots and lots of it, really close. I bet it's exerting some kind of force on time, pulling it all over the place.'

'Meaning?'

'Meaning, things have gone mad and I can't make head or tail of them. Is any of this real? Are *we* real? Is this all something to do with Anjula's ritual in the Bar Colombie?'

Just as Andreas was opening his mouth to confess that he hadn't the faintest idea, the cabin door opened and the captain entered. Wisps of fog curled about him like dry ice in a light show.

'You are rested?'

'Yes, but . . .'

'You must rest. Danger lies ahead.' His voice was a deathly monotone, his eyes like black holes in his preternaturally pale face.

'But, captain,' cut in Mara. 'These disturbances in time, the visions of other ships . . . what is causing them, are they the source of danger to us?'

The captain stared back blankly.

'Other ships? My lady, none sail these seas but the *Plaisir de Mort*.'

Andreas nudged Mara and hissed, 'He hasn't even noticed! He can't see any of it.'

'The fog is closing in,' said the captain. His voice seemed very far away, as though his thoughts were elsewhere, or he was listening to something distant and very quiet.

Then a low, tolling sound seemed to fill the air; the low, deep, mournful sound of a bell, far away but getting closer.

Without a word, the captain turned on his heel and walked back up onto the deck.

'What's wrong?' Andreas called after him. 'What's going on?' But the captain did not turn back.

They followed him to the ship's helm, no longer standing steady but spinning riotously in a sudden, tearing gale that lashed the words from Andreas's throat almost before he had spoken them. He and Mara clung together, scarcely able to stand up as the decks tilted first one way then the other.

The captain stood at the helm, his hands touching it but not steering. His eyes seemed glazed over, unseeing, his mind fixed on something in the distance.

'Captain!' shouted Andreas. 'Captain, will you bloody listen to me?'

He put his hand on the captain's shoulder, meaning to turn him round, only there was one small problem; his hand went right through, as though the captain's body were no more substantial than freezing fog or sea spray.

Andreas turned to Mara; but Mara was staring straight ahead of her. And it was in that very same moment that she realised the horrible truth, saw what up till then only the captain had seen.

The *Plaisir de Mort* was heading straight for huge, towering, jagged-edged rocks, and it was much too late to turn back.

She screamed; but the sound was lost in the banshee wailing of the wind in the tattered sails.

It was midday, and the sun was beating down out of a brassy sky.

Andreas and Mara were floating in the middle of a calm, blue ocean, their raft formed from a broken section of the *Plaisir de Mort*'s foredeck. There was no sign of the captain – or the rest of the ship.

'Mara.' Andreas eased himself across the raft to where Mara was sitting. 'Mara, what are you doing?'

She looked up.

'Reading, what does it look like?'

'You don't think it might have been more sensible to salvage another water barrel, or some food?'

'I suppose.' Now she thought about it, it did seem a bizarre choice. She wondered what had made her do it. 'It seemed like a good idea at the time.'

'Huh!'

'Shush. I'm trying to concentrate.' She turned a yellowed page.

'What on?'

'This. It's the log of the *Plaisir de Mort*'s voyage.'

'And?'

'It tells all about the stone . . . How it was stolen from a Zanzibar priestess called . . .' She started, and looked up into Andreas's eyes. 'Anjula.'

Andreas shrugged.

'Coincidence.' He surveyed the raft, weighing up the situation. One barrel of fresh water, another barrel of (yuk) salt herrings, still, beggars couldn't be choosers. Something white to wave if another ship turned up. All in all, things could be worse. 'You know something, Mara?'

'What?'

'This is just like a scene from a Bond movie. Isn't it?'

'I suppose.'

'Well then.' Andreas slipped an arm round Mara's waist. She was terrifically exciting in that sodden gown, all torn up one side and showing her right leg right up to the thigh. And all that creamy antique lace around the neckline had got so heavy with seawater that it had sagged right down, just showing the very edges of her rose-pink nipples. 'Why don't we do what James Bond does with a half-naked blonde when he's got nothing better to do?'

'Which is?'

He grinned and, rolling over, laid Mara down on her back.

'Give me half a chance and I'll show you.'

By the time they hit land, they'd been through all the Bond movies, plus *Emmanuelle*, *9½ Weeks* and *Last Tango in Paris*. It was hardly surprising that they barely noticed the grating of wet sand underneath their improvised raft.

It was Mara who remarked on it first, squirming out from underneath Andreas's probing tongue.

'Andreas . . . land. Maybe it's an island or something.'

'Oh. Good.' He went on licking her inner thighs.

Lying on her back, Mara blinked up into a brilliant sky.

'Andreas. Andreas, look at the sky.'

'I'd rather look at your beautiful backside. And these gorgeous thighs. And this succulent pussy.'

'Look at the sky! There's something weird about it.'

Reluctantly he gave it a squint. It took a second or two for it to register.

'*Purple*? Purple sky? Skies aren't supposed to be purple.'

'Tell me about it.'

'Have I gone colour blind or something?'

'Not unless I have too.'

Mara crawled off the raft onto the shore. The sky wasn't the only peculiar thing about this place. It was like a picture-book desert island, but drawn with dayglo crayons from a child's colouring box. The sand was virulent orange, the

197

leaves on the scrubby trees acid-green. Shocking-pink crabs ambled down the orange shore to an electric blue sea. Restful it was not.

She stood up, stretching her aching muscles.

'Where do you suppose we are?'

'God knows. Timothy Leary's front garden?'

'This isn't real, it can't be. It doesn't feel real.'

Andreas joined her.

'You mean it's a dream? It's a good one. I especially liked the bit with the shagging.'

'I'm not sure what it is. It *might* be a dream . . . Oh hell, I don't know.'

They stood there, side by side, the orange sand hot and gritty between their bare toes. It was just as they were wondering what to do next that the pigeon fluttered down like a piebald brown duster from the freshly polished sky and landed on the sand.

'Hang on,' said Andreas, pointing to the bird. 'I've seen that pigeon before.'

'Don't be silly,' said Mara. 'You can't have.'

Then the pigeon looked up at Andreas and said, 'You two. At last. It's about flipping time you got here.'

Chapter 15

In the Stonehenge Room at Winterbourne, the Master's chosen élite were gathered around a stone altar, watching and waiting.

Upon the age-smoothed plinth lay the naked form of a girl, curled up like a sleeping kitten. To be more precise this was no ordinary girl, this was blonde and vivacious Steffi Deane, miniskirted ex-kids' TV presenter lusted after by fathers – and mothers – the length of the country. The two tiny puncture wounds on her throat had almost disappeared now, leaving only the tiniest of pearl-white scars on her lickable, biteable skin.

Sighs of impatient lust rippled around the watching vampires. The Master glanced at his Cartier watch. Sometimes being leader of His Majesty's Opposition was more of a chore than a power trip. He had Prime Minister's Question Time to deal with at half-past three; still, there was nothing he liked better than to make the PM squirm – unless it was to watch the birth of a new and beautiful vampire.

'How long has she slept?'

Heimdal stepped forward.

'Twelve hours, Master. She will soon awake. See, already she is stirring in her sleep.'

The sleep of the dead, thought the Master. Soon to awake to the far more opulent realm of the undead. I trust she will be suitably grateful.

Steffi moaned in her sleep and uncurled her limbs,

stretching them out on the warm stone and rolling onto her side. A natural blonde, thought the Master with quickened interest. Flaxen curls danced over her pubis, matching the Shirley Temple hair which had fallen in riotous bubbles over one waxy cheek.

Such skin. Flawless and white, tinged only faintly with a soft rose-pink, blushing to a darker rose beneath her maidenhair. The Master licked his lips, imagining the deep damask between the fragrant petals of her sex and the amber kiss of her beautiful arse. A morsel fit for a king; the uncrowned emperor of darkness.

'See, Master, the sleep of death is leaving her.'

The girl's eyelids twitched once, twice, as though she was fighting some unearthly heaviness and desperately trying to open her eyes. Defeated, she sank down onto the stone, now lying on her back with her head arched back and her golden hair dangling down, almost touching the ground.

It was a sight to awaken lust in any man; and for a vampire it was an irresistible call to feed. Steffi Deane lay with her belly and breasts arched upwards, her thighs parted and the white-gold tuft of her pubic fleece unconsciously offering itself to the Master like a pretty garnish on an exotic fruit. Within the lobes of her sex she was glass-smooth with her own secret moisture, tender as watermelon, bursting with juice.

Awake or not, the Master would have her. He craved the sensual energy from her body, knew how it would energise him to slide his dick into her and possess her dead yet living flesh.

But events were conspiring against him. As he was considering exactly how to take his pleasure of the sleeping girl, there was a thunderous knocking at the door and the Ethiopian slave Ibrahim burst in, his oiled chest rising and falling rapidly with exertion.

'What outrage is this!' seethed the Master, dealing

Ibrahim a sharp blow which left the imprint of his signet ring in his flesh. With a groan of appreciative terror, Ibrahim sank to his knees.

'Master, forgive me. Coming here was not of my choosing. The Mistress . . .'

'Do not lie to me, worm!'

'Please, Master, you must listen. Word has been received. Strange and terrible things are happening in France . . .'

'Things?' echoed the Master coldly. 'What *things*?'

'Things that cannot be explained. Time distorted beyond recognition, strange visions, disappearances . . .'

The beginnings of disquiet entered the Master's cold heart. Perhaps there was some importance in Ibrahim's message, after all. Perhaps he had even misjudged the situation.

'What of Weatherall? Dubois? Graveney?'

But Ibrahim was interrupted before he could reply. A voice, drowsy from sleep, hesitant but smooth as blood-red silk, possessed the silence.

'I . . . I . . . hunger . . .'

The Master swung round. Steffi, his new creation, was awake and on hands and knees on the altar, her blue eyes wide in wonderment yet sly with a new and sensual knowledge. She was like a knowing child, innocent yet oh-so-eager to lose that innocence. Corruption would sit as easily upon her as a Versace gown.

'M-master?'

The Master smiled.

'My child. My newborn child of night.'

'Master . . . this hunger inside me . . .'

'You must and shall feed.' The Master snapped his fingers. 'Ibrahim.'

'Master?'

The Master projected his precise intentions into Ibrahim's mind and the slave rose to his feet with a respectful bow.

201

'At once, Master.'

Ibrahim was delightfully receptive to psychic suggestion, observed the Master. Utterly loyal, utterly open to any and every command, no matter how evil, no matter how ingeniously depraved.

He watched with growing satisfaction as Ibrahim took up position behind the girl. She was writhing and mewing like a tiger cub, rubbing her thighs together as though she thought she might find satisfaction from her own resources. Foolish child, she had so much to learn. Mortals existed for the provision of pleasure and the satisfaction of appetite, lesser vampires to satisfy the hunger of the greater and the more important. And all existed to gratify the sensual demands of the Master.

Ibrahim sank to his knees behind the girl. The Master's spirit entered his mind and, with a sigh of pleasure, he began to lick her upraised buttocks. They were certainly an appetising feast, rounded and high set, white and smooth as milk curd. Ibrahim's fingers showed long and black as spider's legs as he took hold of her backside, digging in his nails and holding her very tight as he splayed her wide.

No more secrets, no more secrets ever. And Steffi had been transported far beyond the limits of foolish inhibition. Nothing was shameful now, or forbidden, everything was acceptable and good as long as it provided pleasure, and the sensual energy upon which the Master's followers fed.

He amused himself by allowing his spirit to possess Ibrahim's body, feeling his sensations, experiencing his emotions. How delightfully raw he was, how crude were his needs and his perceptions. Yet there was undeniable gratification in the rough pleasure he was deriving from the girl's body.

Steffi, too, squirmed and howled with pleasure as Ibrahim's tongue darted deep into her backside, taking her last virginity with perfect, savage ease.

'Beast, beast, beast!' she screamed, and the Master knew

that it was a cry of celebration, of the beast awakened inside herself by the kiss of death.

How Ibrahim sighed and moaned as he tongue-fucked Steffi's ready backside, how he delighted in the taste and feel of her, tight and piquant on his tongue. She pushed back, taking every last millimetre of muscular flesh inside herself, and with each thrust the honeydew welled up inside her, until at last it spilled out of her, forming long clear trickles of nectar down the insides of her thighs.

Despite Ibrahim's worrying news, the Master was enjoying himself. Psychic sex provided an agreeable escape from the day-to-day problems of world domination. He played with Ibrahim's mind a little, refusing to let the poor slave climax until he had brought Steffi to a series of gloriously wet, abandoned orgasms. At last he let go and experienced the blood-rush of ecstasy as Ibrahim's magnificent cock spat its venom in pearly gobbets all over the floor.

When he returned to his own body, feeling far more relaxed and invigorated than he had done in ages, the Master saw that his minions had dragged the new little vampire from her plinth and were bathing themselves in the aura of her fresh young sex.

'Feed, my children,' he smiled benevolently. 'Feed and grow strong.'

When he judged that they had enjoyed her as much as they deserved to, he snapped his fingers once again and she crawled eagerly to his side like the pretty pet she was.

'You may suck my dick, slut.'

A smile of complete adoration spread across Steffi Deane's face.

'You honour me, Master.'

Which of course, was true.

It felt extremely pleasant to have the slut's lips about his dick, her teeth grazing his flesh and the swollen dome of his glans bumping against the back of her throat. He glanced down at Ibrahim, who was still kneeling on the ground, considering what the slave had told him.

'Come here.'

'As you command, Master.' The slave drew himself up to his full six foot six, crossed to the Master and bowed.

'I have an important mission for you, Ibrahim.' Steffi's tongue glanced lusciously over the tip of his cock. It was absolute sensual perfection, far too good to interrupt. 'But it can wait.'

Andreas stared down at the pigeon. It scratched its head with its foot, then blinked impatiently.

'Well?'

Andreas took a step forward.

'*Max*?'

'Of course I'm Max. Who else would I be?'

Andreas exchanged looks with Mara.

'Actually,' she admitted, 'we thought you were a pigeon.'

'Well I'm Max Trevidian, Psychic Investigator.' He preened his piebald feathers with his beak.

'But Max . . .' began Andreas, still half expecting Jeremy Beadle to pop out from behind a rock.

'What?'

'You're supposed to be dead, don't you remember? And you definitely weren't a pigeon last time I saw you.'

'I'm not likely to forget being vapourised by the Master, am I? I'd only just bought those trousers. Look, Andreas, I'm dead, I'm a free spirit, I can be anything I want to be.'

'So why a pigeon?'

Max considered for a moment.

'Plenty of sex. Travel. No responsibilities. And it's a great disguise, what with the kind of work I do.'

'You're still working? As a psychic investigator?'

'Of course I am. Only instead of investigating the dead, I'm a dead person who investigates the living. So far I've pretty much cornered the market.'

'I can imagine,' said Mara, who was getting a headache. 'But what are you doing here?'

'And what are *we* doing here?' added Andreas.

'I thought you'd never ask. First of all, I think you'd better get under cover.' Max glanced up at the sky; it was now oscillating between metallic purple and magenta. 'I'm not entirely sure it's safe here.'

Max led the way up the beach, over pink and orange sand dunes and down a gentle slope. A town was laid out before them, some kind of seaside resort thought Andreas, with a bay, a beach and a long promenade.

'Where are we?'

Max screwed his head round one hundred and eighty degrees.

'Dinard.'

'Where's that?'

'Up the top end of Brittany.'

'Oh. So it's not a desert island then?'

'Get real, Andreas.'

Real? Andreas surveyed the scene before him. It had little to do with reality. It wasn't just the shifting, dayglo colours, though they made the place look like a kid's painting. It was the fact that nothing seemed to stay the same for more than a few moments. You'd be looking at a cottage one minute, then it would turn into a casino, then a bit of a castle, then a mud hut . . . it was all very, very confusing.

'Get down,' said Max suddenly. 'Quickly!' Startled, Mara and Andreas fell flat on their faces on the sand.

'What's happening?' asked Mara, peeping through her fingers.

'Keep quiet and don't move, they probably won't notice you.'

A couple of moments later, a squadron of about two dozen Vespa scooters came screaming down the promenade, screeched to a halt a few yards away, then turned and disappeared in the opposite direction with a smell of scorched rubber and exhaust gases.

Mara got hesitantly to her feet, dusting the sand off her tattered dress.

'Who . . . ?'

'Vampire mods. They think they're the Lost Boys, but really they're just plain juvenile. Who ever heard of vampires in parkas? Look, follow me, I'll try to explain when we get there.'

'There' turned out to be a beachside café, overlooking (alternately) a small château, a fishing boat, an amusement arcade and a Breton cottage.

'I don't think much of the clientele,' commented Andreas. He frowned. What exactly was it about them that gave him the creeps? Was it their curiously vacant and docile faces, staring into space like drugged sheep; or could it be the fact that they all belonged to different bits of history? Within a sweep of ten yards, he could make out two French revolutionary soldiers, a couple of Sans-Culottes, Eric Cantona, three women in lacy headdresses and clogs, and a dead ringer for Charles de Gaulle. Looking up at the television above the bar, he noticed that it was playing a football match . . . from 1973.

'Max . . .'

'Yes, all right, I said I'd try and explain. Sit down and have a drink before somebody notices you. And try to look inconspicuous.'

Andreas and Mara squeezed round a table in the corner; Max sat on the table top and dipped his beak into a *citron pressé*. It would have been easier for Andreas and Mara to enjoy their drinks if they hadn't kept changing from glasses of beer to horn beakers full of mead, but they did their best.

'It's like this,' said Max. 'Diana Graveney has Anjula's mask – and it's made out of the magic stone. With me so far?'

Mara nodded.

'The mask has something to do with all of this?'

'More than something. Graveney's an ambitious woman and dangerous with it. She wants power and she doesn't care what she has to do to get it. She's been using the mask to disrupt time and it's affecting most of Normandy and Brittany.

'Anyhow, she's breaking down the normal course of time and the past two or three hundred years have started happening all at once.'

'That's why things keep . . . sort of . . . strobing?' Mara gazed uneasily out of the window, where the sea wall obligingly turned into a wooden jetty and back again.

'And that's why all these poor bastards are here, God knows what they think they're doing. The thing is, normal people can't handle this, it blows their minds, but vampires are immune – hence the vampire mods.'

'Yes, but . . .' hazarded Mara.

Max cocked his head on one side.

'Look. I'm dead, you've got a vampire body and as for you, Andreas . . . well, you were never normal.'

Mara's fingers tightened on the edge of the table. She wished it would stop transforming itself into the roof of a henhouse.

'We've got to stop Graveney!'

'Mara's right,' nodded Max. 'We've got to stop her before she realises how many tones of magic stone are buried under the fortifications at St Malo. Imagine what she could do with that much . . .'

'Oh God.' Andreas rubbed his forehead with the back of his hand. It was hot and sweaty. 'So what do we do?'

'Is there anyone who can help us?' asked Mara.

'There might be.' Max bowed his head. 'But you're not going to like this. The way I see it, the only one who stands a chance of defeating Graveney is the Master.'

Andreas groaned.

'So what do we do now?'

'We go to Carnac.'

'Where?'

'Carnac. It's like Stonehenge, only bigger. Henri's going to drive us there, aren't you Henri?'

Andreas looked round and started. Standing by the bar was the old man he'd seen in St Malo. Only he kept changing into the young man who'd rescued them from jail.

'Henri!' exclaimed Mara, leaping up from her seat.

'It's no use waving your arms about,' said Max. 'He can't see you. It's this time thingy, it's put him into a trance. I'm the only one who can get through to him.' He flew onto Henri's shoulder and pecked his earlobe. 'Come on, Henri, that's right. You're taking us on a little trip.'

'But why?' protested Andreas as he followed Max and Henri out of the café. 'Why would Henri drive us anywhere?'

'Because,' said Max slowly, 'Henri owes you a favour. A very big one.'

The car was a red Mercedes. It was also a pre-war Daimler, a horse and cart and an ancient steam-powered delivery van, depending on when you looked at it. As they rolled on through the ever-changing countryside, Henri kept changing too, from an old man to a young man, then a boy and back again. There was something disconcerting about being chauffeured by a six-year-old, but Henri didn't seem to mind.

'What did you mean?' asked Mara. 'About Henri owing Andreas a favour?'

Max turned round to look at them.

'Remember Gaston Lebecq? From nineteen forty-one?'

Andreas pulled a face.

'I'll take that as a yes. Well, in the war he was a patriotic young man working in a jeweller's shop in St Malo. His friend Henri went out nicking people's jewellery, and Lebecq fenced it to raise money for the Resistance.'

'What's this got to do with me? And why do people keep thinking *I'm* Gaston Lebecq?'

'If you listen you might find out. One night, Henri got overambitious. He stole jewels from the Commandant's wife, Marthe von Kleewort, including a rather nice cock ring set with a piece of unusual greenish-grey stone. Anyhow, after giving the swag to Lebecq, Henri got caught.'

'And?'

'And to save his skin, he turned informant. Lebecq was picked up, roughed up and thrown in the cells. But he denied all knowledge of the jewels.'

'Henri. The double-dealing bastard.'

'Things were looking bad, then Henri had an attack of conscience and sprang Lebecq from jail.'

'And Lebecq ended up on the *Plaisir de Mort* . . . ?'

Max pecked Henri on the right ear and the car executed a smooth right turn.

'No, Andreas, *you* ended up on the *Plaisir de Mort*, but that's where you and Lebecq parted company. He couldn't stay in France; the Germans were on to him and the Resistance thought he was a traitor. So he scarpered across the Channel to England – with a nice little haul of jewellery.'

'And then what happened to him?' asked Mara.

'He "donated" some of the jewels, including the grey-green stone, to the British Government, in return for a new identity. Moved to Croydon by all accounts. Got married in his late forties, had a son . . .'

Hairs stood up on the back of Andreas's neck. Max paused.

'Hunt, he called himself. Matthias Hunt.' He looked round at Andreas's face, completely drained of all colour. It wasn't a pretty sight. 'Worked it out at last, Andreas? Gaston Lebecq was your dad.'

★ ★ ★

It was a good job Carnac wasn't far away. Suddenly discovering that you'd spent time as your own dad could make you feel quite queasy.

'What's so important about Carnac anyway?' demanded Andreas as they left Henri sitting in the car and walked past the Archéoscope towards the standing stones.

Mara sighed.

'Sometimes I'm ashamed of you, Andreas Hunt. There are hundreds, no, thousands of stones here, they stretch for miles. And they have tremendous psychic energy.'

'If you say so,' said Andreas, peering over the railings at the wild flowers rioting around the higgledy-piggledy stones. 'But they don't look like much.'

'Right. I'm off now,' said Max, perching on the railings.

'But you can't!' exclaimed Mara. 'Come with us, it's our best chance of safety.'

Max shook his feathered head.

'I'll be just fine. What more can happen to you when you're already dead?' He fluttered up onto Mara's shoulder and cuddled up, giving her ear an affectionate peck.

'That's bestiality, that is,' sniffed Andreas.

'You're only jealous because she thinks I'm sexier than you.'

'Dream on.'

As the piebald pigeon fluttered off into the metallic pink sky, Andreas wondered if they would ever see Max Trevidian again. And if they would recognise him when they did.

'Come on,' urged Mara. 'There isn't much time. Climb over the railings and open the gate.'

Andreas clambered over and let Mara into the enclosure. There were rocks everywhere, great big monolithic ones, covered with lichen, that towered over you, fat medium-sized ones, broken ones like jagged teeth and tiny ones so thickly covered with wild flowers that you'd tripped over them and cut your ankle before you even knew they were there.

'Most of them aren't even here,' grunted Andreas. 'Are you sure this is the right place?'

'Of course I'm sure.'

'So what now?'

'We walk. Come on. Take my hand. And *trust* me, OK?'

He sighed and took her hand.

'OK. But if we end up dead, I'll kill you.'

He didn't have to trust for long. At the very first step they took, the whole avenue of stones was transformed. There were no more broken stones, no more gaps; even the wild flowers and the tangle of long grass were gone. In their place stretched two miles of standing stones in all their neolithic glory, drawing Andreas and Mara forward, urging them to walk forward and not look back.

'Guess what,' whispered Andreas. He could hardly believe the excitement that was coursing through him, the desperate need. 'I want you.'

'I want you too, that's the power of this place. But not here. We have to find where the magic is strongest.'

That place was an aching, yearning mile further on. It wasn't until Andreas's body was throbbing with an unbearable ache that they saw it: the centre point of the great avenue of stones.

'Here,' whispered Mara, and she stood on tiptoe to kiss him.

They were standing in a grove of trees, carefully planted around a symmetrical circle of identical stones, garlanded with fresh flowers. As they embraced, Andreas realised with a start that they were both naked, save for flower garlands draped around their shoulders. Their bodies felt white-hot, their skin dry and smooth. Together they sank down onto the flat, round stone at the centre of the circle, their bodies instinctively joining, their lust taking over. This was something greater and infinitely more powerful than either of them, a sensual magic which took reality and dissolved it into a sizzling heat haze, obliterating everything else.

When the heat died down and they came back to their senses, they were making love in a very different circle; a circle beneath ordinary skies ... and a red-faced warden was standing over them with a lamp.

'Oi! You two. You can't do that here!'

Chapter 16

'Lick it all up,' commanded Graveney. 'Every last drop.'

She jerked on the choke chain, which tightened about Anjula's throat. Anjula let out a yelp and tried to scrabble at the chain, but her wrists were restrained by heavy manacles. She was in the parlour of the vampire queen, trussed up in a spider's web of chains which hung her, spread-eagled, from the ceiling.

There were chains everywhere. Chains around her arms and legs, chains that wound and slid across her bare back. Tiny chains, delicate as gossamer, connected to rings in her ears, nose, lips, nipples, navel . . .

'Every drop,' repeated Graveney, and pulled the choke-chain a fraction tighter.

This time, Anjula did not dare resist. She put out her tongue and began to lick the cream from Graveney's finger. Her own cream, guiltily shed from her own sex.

The first taste was treacherously enchanting. Anjula moaned and licked again, already wanting more and more and still more. Graveney purred at the touch of Anjula's warm, muscular tongue, winding its way round and round her fingertip.

'Good slut. Well-trained slut. Obedient slut. Continue to obey me and you shall be my pretty plaything.'

Anjula licked the very last smearings of juice from Graveney's finger, and fell back, exhausted. The muscles and tendons in her arms and legs were stretched almost to tearing, veins standing out like blue wires on her shoulders and thighs. Her sex continued to drip juice, pungently sweet and musky, onto the bare stone floor.

'There,' smiled Graveney. 'I knew you'd like that. You see how much more agreeable life is when you are obedient to your mistress?'

Anjula did not reply. How could she? She was too ashamed to admit what she had felt, and could still feel; the terrible, betraying pleasure of submission. She cursed herself for underestimating Graveney's sensual skills.

Graveney's lieutenants watched from the shadows, their eyes gleaming in the faint light from the black candles. Glimmers of moonlight cast curious shadows on naked, oiled young bodies that flickered as time ebbed and rippled about them. A low moaning sound, an agonised keening, rose up from the children of night as Graveney twisted the ring which passed through Anjula's clitoris, making her scream with unwilling ecstasy.

'Mistress . . .' they moaned. 'Mistress Diana . . .'

'Mistress.' Jean-Marie stood at Graveney's elbow. 'Mistress, we can bear it no longer. The need overwhelms us.'

'Soon. Soon we shall all be satisfied.'

Günther, a tall German backpacker with a shock of wild blond hair and a body literally to die for, threw back his head and laughed maniacally. He was a little crazy, but Graveney liked them that way.

'You are a milksop, Jean-Marie,' he laughed. 'Such pleasure I have already known, I shall gladly endure self-denial a little longer. Such beautiful bodies I have possessed, such sweet blood I have drunk . . .'

'There was a girl,' murmured a voice behind him. 'At the train station, she was Russian I think. I took her in the arse and as she climaxed, there on the platform, my teeth pierced her flesh. It was so soft and white and cold . . .'

'A beautiful boy,' sighed a girl by his side. 'Eighteen, a farm hand. His dick was so adorable I took him into my throat then drank the blood from his balls . . .'

'More . . .'

'More, now . . .'

'Mistress, we must feed . . .'

'Enough,' snapped Graveney. 'There will be pleasures for all, very very soon. We shall take Paris – isn't that so, Anjula?'

Graveney jerked up Anjula's head and made her look into her face.

'Answer me.'

But Anjula said nothing. She was marshalling what little strength she had left to resist, to refuse the lure of Graveney's creeping corruption.

'So, Anjula, it seems that I must teach you a lesson yet again.' She ran a sharp-nailed finger down Anjula's belly, making the firm, smooth, coffee-coloured flesh quiver and flinch. A single movement took her down between Anjula's wide-spread thighs and then up again, into the tight haven of her sex. She chuckled. 'How wet you are, my dear. Wet and ready for your mistress.'

Anjula's eyes widened in alarm as Graveney turned to unlock a small cabinet and took out something twisted and knobbly and threatening. As she held it up, Anjula shrank away, knowing now what it was, sensing the pain and the awful pleasure which were soon to be hers.

It was a double-ended dildo, huge and black; a thing of moulded black rubber, with two thick, curving phalluses covered in nodules and firm, rounded spikes. The phalluses were each thicker than a man's wrist.

Graveney strapped the dildo to her belly, buckling it tight so that the two surrogate pricks stood out menacing and proud.

'And now for your lesson, my pretty child. I am sure that you will enjoy it every bit as much as I shall.'

She took Anjula from behind, gripping her arse cheeks and wrenching them open, targeting the twin hearts of

Anjula's sex. With all her strength, Anjula resisted the terrible urge to cry out.

And she remained silent, even when Graveney entered both quim and arse in the same, unforgiving thrust, not even sparing a moment to smear Anjula's pleasure juices over the dry, tight sphincter which resisted penetration to the very last. A tear pearled at the corner of Anjula's eye, but she would not shed it. No, no, no, whatever else befell her, she must resist.

'Sweet fucking,' purred Graveney, squeezing Anjula's breasts as she thrust in and out of her. 'Sweet, sweet fucking. I shall house-train you, and you shall be my pet animal. Won't you love that, my sweet savage? I know you shall . . .'

Anjula stared straight ahead, into the shadows where figures moved, sinister and naked, their eyes watchful, their hands sliding over each other's bodies, their tongues darting like the tongues of serpents.

How long? thought Anjula. How long before the last drop of strength ebbs away from me and I am as much Graveney's plaything as all the rest of them?

But one pair of eyes did not watch her with quite the same covetous lust. In fact, as Anjula looked at Jean-Marie she could have sworn she saw him flinch, trying to look away.

A tiny seed of hope stirred inside Anjula. Crazy as it seemed, Jean-Marie did not look happy to see her like this.

The Master looked from Andreas to Mara and back again.

'Half naked in the middle of runway ten at Heathrow Airport? You two certainly believe in making a grand entrance.'

'Sorry,' said Andreas. It *had* been a bit embarrassing, that airport official recognising him as an MP and having him and Mara arrested.

'We weren't sure where we were going to end up,' said Mara.

'Evidently not,' said the Master drily, his eyes roaming over Mara and Andreas's tattered clothes. 'I take it you are dressed for a fancy-dress party?'

'There's an explanation for all this.'

'Yeah,' nodded Andreas. 'But not an easy one.'

'Whatever it is,' replied the Master, 'it had better be convincing.'

The three of them were standing in the Customs area at Heathrow Airport, conveniently and securely cordoned off by the police on the Master's orders. A scattering of Customs officers were nearby, but they were frozen where they stood, staring blankly ahead of them without seeing or understanding anything. The Master had thought of everything.

It was Mara who began the story of what had happened to them.

'We couldn't contact you, Master. The fabric of time has been so distorted that we found ourselves shifting between different periods.'

'First we were in the present,' agreed Andreas, 'Then in nineteen forty-something, then we were on this weird ship . . .'

'What kind of ship?'

'It was ancient, practically falling to bits. The *Plaisir de Mort*, it was called . . . and you should have seen the state of the captain.'

To their surprise the Master chuckled delightedly.

'The *Plaisir de Mort*?'

'Well, that's what it was most of the time. Sometimes when you looked out of the cabin porthole it was the first-class cocktail lounge on the *Titanic*.'

'There was a storm,' added Mara. 'We ran up on deck and the captain was standing at the wheel. It was spinning round and round but he was just staring into space. We were heading straight for these enormous rocks.'

'And the next thing,' concluded Andreas, 'we were

shipwrecked in an orange sea, on a bit of the *Plaisir*'s foredeck.'

'I managed to salvage the logbook.' Mara handed it over, water-stained but still intact. 'It tells everything about the ship's voyages for the last five hundred years.'

'I see.' The Master considered for a moment, eyes closed, drinking in the vibrations from the logbook, skimming its content and lingering on an ancient, hand-drawn map. Then he directed his attentions towards Mara. 'Tell me, slut, was the captain a tall fellow with long black hair and a look of the Devil?'

'As a matter of fact he was,' replied Mara. 'You once knew him?'

'Well, well,' said the Master softly to himself. 'Esteban. He was first mate on the *Plaisir de Mort* when she was the pride and joy of my slaving fleet.' He stroked the warped and cracked leather binding of the logbook. 'Poor, unfortunate Esteban.'

The Master's face darkened, the smile disappearing from his lips.

'He betrayed me, the ignorant fool, fancied he had the cunning to usurp my power. Who would have thought that fate could doom him to such a fitting punishment? Condemned to relive his last, terrible moments for all eternity . . . How delightfully appropriate.'

'Master,' cut in Andreas, hardly daring to break into his reverie but only too aware that time was ticking away. For all he knew it was ticking back to front and inside out as well. You just couldn't be sure of anything any more.

'What is it, Weatherall?'

'Diana Graveney, Master. She is behind everything.'

'Graveney?' hissed the Master. 'So. The bitch has developed ideas above her station.'

'She has obtained some kind of mask,' explained Mara. 'Made of the magic stone. Evidently it has the power to

218

disrupt time. So far her influence has spread over Normandy and Brittany, but soon . . .'

'I think, Master,' hazarded Andreas, 'that she believes she can defeat you and make your empire her own.'

'Esteban believed he could oppose me,' snapped the Master, 'and he is doomed to exquisite eternal torture. I feel sure we can arrange something similar for Doctor Diana Graveney.'

For once, Andreas hoped the Master was right.

'What must we do, Master?' asked Mara.

The Master glanced down at the logbook in his hand, then cast it aside. He had drained it of its information, as efficiently as he might drain a body of its life-energy.

'You shall fly to Mombasa. When you arrive you will receive further instructions.'

'Mombasa!' gaped Andreas. 'But we haven't got visas . . . and aren't I supposed to be chairing a cross-parliamentary committee on inner-city redevelopment on Friday? What if the Chief Whip . . . ?'

The Master stared at Andreas as though he had suddenly turned into a giant chicken. Then laughed and clapped him on the shoulder.

'Good God, Weatherall, you seem to have developed a sense of humour. I like it. Now . . . a little entertainment before you leave.'

It was an offer they couldn't refuse. The Master surveyed the Customs officials standing around, their eyes glazed, their limbs stiff and frozen.

'Choose whichever will satisfy your craving. Perhaps the large-breasted blonde for you, Weatherall? And for you, Dubois . . . the Asiatic has a good body, but maybe you prefer the thin and hungry look?'

He took his time choosing his own sweetmeat, at last selecting an athletic-looking redhead with high-set breasts and skin like alabaster. Snapping his fingers, he brought her out of the trance.

'Make your choices. Myself, I have an appetite for red.'

The Master's private jet rose high in the sky above the English coastline, its silver and black fuselage gleaming in the summer sunshine.

Andreas and Mara were far too busy to spend time admiring the view. They were fully occupied rediscovering the pleasures of total luxury.

'More wine, Mistress Dubois?' enquired a young male attendant with a bow tie and very little else. The chain leading between his cock ring and his wristlet jingled prettily as he bowed, offering chilled Muscadet on a laquered tray inlaid with abalone.

'A little. You may top up both glasses.' Mara winked naughtily at Andreas. 'And mind you don't spill any, or I may have to punish you.'

The slave's cock twitched and stiffened at this lustful thought, as Mara had known it would. There was nothing the Master's slaves loved more than the promise of pain.

Andreas leant back in the sunken bath, watching the slave boy's tight backside swaying off into the galley and relaxing as a Chinese girl's small, white fingers kneaded the tension from his shoulder muscles with warm jasmine oil.

'Prick-tease,' he scolded, reaching out with his right foot and sliding it up Mara's thigh. She laughed.

'He loves it.'

Wriggling in the rose-tinged, foamy water, she slid down until only her face was above the surface. Looking down at her body was like looking at a wonderful tropical island, now hidden, now revealed by shifting clouds of creamy foam. She reached out and took a sip from her glass of wine.

'Perhaps I'll tell him the wine's not the right temperature,' she teased.

'He'll spurt at the very thought of a good spanking,'

retorted Andreas. 'Come to think of it, that's what you could do with too.'

'You wouldn't dare!'

Andreas waved away the doe-eyed Chinese girl and lunged forward, making a grab for Mara. But it was a large pool, and she slid easily out of his grasp, laughing as he floundered in the foamy water, wiping the soap out of his eyes.

'Just come here and let me teach you a lesson.'

'Come and catch me. If you can.'

She jumped up lightly onto the edge of the bath and stood up, dripping suds onto the black onyx tiles. Slithering tongues of soapy foam crept down over her shoulders and her breasts, dripping from the crested tips like warm, wet snow.

It was more than Andreas could stand. A lot more. As she turned away, he reached up and grabbed her by the ankle. Laughing, she kicked out at him but as he slipped backwards he kept hold of her and she tumbled in on top of him with a tremendous splash. Water slopped over the edge of the bath, soaking the pure-white carpet, but the Master's attendants mopped it up discreetly, never interfering with the sensual pleasures of their betters.

Andreas and Mara floundered in the water, coughing and spluttering as they rose to the surface, each still struggling to outdo the other.

'Pig,' said Mara, fighting back a smile.

'Oink,' said Andreas, his hands securing a firmer grip on Mara's wriggling body.

'Let go.'

'Not a chance.' Slipping his index finger between Mara's buttocks, he eased it into her anus. It dilated to welcome him in, then contracted about his finger, as if coaxing him in further.

'That's cheating,' moaned Mara, the moan turning into a sigh of excitement.

'I wonder . . .' murmured Andreas, working his finger

221

in and out of Mara's backside. 'I wonder if we're a mile high yet.'

Mara startled him out of his complacency by suddenly breaking free, leaping out of the bath and running away towards the main cabin. She was laughing as she looked back at him over her shoulder.

'Come back here – I'm going to teach you a lesson!'

'You'll have to catch me first.'

It was a challenge, and Andreas liked challenges. In a moment he was up and running, his dripping body leaving soapy patches and wet footprints all over the Master's exquisite carpet. He noticed that Mara wasn't exactly exerting herself to get away from him – besides, where was there for her to run to?

Sure enough, he cornered her in the galley, her back to the microwave oven, her breasts and chin thrust out defiantly at him. There was a bottle of olive oil in her hand.

'Come any closer, and I'll pour this all over you.'

'Promises, promises.'

He made a grab for her and she carried out her threat, lifting up the bottle and letting the oil cascade down over his hair, his face, his shoulders, his back. It was lukewarm and sticky, but he didn't care. With his slippery fingers, he caught Mara and flipped her over like a pancake.

'I promised you a good spanking, didn't I?'

She was silent, but he could feel her body shaking with laughter; spasms of mirth which gradually subsided to the quickening rise and fall of her breathing. He knew she was excited. He could smell her excitement. She was leaning forward over the worktop, her arms above her head, her backside pushed out toward his crotch. A few trickles of greenish-yellow oil had found their way down his belly and were dripping onto her buttocks. He amused himself by rubbing the oil into her skin, with broad circular movements.

The flesh of Mara's buttocks was firm and smooth. It

stretched and sprang back at his touch, and he felt her body alternately flex and relax with each slippery stroke. Pulling back his hand, he contemplated her backside for a few, luxurious moments. It was glistening with oil now, smooth and shiny and inviting as the skin of a polished apple. He simply couldn't resist.

Thwack!

'Ouch!'

Slap!

'Beast!'

She was laughing and shrieking, swearing and sighing; and Andreas was loving it every bit as much as Mara was. The way her buttocks danced and sprang back from each blow of his hand; the way her flesh pinked and then reddened, until it glowed and felt hot to the touch.

Andreas had never been particularly into spanking; now, he was beginning to see its appeal. There was something exceptionally stimulating about the sight of a well-rounded bottom, cheeks quivering and slightly spread, flesh firm and reddened until it was as toothsome as a ripe, sweet plum.

Mara shuddered and sighed, pushing back onto his dick, well oiled and now inundated with the slippering oozings of her pussy. Luxury; pure, sensual luxury. Tomorrow, they would be in Mombasa. Tomorrow, they would worry about magic stones and vampire queens.

Today, they would simply luxuriate in pleasure.

Mara lay dozing on a pile of soft, white pillows. Idle, dreamy thoughts fluttered like butterflies around the emptiness of her mind.

Andreas. Where was he? He must be somewhere about . . . but she was far too pleasantly sleepy to wonder where. They had fucked all afternoon, and she was utterly exhausted. She would just lie here and let herself drift off . . .

But wait. She might be sleepy, but somebody else definitely wasn't. As Mara lay there, eyes closed, she felt a tongue on her breast, fingers pinching and teasing her nipples, other fingers sliding between her parted thighs and rubbing her clitoris.

Her eyes were heavy. Sooo heavy. But the pleasure was irresistible. She sighed, and stretched out her limbs, offering herself to her lover's kisses and caresses.

'Andreas . . .' she giggled. 'You bad boy . . .'

He didn't reply, but it went on. The sensations were incredible, even though Mara had thought she was too tired to feel anything more than the need for sleep. Waves and waves of pleasure washed over her, bringing her expertly to a crashing, overwhelming climax.

As the last waves of orgasm died away, Mara sank back onto the pillows and fell deeply asleep, her hair spread out about her face like damp auburn sea wrack. She lay stretched out on her back, one hand on her breast, the other still resting between her labia, index finger on the wet nubbin of her swollen clitoris.

And she was smiling. Not like Mara Fleming, but like Anastasia Dubois.

Chapter 17

Anastasia Dubois was triumphant. At last.

She smiled the smile of the tigress as her fingertips explored her body. *Her* body, no one else's. And certainly never the body of Mara Fleming.

Anastasia chuckled as she caught sight of her reflection in a gilded, circular mirror beside the sunken bath.

'You are as beautiful as ever,' she purred contentedly. 'No, *more* beautiful since you overcame the spirit of that upstart, body-stealing bitch Mara Fleming.'

She glanced about her. The attendants had withdrawn discreetly, and that fool Andreas was still deeply asleep, his body sprawled untidily across the pile of damp satin cushions. For the moment she was alone; excellent. But she must work quickly, fashion herself a disguise before Andreas awoke and saw what she had done to his precious Mara.

The crystal necklace was lying on one of the cushions. Anastasia contemplated it with distaste. It was such a tacky, nasty little thing, with its rough crystals hanging in little spiral cages of silver wire, not to her taste at all . . . and dangerous too. It had bound her powerful spirit for an inconveniently long time, and she must be certain that she was rid of it.

A young male attendant was hovering close to the door of the main cabin. Anastasia summoned him with a toss of her auburn tresses and he came padding barefoot across the soft white carpet, his semi-erect dick invitingly accessible beneath a tiny apron of raw white silk.

He bowed.

'Mistress?'

'Softly, slave. If you wake my companion you will feel my anger.'

The youth's eyes looked down into hers, longingly, lovingly. Poor darling, thought Anastasia; you are in love with pain and punishment, and I, alas, am far too busy to waste time on your gratification.

'Get down on your knees.'

He obeyed, the muscles in his long, athletic legs flexing beneath the tanned skin. Anastasia indicated the necklace.

'Pick it up. Now remove the crystals.' She waited until his fingers touched the silver casing, then seized his balls in a crushing grip, squeezing them hard through the silk apron. Tears flooded the slave's soft grey eyes, but he made no sound except for a soft, fluttering sigh. He dared not scream out his pain. 'Not with your fingers, imbecile. With your teeth.'

He was a willing enough slave, if a little slow on the uptake. But once he had grasped the idea, he succeeded in prising out the crystals with surprising dexterity. Had time been hers to toy with, Anastasia might well have frittered away a few hours commanding this comely youth to pleasure her with his tongue and teeth.

But – for now at least – time was her enemy. As soon as the slave had completed his task, she sent him away with no more reward than the discarded crystals and the lingering sharpness of her nails, digging deep into his softly yielding testicles.

What now? Ah yes, the very thing. A collection of glass bowls stood on a nearby table, some laden with exotic fruit, others filled to the brim with scented oils or coloured pebbles. She selected a small bowl, made from rose-tinted glass, so close to the colour of the crystal necklace that no one would ever tell the difference simply by looking at it.

Raising her fist, she smashed it with a single blow.

Ah. Ah, bliss. As Anastasia raised her arm, blood cascaded down it from cuts in her knuckles and wrist. She shivered with lascivious hunger and began lapping at the bloody trickles, eager to drink every drop before the cuts healed themselves.

She chose three jagged fragments of pinkish glass and inserted them into the silver cages of the necklace. Perfect. Surely not even the closest inspection could reveal the difference. But there was all the difference in the world . . .

Anastasia purred as she tied the leather thong round her neck; purred with the sublime gratification of knowing that she had destroyed its power, removed the one remaining barrier to regaining complete control of her body.

'You are dead and gone, Mara Fleming,' she whispered to herself, stroking her hands down over the smooth slopes of her flanks. 'May you rot in oblivion for all eternity.'

Andreas awoke with much yawning and rolling about. The body he had stolen from Nick Weatherall was pretty enough, thought Anastasia, but the spirit currently inhabiting it was Andreas Hunt through and through. And that would never do. She would have to see what she could do about it . . .

As he sat up and slipped on a bathrobe, she noticed the dragon's head identity bracelet which he always wore. Of course. The bracelet which Mara Fleming had empowered to protect him against discovery. Anastasia allowed herself a secret smile, suppressing the insane laughter which was bubbling up inside her. Of course . . .

Andreas's hand fell lightly on her shoulder.

'Mombasa soon,' he yawned, idly stroking the nape of her neck. She wanted to bite the fingers that dared caress her with such familiarity, catch them in her teeth and crunch the bones to powder, but she forced herself to turn and greet him with a kiss and a sexy smile.

'I guess I'd better get dressed then.'

'Yeah.' Andreas ran his index finger along the leather thong round Anastasia's neck. 'And whatever you do, don't take this off. We don't want any nasty accidents.'

Ibrahim walked confidently but respectfully into Graveney's underground headquarters. He looked sleek and just a touch exotic in a white linen suit with mandarin collar, two-tone shoes and heavy gold rings that glowed against his ebony skin. From time to time, a ripple in eternity turned the walls of the chamber to rushing water, filled with twisting snakes, but he paid them no heed.

Jean-Marie introduced him, bowing low before his mistress.

'*Maîtresse Diana, je vous présente l'esclave Ibrahim . . .*'

Ibrahim stepped forward. He towered over everyone in the subterranean chamber. He did not bow, but inclined his head slightly forward.

'I am Ibrahim, that is indeed true, but I am no man's slave.'

Graveney eyed him with a mixture of lust and suspicion.

'And no woman's?'

'Madam, I have come to offer my services to you. My services and my loyalty.'

Graveney laughed sardonically.

'You, who swore eternal loyalty to the Master? What value has your loyalty, worm?'

Nothing, it seemed, would disconcert Ibrahim. His steady gaze did not flicker for a second.

'The Master is not what he once was, Madam. His powers are waning, he no longer holds the hearts and minds of the faithful.'

'Why have you come here?'

'I am ambitious, Madam.' His cool, dark eyes rested long on Diana's petite frame, so closely moulded by a catsuit of fine black latex. 'And hungry.'

'And you would serve me?'

'Yes, Madam.'

'You would do *anything* I command?'

'I offer you my complete loyalty, madam. The service of my body and the darkness of my soul.'

Graveney smiled thinly.

'Fine words. But is there substance behind them? If you wish to serve me, you must prove your . . . motivation.' She threw a look at Jean-Marie, watching sullenly from the corner. 'What task shall we set this postulant, my dear child?'

At this invitation, a flicker of interest lit up Jean-Marie's face.

'Perhaps, Mistress Diana, he should prove that he is willing to deny himself completely, through complete humiliation and degradation of the body.'

Graveney gave a throaty chuckle.

'Dear, sweet child. You set such exacting standards. Very well, *cher enfant*, you may humiliate him. If nothing else, it should provide an agreeable entertainment.'

Jean-Marie strutted up to Ibrahim like a bantam cock. 'Strip naked.'

The Ethiopian was a good six inches taller than Jean-Marie, but he carried out the command like a pet lamb. First the jacket, then the collarless silk shirt, the platinum Rolex, the crocodile belt . . .

'Quickly now, you are trying my patience!'

Ibrahim continued to undress with a kind of sensual slowness, only too aware of the sensation he was creating with his muscular perfection, his toned boxer's body rippling with strength and symmetry. As he stepped out of his trousers and grey jersey shorts, the sleeping viper of his dick sprang to the alert, rearing its cloven head as though at any moment a forked pink tongue might spit a deadly venom.

Jean-Marie ran the tip of his tongue nervously over parched lips. His eyes ran down Ibrahim's body, taking in the powerful shoulders, the muscular arms and washboard stomach, the polished ebony thighs. And that mesmerically beautiful dick, arching and dancing above the aubergine ripeness of large, full, shaven testicles.

At last he found his voice.

'To your knees.'

Ibrahim knelt, but there was a distinct lack of submission in the set of the head, the slightly bowed shoulders.

Jean-Marie took a naked teenage boy from the watching throng and pushed him in front of Ibrahim.

'Lick out Pierre's arse.'

Ibrahim did not reply, but simply took the youth by the buttocks and pulled him hard onto his face. Pierre's eyes closed and he let out a sudden gasp of breath at the brusque, slicing thrust of Ibrahim's tongue, pushing its way into the heartland of his anus.

He began by keeping silent, his teeth biting into his lower lip in an effort not to cry out; but Ibrahim had spent a long time studying the fine art of rimming and his exceptionally long tongue gave him a natural advantage. As he tongue-fucked Pierre, his fingers slid between the youth's thighs and started rubbing the secret place between balls and anus, the place which could bring complete joy if touched by an expert hand.

Ibrahim let it last. The youth was clearly beside himself with uncontrollable sexual need and was now weeping and wailing in a very undisciplined manner (a manner which the Master would certainly not have tolerated). He allowed the boy to disgrace himself a little longer, then pushed his tongue into him, right up to the root, at the very same moment squeezing his prostate gland between finger and thumb.

Pierre's scream reverberated off the walls of the underground chamber, the echoes chasing each other round and round for many a long moment. When Ibrahim sat back on his haunches, licking the last of Pierre from his lips, the stone floor was spattered with the youth's copious seed.

'Lick it up,' said Jean-Marie, placing his hand on the back of Ibrahim's neck and forcing it down towards the dirty flagstones. 'And don't leave any. Unless of course you *want* to be punished.'

With perfect serenity, Ibrahim lapped at the opalescent pools of semen, his tongue curling and cupping to lick up the cooling, salty fluid. He took his time, judging thoroughness more impressive than speed; and when he had finished, he began licking the shiny toecap of Graveney's patent-leather boot.

'Filth!' screeched Jean-Marie, catching Ibrahim in the chest with the sole of his shoe. Ibrahim judged it wise to allow himself to topple sideways. 'Filthy scum! How dare you touch the Mistress without permission!'

Ibrahim lay still, awaiting the decree which would decide his fate. He was in no hurry.

Graveney smiled.

'My impetuous children,' she murmured delightedly. It was not clear whether she was referring to Jean-Marie or Ibrahim, or both. 'You must learn the arts of self-discipline. Pierre, Charles, Madeleine, prepare the cabinet.'

The cabinet stood behind a dark brocade curtain. It was a huge, dark, medieval creation in the shape of a black devil, with a grinning face and red eyes painted onto the heavy iron shell.

'Open it.'

It swung open on oiled hinges, revealing a cavernous interior made narrow by a forest of evil iron spikes, sharp as devils' teeth. Spikes which, when the cabinet was closed, would interlock, piercing and tearing flesh.

Graveney nodded to Jean-Marie.

'You may place the postulant inside.'

Jean-Marie was almost weeping with joy as he half pushed, half kicked Ibrahim into the cabinet. Not that he needed to play-act the heavy-handed torturer; Ibrahim was more than happy to get inside. In fact, as the cabinet clanged shut and the spikes bit deep into his body, Ibrahim was smiling.

Stepping off the plane at Mombasa was like stepping into an oven. The tarmac under Andreas's feet was so hot that it stuck to the soles of his shoes. He was glad to get inside the air-conditioned terminal.

'Are you all right?' He looked Mara up and down. Now, he wasn't the most intuitive of men, but he could have sworn there was something different about her. Still, at least she was wearing the necklace and that floaty scarlet thing she'd chosen to wear was pure sex on legs.

'Why shouldn't I be?'

'I don't know really. I just . . . worry.'

'Well don't. OK?'

'OK, keep your hair on. So what now?' The words were scarcely out of Andreas's mouth when a steward came forward and guided them towards the VIP lounge.

'I will leave you here to wait, sir, madam. There is a message for you from England.'

The door closed. Andreas crossed to the fax machine.

'It's from the Master!'

Mara snatched it out of his hand with uncharacteristic rudeness, scanned it and gave it back to him. He read it.

'Anjula, Mistress of the Stone, once held sway from a palace at the northern tip of Zanzibar.

'Go and find it.

'M.'

'But *how*?' wondered Andreas out loud.

'We go to Zanzibar and then we look.'

'Oh,' said Andreas.

'Oh what?'

'Where exactly *is* Zanzibar?'

'You're completely useless, do you know that? Useless, incompetent scum.'

Mara flounced out of the VIP lounge, banging the door shut behind her. Andreas sighed, picked up his suitcase and followed. He was beginning to think that the heat didn't agree with Mara. And now all this business about Zanzibar. He wasn't sure he wanted to go somewhere he'd never heard of outside bad pirate movies.

Mara was sitting on a bench outside the terminal, elbows on knees and chin in hands. She looked pissed off. Andreas sauntered over, as casually as he could.

'Sorry,' he said. She glanced up.

'It's not your fault you're a cretin,' she conceded.

Andreas was about to sit down next to her when he noticed the guy in the beaten-up fedora and safari suit. Indiana Jones's seedier brother, with three days' growth of beard and a mahogany tan so deep you'd swear it was Ronseal.

'Look!'

Mara looked.

'So? It's a smelly old guy.'

'A smelly old guy with a piece of cardboard. Look what it says.'

It read: 'ZANZIBAR GEOLOGICAL SURVEY'.

'Bit of a coincidence, huh? He's obviously waiting for them – I wonder where they've got to?'

All of a sudden, Mara laughed and sprang to her feet.

'Got to, Andreas? They haven't got to anywhere. *We're* the Zanzibar Geological Survey!'

'What? But . . . !'

It was no good trying to make Mara see reason. She was already running across the forecourt, waving her arms at the old guy, like he was some long-lost friend. Andreas felt obliged to follow. He wished he wasn't quite so sure it was a bad idea.

* * *

Heading across tropical seas in a very tiny, very old boat was not Andreas's idea of a good time. The waves were big, there were things in the distance that looked like sharks' fins and the crew looked more like drug smugglers than scientific researchers.

'That must be Zanzibar in the distance,' commented Mara, looking out of the tiny cabin through the even tinier porthole.

'What, that there?'

'No, that's a smudge of dirt. There, to the right.'

He gazed out at it, torn between pleasure at the thought of getting off this boat and the nagging feeling of unease in his belly.

'There's something we should do before we get there,' said Mara.

Andreas perked up.

'I thought you'd never ask.'

'Not that. Well, not exactly.' Mara pushed up Andreas's sleeve. 'Your bracelet, the talismanic power's running low. It needs renewing.'

Puzzled, Andreas looked down at the bracelet on his wrist. The dragon's ruby eyes were glittering as brightly as ever.

'It looks all right to me,' he said. But Mara laid her hand over it.

'Believe me, Andreas, it has to be renewed or you'll lose the protection.' Mara stroked her fingers over the dragon bracelet and slipped it gently off Andreas's wrist, cupping it in her hand. 'And without it, the Master would be able to tell that you're not really who you're pretending to be. We have to perform the ritual of empowerment, right now.'

Andreas thought of the probable consequences of the Master finding out that he wasn't, after all, Nick Weatherall MP but the late Andreas Hunt, not quite as late as he was supposed to be. If he was lucky, he might just get away with having his heart ripped out, his eyeballs pickled and his chargrilled dangly bits served up as hors d'oeuvres at the next Winterbourne orgy.

'The thing is, Mara . . .'

'You're not afraid, are you, Andreas? Surely you trust me after all this time?'

'Yes, of course, but . . .'

'Come on, we're wasting time.'

'Well, if you're sure . . .'

Mara smiled.

'Of course I am. *Very* sure. I mean . . . you wouldn't want anyone discovering who you really are, would you?'

Too flipping right I don't, thought Andreas. Everything Mara said made perfect sense. So why did he feel so uneasy?

Chapter 18

When Jean-Marie descended to the dungeon – through a door which kept changing its shape and size – he found Anjula writhing on the floor, her eyes wild and her teeth and nails scrabbling to free her wrists and ankles from their chains. She was shaking and moaning, staring unseeingly ahead of her as her body twisted in unspeakable agony.

Graveney would have been delighted to see her captive in such obvious distress, but Jean-Marie was not so sure. He had been sent – as a privilege from his mistress Diana – to inflict new and ingenious tortures on the Zanzibar priestess. Little by little, Graveney had told him, they would break what remained of Anjula's spirit and she would be their pretty plaything for all eternity.

Jean-Marie stood in the doorway, blinking in horror. Such suffering. He thoroughly enjoyed pain – in moderation – but this wasn't play-acting, this wasn't sensual torment, this was real agony, so deep that it transcended the purely physical.

He took a step towards Anjula, the heavy rice-flail hanging useless in his hand.

'Slut.'

She did not look at him; just kept on twisting and writhing and crying out, in the grip of her own private torture.

'Anjula. Look at me. What ails you?'

This time, as though by some supreme effort, Anjula

succeeded in screwing her head round. Her face and lips were glossy with perspiration, her eyes swollen and moist with tears. She struggled to speak.

'Pain. Such pain.'

'What is wrong? What is doing this to you? Tell me.'

He knelt beside her and she forced herself into a sitting position, her whole body trembling with the effort.

'The . . . stone. I need it.'

'But . . .'

Anjula's hand caught, claw-like, at his forearm.

'I need it, Jean-Marie. My life . . . my life depends upon it. Please . . .'

Jean-Marie edged away, shaking his head.

'I cannot. The Mistress's anger . . . no, I cannot.'

'Please, Jean-Marie. Without the stone I will die. The pain is tearing out my soul . . .'

Guilt attacked Jean-Marie from within. His own soft heart had always been his foremost weakness, he was well aware of that, but that didn't make the guilt any easier to bear. His hand slipped to the inside pocket of his white denim jacket. Surely. Surely there could be no harm . . .

'I saved this for myself.' He took it out of his pocket; it glowed unimportantly in the centre of his palm. 'A piece of the stone.'

Anjula's eyes narrowed with desire; the pupils were large with loving hunger.

'Oh Jean-Marie, Jean-Marie, I knew you would not fail me.'

Her fingers stroked him, caressed him, her lips roaming all over his body as he curled his fingers about the tiny fragment of grey-green stone, still not quite certain that he ought to give it to Anjula.

'Already the pain is fading, Jean-Marie. Touch me with the stone, revive me.'

Kneeling beside her, he slid the stone over Anjula's body, tracing secret paths that ran over her back and shoulders, the kiss of her breasts and the tight embrace of her strong, smooth thighs. And Anjula whispered in his ear.

'Unlock my chains.'

'I cannot,' he protested, but it was a very feeble protest. Anjula's fingers had found their way between his legs, to the secret, white-hot wand of pleasure that burned like the fuse on a stick of gelignite. 'The Mistress has commanded . . .'

'Forget the Mistress,' soothed Anjula. 'I won't run away. All I want to do is *thank* you . . . for your kindness.'

Before he knew it, Jean-Marie had taken the keys from his belt and was unlocking the shackles about Anjula's wrist, throat and ankles. They snapped open with a satisfying click and Anjula slid out, serpentine and beautiful.

'You see, Jean-Marie? That's all I want to do. Just thank you.'

He murmured some kind of inarticulate protest, but she stopped his mouth with her tongue and he sank down onto the cold flagstones, his body submitting with disgraceful willingness to the subtle insistence of her exploring fingertips.

Mistress Graveney knew all the secrets of pleasure, or at least that was what Jean-Marie had thought. But Anjula knew other ways, secrets that took a man to the edge of madness, whilst only the faint promise of ecstasy kept him hanging on to the last threads of sanity.

Her sharpened fingernails slid underneath his silk pants and dug deep grooves into the flesh of his buttocks. It was like being caressed with flick knives, exhilarating and dangerous and breathtakingly painful. More painful still was the sensation of her index finger, pushing through the tight membrane of his anus and tormenting the soft membrane within. It felt shameful and unbearable and wonderful, all at once.

'Anjula . . . no, we shouldn't.'

'Hush.'

'If the Mistress comes . . .'

'Hush, child.' She pushed up his tee-shirt and fastened her lips round his nipple, biting and licking it as though she were the man and he the yielding girl. The sensation wasn't like anything Jean-Marie had experienced before. He had no idea that it would feel so strange and so good, having his nipple in a woman's mouth and her finger waggling and scratching inside his anus.

Keeping her finger inside him, she squatted over him and pushed the tip of his dick between the plump folds of her labia majora. Glassy-smooth, her pussy sheath slipped down over his penis and guzzled it up, sending tingles of longing through Jean-Marie's body.

It was wrong. Wrong to disobey the Mistress's commands, wrong to allow the prisoner to fuck him with her strong thighs and her silken pussy. But frankly, Jean-Marie was beyond caring. He was his mistress's creation: and she had created him to be a creature of pure pleasure.

'I'm going to make you come,' breathed Anjula through sultry kisses.

'Oh. Not yet. Not yet.'

'I'm going to make you spurt. Right inside me. You're going to empty your balls into me till I've drunk you dry.'

He groaned. His head was spinning, his groin was on fire, his dick was pumping in and out like a piston rod in some crazy, run away machine.

'No, please. It's too much. I can't bear it.'

Panic rose inside him. Whatever it was that was happening to him, it was too much for him to stand. The pleasure that was building up inside him was too savage, too darkly powerful, like a colossal tidal wave threatening to engulf a whole continent.

'Please!'

If Anjula heard, she paid no heed. Her backside went on pumping up and down on Jean-Marie's dick, her strong thighs wet with perspiration as they alternately flexed and tensed.

He was very close to coming, that much was obvious. His eyes were closed and his breathing had become a shallow, harsh gasping, dragging the air painfully into his lungs. And as he got closer to the point of orgasm, something very curious began to happen. It was as though he was filled with light, a great glowing ball of flame that had settled in the heart of him and was radiating out, flooding out of every orifice and pore.

Closer still. Almost there now. The light was so brilliant that it was almost too powerful to look at.

Jean-Marie juddered; cried out; and spurted, his body jerking forward as the semen left his body. And a split second later, his entire self simply dissolved.

And vanished.

Anjula contemplated the bare patch of stone-flagged floor where Jean-Marie had knelt. Now all that remained was the tiny stone fragment, glowing a dull red. Reaching down, she gathered it up and parted her thighs, pushing the stone deep inside her.

Then she slipped her hands and feet back into the unlocked shackles. And settled down to wait.

The little survey boat landed on a rocky beach at the northern end of Zanzibar.

'I'll be back for you first thing tomorrow then,' said the captain, scratching his stubbly chin. 'If the weather holds out.'

'You'll be back whether it does or not,' snapped Mara.

Andreas looked at her uneasily, then nodded at the captain and slipped a couple of banknotes into the top pocket of his safari suit.

'Do your best, mate.'

The captain winked.

'What's up – scared of being left alone with her?'

Andreas laughed. Weakly.

'See you tomorrow then, captain.'

'Aye, tomorrow. Make sure you're ready and waiting, the tide won't wait. Oh – and watch out for creepy-crawlies. Last scientist I brought here went back in a wooden box.'

Andreas felt suddenly sick.

'You mean . . . he . . . ?'

'Stepped on a poisonous spider. He was dead within half an hour, by all accounts.'

'Nice place,' commented Andreas, glancing around him.

Andreas and Mara spent the next three hours hacking their way through tangled undergrowth and tall, twisted trees that dripped sweet, sticky sap and insects so brightly coloured Andreas was convinced they must all be deadly poisonous.

'It doesn't look like anybody's been here for years,' commented Mara as they waded round the margins of a saltwater swamp.

'Don't suppose the urban cowboys reckon much to the poisonous spiders. *And* it's miles to the nearest McDonald's.' Andreas paused, stretching his aching back. You couldn't see more than a few yards in front of you, what with all the tangled vegetation and the fallen trees. 'Can you feel anything?'

Mara met his gaze with initial puzzlement.

'Feel . . . ? Oh. Oh, you mean vibrations.'

'Yeah. Vibrations. That's what you usually do, isn't it? Touch things and see what psychic auras they give off and all that.' Andreas flicked a bug off the end of his nose. 'You *sure* you're all right?'

'Of course I am.' Mara closed her eyes and raised her arms. She stood like that for several long moments, apparently lost in astral contemplation.

'Well?'

'Nothing.' She dropped her arms and picked up her rucksack.

'What, nothing at all?'

'What are you Andreas, a parrot or something?'

He followed Mara in silence through the thickening forest, trying to stifle the worries that kept on nagging at the back of his mind. The same sort of worries he'd had when Mara turned peculiar on him, at the Eiffel Tower reopening ceremony. If it hadn't been for the necklace, he might almost have thought . . . but no, she was still wearing it all right, he must just be paranoid.

'Look!' A few yards up ahead, Mara gave a triumphant shout.

'What is it?' Andreas fetched up in her wake and peered through the gap in the trees. 'Wow.'

Before them, nestling among the interweaving vegetation, lay a complex of six or seven ruined stone buildings. The shapes of other buildings could be glimpsed in the distance through the dappled greenish twilight, some almost intact, others little more than organised heaps of rubble.

'It's . . . a town or something.' Andreas took a few steps nearer the ruined buildings.

Mara turned and smiled.

'Or a palace. *Anjula*'s palace.'

Andreas whistled.

'You reckon this is the one then?'

'Come on, Andreas, how many other ruined palaces are there in northern Zanzibar?'

'How should I blooming well know?'

It seemed a perfectly reasonable reply, but Mara took offence and strode off, Andreas following less than enthusiastically in her wake. It paid to look where you were stepping. Mara had the fringe benefits of a vampire body, but Andreas didn't, and he'd heard some terrible stories about bugs that crawled up the inside of your trouser leg to munch on your dangly bits. He wasn't in a tearing hurry to discover the secret of this place . . . whatever it might be. Frankly, it gave him the screaming abdabs.

'Funny place this,' he commented, more to himself than to Mara, who was running about all over the place. 'I mean, look at those paintings. They're just plain . . . weird.'

He peered up at the exposed internal wall of what must once have been a very large and impressive building, resplendent with crumbling statues and the remains of painted columns. Inside, the wall was decorated with a huge and elaborate fresco, depicting a series of erotic scenes in which beautiful, caramel-skinned people screwed imaginatively under a jet-black sun.

Black? Was that intentional, or had the artist just run out of Sunshine Yellow? Apparently not, as the screwing-under-a-black-sun motif was repeated everywhere he looked. The people who had once lived here, whoever they might be, had certainly enjoyed screwing. Twosomes, threesomes, fivesomes and sixsomes: in some pictures, you could only tell how many people there were by counting the number of tits and dicks.

'There are more buildings over there,' called out Mara, and Andreas reluctantly tore himself away from a very fetching portrait of a woman having intimate things done to her between the shafts of an ox cart. It wasn't easy. Andreas Hunt might know sod all about art, but he knew what he liked – and this was right up his alley.

About two hundred yards further on, the forest came to an abrupt and unexpected end. It didn't just peter out, it was as if someone or something had taken a great big circular bite out of it, leaving a sizeable clearing which was almost devoid of vegetation. Around the edges nestled a few stone buildings, smaller but more intact than the others, and still displaying vestiges of gold and jewelled ornamentation.

But neither Andreas nor Mara was looking at the buildings, or the curiously stunted and blackened trees around the margins of the clearing. They were staring at the gigantic round crater, and the blond-haired youth standing at the edge, gazing down into its depths.

Andreas opened his mouth to speak, but nothing came out. A bizarre and frighteningly powerful force had caught hold of him like a cartoon magnet and was dragging him towards the edge of the crater. Towards the blond youth who had turned to face him and was smiling, holding out his arms.

'Welcome,' said the youth. And at that word, shivers of unwilling, guilty interest rippled through Andreas's body. What was happening to him? Panic washed over him, yet there was nothing he could do to resist these feelings of brutish, unsophisticated lust.

He kept on walking, because there was nothing else he could do. And he saw out of the corner of his eye that Mara was also walking towards the edge of the crater, towards the blond youth whose moist-lipped, tight-arsed smile was filled with the promise of every depraved pleasure you could ever want in your whole life.

Want. Want. Want. There was nothing rational about it, just an incredible and primeval urge.

'Come,' said the youth. 'Can't you feel it? Pleasure is all around us.'

And it was true. You could feel it in the air; rising up like curls of warm, fragranced smoke from the depths of the crater, curling about you, caressing you with invisible fingers. Making you yearn to be naked and free.

Andreas walked on, stumbling as his own hands tore off his clothes and left them on the ground where they fell. The only thing he cared about now, the one thing that was more important even than breathing, was sex. He had to have it. Now.

Now just you hang on a minute, squeaked a protesting voice somewhere in the dark confusion of Andreas's thoughts. Hang on Hunt. He's a bloke, you're a bloke, you fancy *girls*, don't you remember?

He remembered. Only right now it didn't seem to matter that much.

The youth stepped forward, pulling his collarless shirt off over his head, then sliding down his white denims and Calvin Kleins. Underneath, his body was golden and smooth, with the absolute perfection that only youth can possess.

His dick hung semi-erect between his supple thighs, its tip bulbous and glossily inviting; and all of a sudden, Andreas felt the unaccountable urge to take that dick into his mouth and suck on it until it spurted. The very thought of it made him hard, making his dick rear up. Automatically, his hand moved to it, cradling it and gently stroking it. He fantasised. That long, thick penis swelling on his tongue and his own dick in the youth's slim fingers; and all the time Mara's tongue working its way in and out of his arse.

A wet dream of perfect pleasure.

Mara laughed as she slipped her arms about his waist and slid down his back, her tongue skating wetly down from between his shoulder blades to the shallow, sweat-filled well at the base of his spine. He shivered. Somewhere, miles and miles away, he could hear himself laughing too; his whole body shaking with spasms of delighted laughter as the blond youth knelt before him and took his dick between those perfect, rose-soft lips.

Oh yes, oh yes, oh *yeeees*. Andreas drew in breath sharply and let it go in a series of juddering gasps. The sensations were intense, way, way beyond 'good' or even 'bloody fantastic'. A moist tongue was wriggling over his glans and another was lapping between his arse cheeks, darting in and out of his anus with reptilian precision. Fucking *yes*.

As the three bodies writhed and rioted, coupling at the crater's edge, Andreas was vaguely aware of something that lay beneath him, many feet below at the bottom of the crater. Something big and grey, rough and lumpy, and lustrous where its abrupt descent from the skies above had splintered sharp shards from its surface.

It looked remarkably like the remains of a meteorite. A

flipping enormous meteorite, composed entirely of the magical grey-green stone.

The Master stood in the Great Hall at Winterbourne, inspecting the mound of grey-green rubble which lay before him, almost filling the drained sunken pool.

Stooping, he stroked his fingertips over the glass-smooth surface, exposed where a flake of stone had been splintered off. He smiled, feeling its power ooze into him, filling him with a sudden, savage joy. With knowledge too, an astral insight which made him wonder how he could have been so blind for so long.

He turned to Heimdal.

'Send them to me. Now.'

'At once, Master.'

Heimdal returned a few minutes later with Andreas and Mara. Mara looked chicly carnivorous in figure-hugging black rubber and silver chains: hardly her usual choice of garb, thought Andreas, but no doubt she was out to impress the Master. Andreas felt stiffly conventional in his nicely cut suit and kept glancing down at the identity bracelet around his wrist. Not so much an ID bracelet as a security blanket, he thought ruefully. Was he imagining it, or were the dragon's eyes a different shade of red and sort of . . . flickering?

Pull yourself together, he told himself. The Master's smiling. He's pleased with you, you got him what he wanted.

'Master?' Andreas shuffled uneasily in his handmade black brogues. At heart he was still the scruffy hack with a taste for the tasteless things in life.

The Master contemplated the meteorite for a few seconds, then sat down on his throne, fingers tapping idly on the carved arm rests.

'You have done well,' he commented. His eyes moved from Andreas to Mara and back again. 'Both of you.'

'Thank you, Master.'

'Though I confess,' continued the Master, 'that I was beginning to have severe doubts about your loyalty.'

The smile had slipped, and there was something steely in the Master's gaze; something that Andreas didn't like one little bit. He forced himself to meet that gaze head-on.

'We did everything in our power to contact you. There were . . . complications.'

'Indeed.' The Master's lip curled. 'Tell me about these *complications*.'

Before Andreas had opened his mouth, Mara – to his complete astonishment – flung herself onto the black marble steps which led up to the Master's throne.

'Oh Master,' she purred, her voice kitten-soft with sweet poison. 'My beloved Master, your loyal slut Anastasia returns to you from the dark void of captivity. For many long months my body was possessed by the spirit of the white witch Mara Fleming, but I have cast out her soul into the blackness, and she will never return.

'I return to you now, oh Master; and I bring with me a tribute.'

She raised her face to the Master's, entreating him to give her some sign of surprise or approval. He looked down at her, expressionless. Her eyes gleamed.

'I bring you the traitor, Andreas Hunt.'

Andreas felt as if he had suddenly been plunged into iced water. Rooted to the spot, he stood open-mouthed as a frozen finger of horrible realisation slid all the way down his spine from head to tail. No. Oh God no, not this. Not the thing he'd dreaded ever since he had taken up residence in Nick Weatherall's body. He'd been tricked, rumbled, betrayed.

How the hell was he going to wriggle out of this one?

He tried to speak, but his whole body was shaking and he couldn't make the muscles in his face stop twitching.

'M-master . . .' he managed. 'It's . . . she's lying.'

The Master glanced at Andreas, then back at Mara. No, not Mara, thought Andreas bitterly. Anastasia Dubois. Somehow, he couldn't think how, the vampire slut's spirit had overcome the power of the crystal necklace and retaken control of her body. Leaving Mara . . . where? Dead? Lost in some astral limbo? His head reeled.

Still lying on her belly on the steps of the throne, Anastasia reached up with her claw-tipped fingers and pawed gently at the Master's feet, kissing them and fawning in sycophantic bliss.

'Master . . . beloved Master . . . let me pleasure you . . .'

The Master let out an impatient sigh and, extricating his foot, used it to push Anastasia away. She rolled down the steps and sprawled at the bottom, her tousled hair falling sluttishly across her heavily painted lips.

'Imbeciles,' spat the Master. 'Did you really believe you could deceive me for ever?'

'Deceive you?' gasped Anastasia, on her knees and reaching out imploringly. 'Never, Master, never! I am your loyal slut, I was betrayed and imprisoned by Mara Fleming . . .'

'So you say,' commented the Master coldly.

'It is the truth, Master! And to prove my loyalty I have brought you the traitorous Hunt, the arch-deceiver . . .'

'Be silent, slut!'

The Master turned his attentions to Andreas.

'Hunt.' He spoke the word as though it began with a C rather than an H.

'Yes.' Somehow there didn't seem any point in trying to deny it. So. Andreas Hunt was finally going to die. They might as well get it over with.

'Not dead, I see.'

'Not quite.'

'Evidently I underestimated you.' A bit of a backhanded compliment, thought Andreas, but hey – little things mean a lot. 'Slightly.'

'You say the nicest things.'

'The talisman bracelet was an ingenious idea, but its flimsy power cannot protect you now. Nor can that foolish bitch Mara Fleming. I have seen you for what you truly are.' The Master's even tone took on an edge of anger. 'You have caused me a great deal of inconvenience, Hunt.'

Andreas shrugged.

'Don't mention it.'

'You have tried my patience far too long. And now you are going to pay dearly.' The Master's eyes narrowed. 'Both of you.' He snapped his fingers and guards stepped forward into the centre of the Great Hall. 'Take them.'

Anastasia screamed as rough hands dragged her to her feet and forced a rope about her wrists.

'Master, why? Master, I am Anastasia, your loyal slut, I seek only to serve you . . .'

'You expect me to believe your feeble protestations?' The Master laughed drily. 'Perhaps the milksop soul of Mara Fleming is still within you . . .'

'No! No, Master, you cannot!'

Oh yes he can, thought Andreas. And he felt some slight satisfaction in seeing that cheating, treacherous, poison-tongued slut Anastasia Dubois getting a taste of her own medicine.

'Take them away,' commanded the Master. 'Lock them in the Medieval Suite. Later, I shall enjoy deciding exactly how to annihilate them.'

Chapter 19

The cell door swung open and Graveney strode in, her petite body clad in tight-fitting leather and thigh-high boots. Her six-inch spike heels struck angry sparks from the rough stone flags. Behind her, the scene switched intermittently between solid rock, cascading water and a forest glade; but Graveney was serenely aloof from all the vagaries of time.

She stopped before the slumped body of the sleeping Anjula and contemplated her for a few moments; then took off one of her studded leather gauntlets and swiped it hard across the Zanzibar priestess's face.

Anjula whimpered in her sleep, then started awake, her hand moving instinctively to her injured cheek as her eyes snapped open.

'Mistress. Mistress Diana.' The words were a scarcely audible whisper.

Graveney took the chain which led from the rusty wall ring to the iron collar about Anjula's neck, and jerked it tight.

'That is no fitting way to greet your beloved mistress. Do it again. Properly.'

To her immense satisfaction, Anjula's dark eyes filled with tears of joy as Graveney's spiked heel dug vengefully into the flesh of her upturned backside. Her curled mane dragged in the dust as she showered tears and kisses on Graveney's feet.

'Mistress. Oh my mistress Diana. Forgive me.'

Graveney considered Anjula for a few moments. She was playing the contrite slave to perfection; so perfectly in fact, that Graveney was tempted to believe that she had at last broken the bitch's spirit. Pride swelled within her. The bitch was hers. Another step on the road to invincible power. And yet . . .

'Enough.' She kicked the bitch away.

Anjula looked up at her with wide, fearful eyes.

'I have angered you, Mistress?'

'Jean-Marie. Where is he?'

'Mistress . . . I have not seen him since . . .' She cast down her eyes. 'Since he came to punish me.'

'As I commanded him to. You have been a very disobedient and troublesome slut.'

'I know that now, Mistress. And I will do anything to earn your forgiveness.' The dark eyes dared to travel upwards once more. 'And your love.' Graveney was pleased to see that Anjula's gaze was filled with sexual yearning. It awoke pleasurable shivers of anticipation within her, almost dispelling her irritation with the errant Jean-Marie.

'Where did he go, slut?'

'He did not tell me, Mistress.'

'Damn him,' Graveney muttered under her breath. She had work for Jean-Marie to do, important work. Ultimate power was almost within her grasp and Jean-Marie had chosen this precise moment to go missing.

'Mistress. Let me comfort you.'

Anjula's fingers were soft and coaxing on Graveney's thigh, kneading and stroking the flesh through the tight thigh boots; exploring a little higher, discovering the bare skin beneath the micro-skirt which only just covered her knickerless backside.

'You are a presumptuous and impertinent slut.'

Anjula hung her head.

'Mistress.'

'But I am pleased with your progress. If you continue

252

in your obedience I shall perhaps remove your chains.' She stroked her fingers down the long, smooth slope of Anjula's bare back. It quivered at her touch, tense with joyous anticipation. 'Very well, slut. As a special mark of my favour, you may lick me out.'

'You honour me, Mistress Diana.'

'Then you must strive to deserve that honour.'

Anjula knelt before her new mistress, every inch the complete submissive, the picture of blithe contentment in her willing slavery. Her lips followed the course of her fingers as she pushed up Graveney's skirt, baring the last inches of her thighs and the tempting, glossy moss of her pubic hair.

She breathed in deeply. Hands on Graveney's buttocks, she pushed her mouth and nose into the plump triangle at the apex of her mistress's sleek, taut thighs. The scent was pungent and sweet; and the first drops of moisture which trickled onto Anjula's tongue were sweeter still. For in them was distilled the sweetness of victory.

She was grateful for the soft wetness of Graveney's pussy, and for the dark, tumbling fleece of her own hair, which so effectively masked her triumphant smile.

Graveney was well pleased. Jean-Marie might have done a disappearing act, but it hardly mattered, not now that she had Anjula and the stone mask, and the promise of yet greater power.

All time would do her bidding. For Anjula had finally submitted to her will.

Unchained now, the Zanzibar priestess knelt on the floor of Graveney's throne room, naked save for the iron collar which Graveney had decided to leave in place, as a perpetual token of her possession. She fought to conceal her impatience as she paced the room.

'You will tell me everything, slave. Everything, do you hear?'

'Everything, Mistress. The last secrets of the stone.'

Graveney's eyes glittered with avaricious glee. She had always dreamed of riches, but what greater wealth could there be than this? Somewhere above her head, in the blackened roof beams, something stirred briefly, then was still. An odd-looking piebald pigeon, roosting in the rafters. But neither Graveney nor Anjula noticed it watching them. Both were far too absorbed in their own preoccupations.

'Tell me. Now. About the stone.'

Anjula was looking straight into her eyes.

'The stone increases sexual desire and potency beyond the realm of mere human pleasure. Also, it gives the possessor the power of unlimited astral travel.' She paused, perhaps for effect. 'And it grants mastery over time and space.'

Graveney's throat was dry. She swallowed, but excitement seemed to have closed her throat.

'Explain.'

'Mistress, in the hands of one who knows its power, the stone grants the ability to travel in the past or the future. To change what has happened, or what is still to come.'

Graveney seized Anjula by the collar and dragged her to her feet.

'How is this done, slave?'

'Mistress, you must be guided by me.' The dark eyes narrowed slightly. 'For the full power of the stone can only be harnessed if you are willing to embrace true evil for all eternity.'

Gripping the iron collar, Graveney jerked Anjula towards her and placed a long, all-consuming kiss upon her lips. She was laughing as she pushed her away, panting and moist-lipped with her spittle.

'Foolish slut,' she chuckled. 'True evil? Whatever do you think I have been doing? Evil has nothing to teach me.' She lowered her voice. 'Unlike you. Tell me what I must do.'

'There must be a ritual.'

'It shall be done.'

'There are . . . certain requirements.'

'Name them.'

'You must have a sexual partner.'

'I have more than I know what to do with.'

'Yes, Mistress.' Anjula paused. 'But this partner must be . . . disposable.'

'He is to be destroyed?'

'Reduced to dust, Mistress.'

Graveney smiled. Turning to one of her flunkeys, she snapped her fingers.

'You. Boy.'

'Mistress?'

'Bring Ibrahim to me. Now.'

Andreas got bored with counting the number of water drops plinking onto the sodden floor and screwed his head painfully to the right, to glare venomously at Anastasia Dubois. It wasn't easy, but then again it wasn't easy to do anything with your head and wrists imprisoned in medieval stocks and both feet chained to the floor.

Anastasia hadn't fared much better. Mind you, she probably enjoyed being strapped to a rack with rough hempen cords that stretched her out like a starfish. At any rate, the moment she caught him looking at her she managed to raise a sneer.

'What's up, Andreas? Still trying to work out what I did to your precious Mara?'

'Bitch.'

'You say the sweetest things.'

Bile rose in Andreas's throat. He didn't much care about himself any more (he was as good as dead, so why wriggle?), but he surprised himself with the power of his loathing. Anastasia Dubois had tricked, cheated and betrayed her way back into that body; she had as good as killed Mara and if there was anything Andreas could do to make the rest of her life a complete misery, you could bet your sweet bippy he'd be signing up for a double portion.

'Why don't you just fuck off and die?'

'Ah yes, Hunt, always the English gentleman. No wonder you never made it past page five on a two-bit tabloid.'

Andreas snarled his frustration.

'What have you done with her? What have you done with Mara?'

Anastasia laughed. It was a bitter, twisted kind of laughter and Andreas wondered how the Master could possibly doubt her loyalty to his repellent cause.

'She's dead, Andreas. I killed her, can't you get your tiny brain round that? The stupid slut used so much psychic power to protect you, she lost concentration. And when the Master touched her flesh with the stone, he released me from my prison. It was easy for me to overwhelm her and destroy that trashy necklace you gave her to wear. Easy, Andreas. Almost as easy as it was to deceive you.'

A horrible thought struck Andreas.

'When . . . ? I mean, how did you . . .'

Anastasia mocked him with her smile.

'I never really went away, Andreas. I never left my body, even when Mara had stolen it and thought she had destroyed me. I was always there, Andreas. Yes, that's right. Whenever you were screwing Mara, you were screwing me too . . .'

Andreas felt sick. Sick and mad as hell. If only, just for a few moments . . . but there was no escape. It was just a question of waiting. Waiting to find out how he was going to die.

A key turned in the door and Heimdal entered, blond and massive in a black suit and crisp white shirt. Anastasia greeted him with fawning, pouting smiles.

'Heimdal, my lord! You have come to free me! The Master has granted me his pardon!'

Heimdal stood, arms folded, and observed the two captives. It was pretty obvious to Andreas that he wasn't here on a mission of mercy. He'd come here to gloat.

'Well, well,' said Heimdal at last. 'How are the mighty fallen.'

'Up yours,' snarled Andreas, master of the witty epigram. But Heimdal didn't take the bait. He was far more interested in Anastasia's sprawling, naked body, stretched so taut on the rack that every vein and sinew seemed visible beneath the smooth, white-gold skin.

'Anastasia Dubois. What a treacherous little slut you are.'

'No!' Anastasia tried to squirm and free herself from the ropes, but they held her fast. Only her head was free to move, tossing from side to side as she fought against her bonds. 'No, Lord Heimdal, I am a loyal slut. Loyal to the Master.'

Heimdal ran his fingers lightly down her belly, until the very tips rested between her outspread thighs, almost but not quite touching the bursting bud of her clitoris. She squealed with frustrated need.

'My lord! Touch me, I can't bear it. Satisfy me.'

Heimdal's fingers stayed exactly where they were. A sticky ooze of clear fluid crept from between Anastasia's plump, blush-pink labia.

'And what about me, slut? Are you loyal to me?'

'Yes. Yes! Always.'

'You would do anything to serve me?'

'Anything, Lord Heimdal. Give me one chance to prove my loyalty, and I will show you . . .'

'Very well then. Since you are so eager to prove your worth.'

He climbed up onto the rack, straddling her as he unzipped his fly and took out his cock. The jade serpent ring that pierced his cock-tip gleamed darkly.

'Suck me, slut. And mind you do it well.'

Andreas watched Anastasia open her painted lips and take Heimdal into her mouth, greedily engulfing him, straining to take the very last millimetre of hard flesh. No mean feat, since, of all the Master's well-endowed henchmen, Heimdal was one of the most impressive. Only Ibrahim boasted a longer cock and Heimdal's was so thick that Anastasia's mouth had to stretch to accommodate it.

As Heimdal pushed in and out of Anastasia's mouth, Andreas noticed something rather peculiar. She looked . . . well . . . *blurred*. He closed his eyes and shook his head as best he could, then opened them again. She still looked blurred, in fact he could have sworn he was looking at a double image. Had years of lager and self-abuse finally taken their toll? If he got out of this, he was going straight down the optician's.

Anastasia was certainly giving it all she'd got. Her cheeks hollowed as she sucked hard on Heimdal's cock, and her head rose and fell, meeting his rhythmic thrusts. The rhythm was speeding up now. In a few moments, Heimdal would climax and spurt down Anastasia's throat.

Or at least, that was what Anastasia was expecting. But at the very last moment, Heimdal pulled back, withdrawing his glistening cock and taking it between his fingers. Anastasia whimpered and writhed beneath him.

'Heimdal . . . my lord . . . please . . . please, don't take it away from me, no, no, no.'

He gave it three more strokes, maybe four, and a creamy jet of semen spurted out from between his fingers, spattering all over Anastasia's face. Her tongue darted out, desperate to lap up the cream, but it was out of reach and trickled in pearly runnels over her nose and forehead and cheeks and throat.

'Please . . .' she moaned. 'Don't . . . don't leave me like this.'

But that was precisely what he intended to do. He laughed as he stood up and zipped away his cock.

'Stupid slut. Vain, foolish, empty-headed little slut.' He glanced round at Andreas with a look of supreme indifference. 'The Master will be well rid of you. Both of you. I look forward to watching you die.'

'The preparations are complete, Mistress.'

Anjula sprinkled the rest of the salt on the ground and turned to bow to Mistress Diana. Graveney observed her handiwork. The floor of the throne room had been transformed into an intricate maze of patterns: pentograms, circles, stars and whorls, drawn in white sand, salt and powdered crystal. At the very centre of the maze rose a low dais, with incense burners at each corner and a carved bed garlanded with madonna lilies.

'This *is* going to work?'

Anjula concealed a traitorous half-smile.

'Oh yes, Mistress. It will work perfectly.'

'Then let the ritual begin.'

She walked to the dais, Ibrahim following a few steps behind, magnificent in his nakedness; his only ornamentation the harness of fine golden chains which enclosed his cock and balls and jingled between his firm young buttocks as he walked.

At a sign from Anjula, the chanting began; Graveney's acolytes murmuring the words and harmonies they had been taught. Others accompanied them on African drums, setting the beat, slow and stealthy and somehow menacing.

Thump. Thump. Thump.

Anjula's heart was thumping too. This was it, the key, the moment she had prayed would come. There was still time for her to make everything as it had been, as it should be. The bitch-queen Graveney might still be outwitted, cheated of the power she had usurped.

Ibrahim was lying on his back on the bed, his beautiful cock soaring gracefully upwards through the fine mesh of gold. Graveney was standing over him, the stone mask on her face, swaying in time to the drums.

Thump. Thump. Thump.

Yes! The excitement entered Anjula and she began to chant, her voice rising to a high song of exultation as Graveney sank down onto Ibrahim's upraised prick. Inside her, the fragment of stone began to resonate, answering the drumbeats, echoing the distant resonance of the stone hidden in the very foundations of St Malo.

Yes, yes, yes. The moment was now!

In the Great Hall at Winterbourne, the Master contemplated his craftsmen's handiwork. The mask was almost finished, a work of art in polished grey-green stone.

He reached out and picked it up. Something compelled him to raise it to his face, its surface strangely warm and yielding to the touch. Hidden fires danced within it, and all of a sudden it seemed that the air about him began to thicken.

Thump.

The Master looked round, certain that he had caught some distant sound. What was it? A drumbeat . . . He listened for a few moments but heard nothing, and returned to his contemplation of the mask. To the extremely satisfying sight of his own reflection.

But this time, the face he saw reflected in the mask was not his own.

Andreas slumped in the stocks. His head ached abominably. Thump. Thump. Thump. It was just like a drum, pounding in his head. Bloody hell but it hurt.

He looked across at Anastasia and through the pain he saw that she was thrashing about. No, wait a minute. *She* wasn't thrashing about, *they* were.

There were two of them on that rack, fighting like tiger cubs. It was crazy, he knew that, but that was what his eyes were telling him. At first, all he saw was a blurred double image; but as he stared, it seemed to solidify, to become more and more real.

Thump.

Andreas wasn't sure how much more of this he could take. His head felt like an overblown beachball and now he was seeing things as well.

Thump.

There really *were* two women on that rack. They were quite distinct now, two Anastasias fighting each other. No, Andreas you plonker, he corrected himself, that's not two Anastasias; that's one Anastasia and one Mara!

Thump. Thump. Thump. The drumbeats seemed louder and closer now, so all-consuming that the whole room seemed to shake. Andreas couldn't see anything properly, couldn't focus, couldn't be sure that any of this was real. Queasy with vertigo, he closed his eyes.

But that was just the beginning.

Andreas was falling. No, spinning. Rotating very, very fast, like a ball on a roulette wheel, bouncing and spinning and jolting, not knowing which hole, if any, he'd end up falling into.

Thump.

He was standing in the Head's office at Gas Street Comprehensive. He was fifteen years old and his backside smarted like someone had set it on fire. Hang on, he remembered that day. It was the day he'd been caught giving the gym mistress one in the girls' showers. Not really the kind of day you'd ever forget.

' . . . deplorable behaviour.'

'Yes, sir.' He was looking up at the Head, trying not to smirk.

' . . . hope you're ashamed of yourself. Your parents will be mortified . . .'

Of course they hadn't been. In fact, his old dad had given him a pat on the back and a packet of three. His dad. Gaston Lebecq, alias Matthias Hunt. Funny, the things you remembered when somebody was about to kill you. Maybe it was like drowning.

Thump.

'Hunt, you useless fucker, I want a word with you.'

He was sitting at his desk in the newsroom at the *Daily Comet*. Good God, it was exactly how he remembered it. Half-eaten pork pie, girlie calendar, phone ringing and the Editor shouting at him over the top of it all.

'Where's that story for page nine?'

'Nearly finished. Just waiting for a few quotes.'

'You're a bloody liar, Hunt.'

'But you love me.' He blew the Editor a kiss.

'Don't push it.' The Editor threw a file across the desk at him. He remembered that file, it was the cuttings file with all the weird stories about 'vampire' sex-killings, 'bizarre disappearances' and 'political corruption in high places'. 'Get your arse up to Whitby. Pronto.'

Whitby? Andreas's mind whirled. He was reliving a day he'd never forget. The day he'd been sent to cover some crazy vampire story to fill the pages of the *Comet* in the silly season. Which was how come he'd met Mara Fleming, and then the Master . . .

And his own destruction.

Thump.

What on earth was happening to him? He was spinning again and then falling, plummeting until his stomach caught up with him and his eyes flicked open.

This time he was looking at a girl, sitting at a table in a library. A girl with long, lustrous hair, wicked eyes and pillow-soft breasts. He heard himself speak, his voice hoarse and trembly.

'My name's Andreas Hunt, and you're not moving an inch until you tell me yours.'

The eyes met his.

'Mara. Mara Fleming.'

Whitby library. Four years ago, almost to the day. Mara was sitting opposite him, irresistible in no bra and one of those thin, semi-see-through peasant blouses. And it was Mara as he'd first known her, Mara in the body Sedet had stolen; dark-haired and violet-eyed, busty and beautiful and wild.

Now her bare foot was sliding up his dick and it was all he could do not to shout out loud.

'I . . . er . . . came here to do some research.'

'Really? And there was I, thinking you'd come here to find me.'

Thump.

The falling and the spinning seemed to go on for ever, until Andreas began to believe that they would never end. He would be caught in this vertiginous limbo for ever, forced to watch a cosmic slide show of his own life. Was this the Master's idea of a joke?

Thump.

He opened his eyes. This time, he wished he hadn't. It wasn't a pleasant scene, and certainly not a memory he'd ever wanted to relive. He was standing in the cellars at Winterbourne Hall. It was dark, save for the flickering light of black candles, and the air stank with the mingled scents of stale blood, incense and musk. Wisps of greyish-white smoke curled about him like dry ice in a low-budget horror film.

He was shaking. Why? Because he was shit-scared, that's why.

Mara was walking towards him. She was looking straight at him, but he knew she couldn't see him. Something – or someone – had taken control of her mind. Oh shit no. Not this memory, not this one. Not the one where the Master took control of her mind and made her come at Andreas with a crystal dagger, aiming it right at his heart.

'Mara! Mara, it's me!'

She said nothing. Just kept on walking, slowly and

deliberately, the silver-handled dagger held in both hands and its crystal tip glittering wickedly in the half-light. Somewhere close by, Andreas could have sworn he heard demonic laughter; the Master's laughter.

'Mara, don't do it.'

He backed away, but he already knew what was coming next. The stone sarcophagus behind him prevented him getting away and there was quite simply nowhere left to hide.

'For God's sake, Mara, don't you remember? The Master made you stab me through the heart. He stole my body. That's what *started* this whole fucking mess!'

She was right in front of him, tears streaming down her face as she raised the dagger, reversing it suddenly so that its point was towards him, her two hands white-knuckle tight about its hilt.

'Andreas . . .' she whispered.

And then the dagger came plunging down.

Thump.

Andreas was no longer sure if he was alive, dead, or even the person he'd always thought he was. Was he Hunt or Weatherall? Was Mara Mara, Anastasia, or just plain dead?

Darkness and light spun around him in a coloured swirl. He was on a cosmic helter-skelter, going faster and faster and faster. Down, down, down . . .

Thump.

This time it was a real effort to open his eyes. They felt weighted down and gummed together. The lurching queasiness didn't help, either. It was all he could do not to fall over. Slowly, his heart stopped pounding and he forced his eyes open again, struggling to make sense of what he saw.

One thing at least was obvious: Andreas was no longer at Winterbourne. Not that he had much idea where he might be, though the big hall looked a bit like Fu Manchu's front parlour, what with all the gilding and the red velvet drapes.

Well, at least he wasn't going to be lonely. He certainly wasn't alone, far from it. As Andreas gazed about him in bewilderment, he saw that they were all here: Ibrahim, Graveney, Anastasia, the Master . . . and Mara. None of them looked as if they knew what was going on. They were all frozen to the spot, staring at each other the way Andreas was staring at them.

Before anyone had a chance to do or say anything, torches blazed and flared around the walls of the chamber and the red velvet drapes swept back.

'Welcome.'

Anjula was seated on a carved and gilded throne, resplendent in shimmering golden robes. Jean-Marie sat at her feet, naked but covered from head to foot in gold body paint, a giant ruby set into his navel.

'Welcome to my home.' Anjula rose from her throne, her eyes sweeping around the ranks of her 'guests'. 'Welcome to Isla Venemo, the poisoned isle. Here, you will learn that space and time have no meaning, and my command is the only law.'

Chapter 20

Anjula's beautiful face contorted with malicious pleasure as she threw back her head and laughed. The lily between her fingers crumpled and shed bloody petals, one by one, as she crushed them in her fist.

'You are fools, all of you,' she exulted. 'Every one so arrogant, so self-assured. So certain that you could command all the forces of eternity.'

She lowered her voice to a gloating whisper, her glittering eyes searching the frozen, startled faces of those about her. Her fingers stroked sensuously down over Jean-Marie's cheek, leaving a dark and bloody smear on the gilded skin.

'Imbeciles. The secrets of the stone shall be safe, and you, my poor fools, will be no more.'

Andreas tried to move, tried to speak, but some invisible force kept him rooted to the spot. It was all he could do to breathe. He could not even turn his head away; his gaze was frozen straight ahead, fixed on the chilling sight of Anjula's unfettered delight.

As she raised her arms, her golden bracelets jingled about her wrists and the cut stones in her rings flashed a silvery, green-grey fire. In that same instant, a whirling curtain of wind rose up and filled the whole chamber, sending everything into a dizzy spin, sucking out breath, obscuring sight, leaving Andreas so disorientated and sick that he longed to close his eyes and escape into darkness.

The wind pulled and sucked at him with unseen fingers, tore at his hair and his clothes, finally plucking him off the ground and flinging him into the air. It spun and tossed and buffeted him, slamming him against the walls, the floor, the ceiling; bouncing him and twisting him half inside out.

He no longer knew which way up he was, let alone what had happened to the others. He couldn't even see straight, everything had degenerated into a nauseating blur of red and gold. If the Master ended up with his head rammed up his own arse and his goolies in a reef knot, then so much the better, but Mara . . . ? That fleeting, tantalising glimpse of Mara had brought out a surprising streak of nobility in Andreas Hunt. Somehow it didn't matter what happened to anyone else, not even himself – well not much – if only Mara could be all right.

The whirling tornado stopped as suddenly as it had begun, depositing Andreas like a sack of potatoes on the floor. Winded, he took a few seconds to get his breath back before he opened his eyes.

Uh?

He blinked in disbelief. Was this really the Roman forum, or just a scene from *Carry on Cleo*? Well the toga and sandals were real enough, and so, apparently, was the rank of Roman soldiers with their big swords, and muscular kneecaps peeking out from under natty little leather tunics. A top-notch homoerotic fantasy.

Right in the centre of the forum, playing to the crowd, was the Master. On one side of him knelt three semi-naked beauties, dressed only in the briefest of tigerskin loincloths and hobbled by ankle chains. But these were no ordinary slave girls; these were Anastasia Dubois, Diana Graveney . . . and Mara Fleming.

Andreas found himself walking up the steps and pushing his way through the crowd. The Master hailed him with a smile.

'Ah, my dear friend. You have come to view the captives?'

'Yes.' Have I? thought Andreas. The script seemed to be writing itself.

'They must be punished and humiliated for their treachery, of course. One cannot allow these barbarian tribeswomen to incite their people to resist the might of Imperial Rome.'

'No. Of course.'

Andreas's mouth was dry. He wanted to seize Mara by the hand and drag her away from this place, but she was staring ahead and smiling, a vague sort of drugged smile, as if she couldn't even see him.

'Which one shall I choose first? Why don't you choose for me?'

The Master's smile was reptilian in its repulsiveness. Andreas tried to tell him to go to Hell but the right words wouldn't come. He was caught in a scene that someone else had written, and to his horror he heard his own voice say, 'Why not begin with the white witch Mara?'

The Master's smile grew broader, more satyric. He had Mara by the wrist, was flinging her onto her belly on the ground, tearing off her loincloth as the crowds cheered and bayed for more, more, more. And now she was squirming and crying out, and he was pulling apart her arse cheeks, forcing himself upon her.

It was in that moment that Andreas found his voice. All at once he was running towards Mara, fists flailing, shouting out at the top of his voice, 'No, no, no!'

And in the next moment, everything changed.

The semi-darkness came as quite a shock after the brilliant sunshine of the forum. It took a few moments for Andreas to come to terms with his new surroundings, the new part he was now obliged to play.

He'd seen pictures of the Bastille, around the time of the French Revolution. He'd seen Anton Rogers in *The Scarlet Pimpernel*, and drooled over peasant wenches in low-cut designer rags. But he was definitely not Sir Percy Graveney, nothing so chic. To put it bluntly, he stank like he hadn't washed for a year and there was a big bunch of keys hanging from his massive leather belt.

Mind you, there were compensations in being one of the great unwashed. He might be lying on a stinking straw palliasse in a foetid guardroom, but there was a naked woman lying on it next to him, her back towards him and her well-rounded rump within easy groping distance. By his own dishevelled state and the agreeable tingling in his balls, Andreas guessed that he had just – but only just – missed the main event. Still, there was plenty of time for an encore . . .

As he touched her delicious backside, she growled with pleasure and wriggled round to face him. It was then that he realised his mistake. This was no ordinary slut. This was Anastasia Dubois, sharp little teeth glittering between luscious crimson lips.

'*Encore, chéri*?' she purred, and Andreas was off that palliasse like snot off a slate.

Just as he was debating what to do next, he heard screams. A woman's screams. Worse than that – it was Mara screaming.

He ran out of the guardroom towards the sound of the screams. A cell door barred his path: four inches of solid blackened oak. He fumbled with the bunch of keys, swearing under his breath as again and again he failed to find the right one.

'Help me. Help, please help me!'

'Mara, hold on. Hold on, I'm coming.'

There was a tiny iron grille in the door. He slid it back, and horror hit him like a sledgehammer. The Marquis de Sade was inside the cell, his breeches open and a bullwhip in his hand. Bent over a rough wooden table was a kitchen maid, bare-arsed with her skirts up round her waist and dark red welts appearing on her flawless white skin. Her mouth opened in a scream as the whip fell again, and her eyes implored.

'Help me. Andreas. Help me.'

The Master. And Mara Fleming.

'No!' shouted Andreas, trying to force a rusty key into the lock. It wouldn't turn. He knew it was the right key, but somehow he just couldn't make it turn. And tears of fury began to course down his cheeks.

The next thing he knew, he was tripping over his own skirts. Not surprising really, Andreas Hunt wasn't used to being dressed in a black frock, or running down the corridors of Pope Alexander VI's Vatican. Bugger this cassock, bugger this daft little square hat that kept slipping down over one ear.

In the end he let it fall off and just kept on running, racing desperately towards the sound of the screams. Mara's screams. Something terrible was happening to Mara and he had to stop it.

As he was rounding the corner of yet another endless corridor, a hand landed on his shoulder and stopped him dead in his tracks. What the . . . ? Heart pounding, he swung round. Standing right in the middle of the fifteenth-century Vatican was a young man with tousled brown hair, a check shirt and baggy corduroy trousers.

Andreas thought he had gone past being surprised. He thought wrong.

'Max?'

'Who else?'

'You're not a pigeon.'

'Nothing wrong with *your* eyesight.'

'But . . . you're real!' Andreas reached out and pinched Max on the arm.

'Ow.' Max rubbed his bruised arm. 'Look Andreas, I'm only real here, where time and space don't exist.'

'This is all way beyond me.'

'You don't need to understand. Just listen. You have to stop this, Andreas, in fact only you *can* stop it.'

'But what . . . ?'

'If you don't stop it, you'll be trapped here for ever.

271

And so will Mara. Can you get that into your thick head?'

Andreas nodded glumly.

'I don't know what to do!'

Max sighed.

'Honestly, Andreas, sometimes I don't know why I bother. The stone is the key. Remember that. The stone.'

Footsteps sounded behind Andreas, approaching along the corridor. He swung round and when he turned back a moment later, Max had gone. The stone? Stopping it with a key? How was he ever going to make sense of any of this?

As the old woman shuffled towards him along the corridor, the screams began again. The old woman raised her face, imploring him with her dark eyes. It was Anjula.

'Please, Monsignor, my daughter . . . Find my daughter before Cesare Borgia kills her.'

It was more than Andreas could stand. And again he found himself running full-tilt through the maze of corridors, searching for Mara, racing against time to find her and save her before it was too late.

The final corridor led through a carved archway into a private garden. There, beneath peach trees and vines laden with fruit, two figures were locked in a mortal struggle. A man and a woman, the woman's clothing torn from her luscious body to reveal the fullness of one perfect, swelling breast.

'Mara!' he shouted, and the man turned towards him. It was not Cesare Borgia but Alexander, the evil pope himself, his familiar face contorted in wicked pleasure.

The face of the Master.

And then, just as Andreas was about to play the reckless hero, everything changed again. This time, when the dizziness passed, he knew exactly where he was. After all, he'd been here before. This was the old town of St Malo, circa 1941. And somewhere in it, he knew without the shadow of a doubt, the Master would be torturing Mara for his own private, perverse pleasure.

The ancient, narrow streets stretched out before him. He knew which one he was supposed to take, could feel his feet being directed down it towards the sound of distant screaming.

'Andreas. Oh Andreas, hurry . . .'

It took all the strength in his body to turn and walk away in the opposite direction. Max's words echoed in his head: 'You have to stop it Andreas, only you *can* stop it.' But stop what? And how? And what if he was making a terrible mistake?

As he rounded the next corner, a young man stepped out of the doorway of the Bar Colombie.

'Lebecq! At last you have come.'

'Henri? What are you doing here?'

The youth held out a canvas bag and smiled. Darting glances to right and left, he beckoned Andreas back into the shadow of the doorway. With certain misgivings, Andreas followed him into the deserted café.

'Well?'

Henri upended the bag, dumping its contents onto one of the café tables. Jewellery cascaded out like a gold and silver waterfall: rings, necklaces, bracelets, brooches. Henri winked.

'Liberated, from the Commandant's wife. For the Resistance. The money this lot fetches will help our cause, we can buy many guns for the Maquis.'

Andreas was not really listening. The Commandant's wife's jewels! His mind whirled as he remembered what Max had told him, about Henri's treachery and the unusual, grey-green stone.

His eyes spotted something distinctly unusual among the jumble of precious metals and stones. Digging into the pile he found it and pulled it out. Yep, unusual all right. It wasn't often that you found a cock ring made of platinum. And there surely couldn't be more than one set with a polished sphere of lustrous, green-grey stone . . .

'Lebecq?'

Andreas stroked the stone. Even the lightest, briefest touch sent shivers running up his whole arm. Shivers of dark and sensual power.

'Amazing isn't it,' said Henri. 'A ring, but never have I seen anything like it . . .'

'No.' I bet you haven't, thought Andreas, closing his fingers over it. And if I've got anything to do with it, you're not going to see it again.

He knew the script, knew what was going to happen next. Lebecq would scarper to England, taking the stone with him. It would ruin the lives of all who came into contact with it. And it would end up as part of a 'donation' to the National Geological Archive, where it would be discovered fifty-odd years later by Diana Graveney – and the Master.

But what if it never made the journey? A smile crept over his lips as he contemplated the possibility. Yeah, why the fuck not? If Graveney never found the stone, Anastasia would never have an opportunity to destroy Mara. If the Master didn't even know it existed, he wouldn't get mixed up in shenanigans that threatened to turn time and space inside out.

And anyway: if a piece of stone could change the future, then why couldn't Andreas Hunt?

He pushed open the door of the café and walked out into the street, Henri trailing in his wake.

'Lebecq? Lebecq, where are you going?'

'Outside. There's something I have to do.'

There was a storm drain conveniently close to the door of the café. Andreas gave the cock-ring a last look. It seemed so innocuous, lying there on his outstretched palm. Who'd have thought a bit of rock could cause so much trouble?

'What are you doing?' squeaked Henri as Andreas held the ring over the storm drain and let it go. It clinked briefly against the iron grille, then disappeared from view.

'Putting things right,' replied Andreas with a sigh of

relief, wiping his hand on the seat of his trousers. 'Now, for God's sake go and put the rest of those jewels back before the Commandant's wife realises they're gone.'

Henri gaped.

'But Lebecq . . . the Resistance needs them.'

'Not this lot, believe me. Just do it, OK?'

'If you say so.'

A sudden surge of bravado overtook Andreas.

'Everything's going to be OK now.'

Henri looked up at him, bafflement written all over his youthful face.

'Really?'

'Trust me.' Andreas gave a cheesy grin. 'I'm a journalist.'

Henri didn't reply, and Andreas realised that time had frozen around him. Everything had stopped: even the terrier with its leg cocked against a nearby lamppost, caught in mid-stream, and the raindrop that would never quite manage to hit the pavement. Andreas scratched his nose nervously. It was like being the only moving thing left in a still photograph.

Then Andreas felt himself freeze too. And as colour faded to sepia and then drained away to uniform grey, he couldn't help wondering if he'd done the right thing.

After all, if Gaston Lebecq was never arrested, he might never escape to England . . . and Andreas Hunt might never have been born.

Epilogue

'You're telling me I did all *that*?' Andreas sat on the edge of the hotel bed, staring at a point somewhere in the middle of the carpet. 'And I don't remember any of it?'

The cockroach sighed.

'Look, Andreas,' it said. 'I've tried to explain, but you're just not trying. None of it happened, that's the whole point. The minute you dropped that ring down the storm drain . . .'

'Yeah, yeah, all right. So the stone never made it to England and the last six weeks never happened.'

'Correction. They haven't happened yet. You're back where you started, before Graveney found the stone – and now, of course, she won't.'

'But Max . . .' Andreas contemplated the cockroach, which had now climbed onto the dressing table and was helping itself to toast crumbs off the breakfast tray. It had been difficult enough getting used to the idea of Max Trevidian as a pigeon. And now this . . .

'What?'

'If Gaston Lebecq never made it to England . . .'

'Lebecq left France at the end of the war, with a very nice little haul of stolen jewellery. He changed his name to Matthias Hunt and opened a junk shop in Croydon.'

'So I . . . ?'

'Relax, Andreas, you still exist.'

'Look, Max, is this on the level?'

'Would I lie to you?'

'Max, you're a talking cockroach. For all I know, you'd sell your granny for the contents of a dustbin bag.'

'Ta very much I'm sure.'

Andreas pulled his bathrobe round him. In the en-suite bathroom behind him, Mara was humming to herself as she splashed about in the scented waters of the jacuzzi.

'I'm getting lonely in here, Andreas. Why don't you come and join me?'

'Be right there,' Andreas called back. 'Do you think I ought to tell Mara? You know, about . . .'

'Better break it gently. It's not every day you find out you were the Paris Vampire.'

'Max . . .' ventured Andreas.

'Hmm?' enquired Max through a mouthful of marmalade.

'Max, what happens now?'

'How do I know? But if I were you I'd count your lucky stars that the Master doesn't remember what happened, either.'

'You're sure about that? I mean, he hasn't twigged who Mara and I really are?'

'If he had, do you think you'd be sitting in a nice hotel room, waiting for a chauffeur-driven limousine to whisk you off to your constituency?'

'Well . . .'

'Relax, Andreas, as far as the Master's concerned you're Nick Weatherall MP, and Andreas Hunt is as dead as . . .' He paused and masticated thoughtfully. 'As dead as I am.'

Andreas sighed.

'So you're still dead and Mara and I are still stuck in other people's bodies.' He shivered. 'And Anastasia Dubois is still locked up inside Mara . . .'

'Lighten up, Andreas, they're not bad bodies. At least, Mara's isn't.' Max wiggled his antennae. 'Anyhow, thanks for the toast, I'll be off now. Got an undercover assignment at the Elysée Palace.'

'So that's it then?'

'Don't hesitate to get in touch next time the universe is in peril.'

'But how . . . ?'

It was too late, Max was gone. Andreas got up and walked across to the window. Outside, the summer sun was climbing in a powder-blue sky; later on, Paris would be sizzling in a July heat haze. The city was waking up and – hey – so was Andreas Hunt. Maybe Max was right, they weren't bad bodies and you could have a lot of fun with two.

Rolling his bathrobe into a ball, he drop-kicked it across the room and sauntered into the bathroom. Mara was reclining like an auburn mermaid in a sea of pink bath foam. She smiled and ran the tip of her tongue over her moist lips.

'I thought you were never coming.'

'Ah, but have you kept it warm for me?'

'What do *you* think?'

Andreas slid into the bath and slipped his hand between Mara's thighs, cupping the plump warmth of her sex.

'Come here, little girl,' he murmured into the nape of her neck as she giggled and squirmed in his grasp. 'I want to tell you a story.'

More Erotic Fiction from Headline Delta

Bonjour Amour

EROTIC DREAMS OF PARIS IN THE 1950s

Marie-Claire Villefranche

Odette Charron is twenty-three years old with enchanting green eyes, few inhibitions and a determination to make it as a big-time fashion model. At present she is distinctly small-time. So a meeting with important fashion-illustrator Laurent Breville represents an opportunity not to be missed.

Unfortunately, Laurent has a fiancée to whom he is tediously faithful. But Odette has the kind of face and figure which can chase such mundane commitments from his mind. For her, Laurent is the first step on the ladder of success and she intends to walk all over him. What's more, he's going to love it . . .

FICTION / EROTICA   0 7472 4803 6

More Thrilling Fiction from Headline Delta

UNDERCOVER

FELICE ASH

Alexa is the twin with a lust for life. Gorgeous, redheaded and irresistible, she has an appetite for sex it takes a string of lovers to satisfy. And, in her work as a private investigator, she'll go to any lengths to get what she wants.

Jess couldn't be more different from her identical twin and her life is going nowhere fast. Shy and inhibited, she can't remember when she last had a good time – in or out of bed.

So when Alexa suggests that her sister take her place while she works undercover, Jess is desperate enough to agree. She soon finds out there's more to it than wearing her sister's clothes – particularly when Alexa's lovers are determined to take them off . . .

FICTION / EROTICA 0 7472 4499 5

A Message from the Publisher

Headline Delta is a unique list of erotic fiction, covering many different styles and periods and appealing to a broad readership. As such, we would be most interested to hear from you.

Did you enjoy this book? Did it turn you on – or off? Did you like the story, the characters, the setting? What did you think of the cover presentation? How did this novel compare with others you have read? In short, what's your opinion? If you care to offer it, please write to:

> The Editor
> Headline Delta
> 338 Euston Road
> London NW1 3BH

Or maybe you think you could write a better erotic novel yourself. We are always looking for new authors. If you'd like to try your hand at writing a book for possible inclusion in the Delta list, here are our basic guidelines: we are looking for novels of approximately 75,000 words whose purpose is to inspire the sexual imagination of the reader. The erotic content should not describe illegal sexual activity (pedophilia, for example). The novel should contain sympathetic and interesting characters, pace, atmosphere and an intriguing storyline.

If you would like to have a go, please submit to the Editor a sample of at least 10,000 words, clearly typed in double-lined spacing on one side of the paper only, together with a short outline of the plot. Should you wish your material returned to you, please include a stamped addressed envelope. If we like it sufficiently, we will offer you a contract for publication.